Sheila Norton was born in Romford, Essex, and now lives in the village of Stock, near Chelmsford, with her husband Alan, two cats and a dog.

She has written avidly since childhood, and won two short story awards in the early 1990s. *The Trouble With Ally* is her first novel but she has completed a second and is currently working on a third.

THE TROUBLE WITH ALLY

Ally Bridgeman is in big trouble. Her career is going nowhere; she has a cantankerous mother, and two daughters with far more exciting love-lives than she ever had. Even her ex-husband has found himself an annoyingly perfect trophy girlfriend. But when she discovers her daughters are about to throw her a surprise birthday party to celebrate an age she'd rather commiserate reaching, Ally decides enough is enough. So she tells a little white lie and gains a year's reprieve . . . And when Ally finds herself attracting the attentions of a younger man, she decides to shed a few more years and have the time of her life . . .

SHEILA NORTON

THE TROUBLE WITH ALLY

Complete and Unabridged

ULVERSCROFT
Leicester

First published in Great Britain in 2003 by
Judy Piatkus (Publishers) Limited
London

First Large Print Edition
published 2004
by arrangement with
Judy Piatkus (Publishers) Limited
London

The moral right of the author has been asserted

British Library CIP Data

Norton, Sheila
    The trouble with Ally.—Large print ed.—
Ulverscroft large print series: romance
1. Middle aged women — Fiction
2. Midlife crisis—Fiction
3. Large type books
I. Title
823.9'2 [F]

ISBN 1–84395–293–9

Published by
F. A. Thorpe (Publishing)
Anstey, Leicestershire

Set by Words & Graphics Ltd.
Anstey, Leicestershire
Printed and bound in Great Britain by
T. J. International Ltd., Padstow, Cornwall

This book is printed on acid-free paper

For my family;
Especially my husband Alan,
daughters Cherry, Jenny and Pippa
and mum Kay.
With thanks for all the years of
encouragement!

1

Rated out of ten on a scale of awfulness, of horrendous happenings that ruin your life, I suppose the cat being sick was only about a two or a three. So it's hard to explain to anyone who didn't know me at the time, why it was the catalyst for a disaster of a magnitude that sent me off the rails, spinning out of control, into a nightmare I could never have imagined in my worst . . . well, in my normal nightmares. Come to think of it, it was hard enough to explain to the people who knew me best in the world, so why the hell should you be able to understand if you've never even met me? Still, I think maybe you will. I think maybe you'll read my story and think to yourself:

'There's the story of a poor, sad, worn-out old cow who'd come to the end of her tether.'

Or perhaps you'll think:

'That's the result of too much freedom in the Sixties, the inevitable consequences of the pop culture and moral dissolution of our society, the breakdown of marriage and the traditional family . . .'

Let me make it clear from the outset that I

prefer the poor sad cow theory. It doesn't offend me one bit, and I think it's pretty accurate. So don't be afraid to apply it at any point in the story that you feel appropriate. Starting on the day the cat was sick.

It was an unusually cold April day, two months before my fiftieth birthday. The central heating wasn't working but I wasn't letting that upset me. I was wearing gloves to eat my breakfast and had accepted with a good grace the fact that the central heating engineer couldn't manage to get out to fix it until the Monday of the next week at the earliest. C'est la vie. A bit of cold never hurt anyone.

'When I was a kid,' I was telling Lucy, my younger daughter, 'we didn't have central heating. Nobody did.'

'And people lived in caves and wore wild animal skins.'

'And we had to scrape the ice off the insides of the bedroom windows, and get dressed under the bedclothes . . .'

'Jesus! Are we getting all that Hard Times in the Dark Ages stuff again?' Victoria asked her sister mildly, ignoring me completely as she appeared in the kitchen wearing two dressing gowns over her pyjamas and grabbing two slices of toast that had just popped out of the toaster.

'That's my toast!' said Lucy.

'Put some more on.'

'Mum! Tell her!'

I'm invisible and not worth listening to, but I'm supposed to tell a twenty-one-year-old not to eat a nineteen-year-old's toast. On your bike.

'Load the dishwasher when you've finished,' I said instead. The cat-flap rattled and Apple Pie galloped in as if all the hounds of hell were after him.

'Cold out there, isn't it, boy!' said Victoria brightly, sitting down at the table with Lucy's toast on a plate, dripping butter down the top dressing gown. Apple Pie jumped up on the table, looked at her as if considering his options for a minute, and then vomited all over the toast.

It wasn't the vomit so much, although it was copious and strangely red in colour. It was the way he looked.

'He did that deliberately!' squawked Victoria, who had jumped out of her chair and backed away from the table, her face screwed up in horror.

'Serves you right,' said Lucy calmly, buttering the newly popped toast.

Apple Pie was lying on his side by the pool of vomit, panting lightly.

'He's not well,' observed Victoria. 'You'd

better take him to the vet, Mum.'

'Is anyone going to help me clear this up?' I asked tersely, looking at my watch. Concern about the cat was doing a fine balancing act in my mind with concern about my job.

Victoria crept back towards the table, looking at it with barely concealed disgust. I handed her a couple of pages of the previous day's newspaper and between us we scooped the contents of the cat's stomach into this and thence into a bin-bag.

'Poor old boy,' she said lovingly to Apple Pie, who watched her with a baleful eye. She picked him up, shushing his angry growl of protest, rocking him like a baby and carrying on a one-sided conversation with him about the possibilities of his having eaten a frog or a mouse that had disagreed with him. Just as I finished swabbing the table with two solutions of disinfectant, he threw up again, this time straight down Victoria's top dressing gown, marginally compromising the inner dressing gown, splashing her New For Christmas silly dog slippers with vivid spots of orange and finally regurgitating the last few mouthfuls onto the table again.

'Fucking hell!' shouted Victoria, dropping the cat.

'Victoria! Be careful with him . . . '

'Careful? Look at me!'

'It'll wash off. Come on, don't just stand there, help me clear . . . '

'Mum, why the hell are you bothering to clear up, when he's quite obviously going to puke again as soon as you've finished . . . '

'He's shaking, Mum!' interrupted Lucy, down on the floor beside Apple Pie, who was lying on his side again and looking distinctly miserable. 'He won't let me pick him up . . . '

'Don't try, then!' I snapped. 'Just leave him alone.'

'I'll get his basket,' said Lucy sadly, 'If you're going to take him to the vet's.'

'I've got to get ready for work,' said Victoria, leaving her two dressing gowns and silly dog slippers in a stinking heap on the floor.

'I've got to get to college,' echoed Lucy, dumping the cat basket on the floor beside Apple Pie's limp form.

They disappeared upstairs to their cold bedrooms (but not so cold that there was ice on the insides of the windows, because I'd plugged in an electric radiator on the landing outside their doors), and I heard the boom-thump-boom of their conflicting CD stereo players rising above the noise of their two-speed two-heat volumising hair-dryers, their nail-varnish dryers and their leg shavers. I looked around the kitchen, at the unloaded dishwasher, the uncleared vomit, the discarded clothes and the general debris of tea bags, butter knives, toast crumbs and marmalade globules on the worktop, and I wished there was something I could plug in, something noisy and effective that would drown out the responsibilities and frustrations of my life, take them over, clear them up and leave me with nothing more pressing to do than shave my legs and curl my eyelashes.

★　★　★

'Apple Pie?' echoed the vet, looking at me over the top of his glasses.

'It's his name,' I shrugged defensively. 'The children were young . . . they liked apple pie . . . '

He was new to the practice. The other vet was used to us. More to the point, Apple Pie was used to him. He dug his claws into this new one's arms as he tried to encourage him out of his basket.

'I think he's in pain,' I said, making reassuring noises to Apple Pie through the side of the basket. 'Come on, baby. Let the nice man . . . '

'Ouch!'

The nice man finally managed to lift Apple Pie on to the examination table at the expense of several centimetres of his flesh. The cat promptly lay down on his side, panting, watching me with accusing eyes.

'He looks really ill,' I said, beginning to feel quite alarmed. 'He's vomited twice, really bad, all over the . . . '

'He's very swollen,' said the vet, pressing his fingers gently into Apple Pie's flank and being rewarded by a howl of pain. 'Has he urinated this morning?'

Urinated? How would I know? I mean, it's not a thing I normally watch out for.

'He goes in the garden . . . '

'I think it's his kidneys. He could be going into kidney failure. He's not a young cat . . . '

'What are you trying to tell me?'

I went to sit down. I hadn't been prepared for this. Something Serious. I thought we'd get some anti-sickness pills, an extortionate bill and some advice about keeping him away from frogs. The vet looked at me over his glasses again.

'I'll have to do some tests. He's dehydrating. He needs to be put on a drip straight away.'

'I'll need to leave him here? Now?'

'Absolutely. He's a very sick cat. We'll give you a call later. We should know the results of the . . . '

'Will he pull through?'

He was Victoria and Lucy's Christmas

present when they were eight and ten years old. I know you're not supposed to give pets as presents, but they were sensible little girls, and they loved animals. We'd had to have our old dog put down a few months earlier and they'd been inconsolable.

'He's so LOVELY!' they'd squealed with delight at their first sight of the little fluffy black and white kitten.

'I'll love him for ever and ever,' declared Victoria solemnly, almost crying with pleasure as she held him on her lap.

'I love him more than anything,' said Lucy, not to be outdone. 'I love him more than . . . more than even apple pie!'

★ ★ ★

The vet lifted the yowling cat gently back into his carrying basket and called for the nurse to take him through to the hospital area.

'We'll do all we can,' he told me with a sympathetic smile, 'Of course.'

''Bye, Apple Pie,' I called after the departing basket. 'Be a good boy . . . '

★ ★ ★

The traffic had built up by the time I got back on the main road into town. I phoned

8

work from my mobile phone as I waited at the first red lights.

'We did wonder what had happened to you,' said Snotty-Nosed Nicola on the reception desk. The sarcasm in her tone was so palpable it felt like it was slapping me in the face with a wet flannel.

'Well, I'm sorry; I couldn't phone before I left for the vet's because it was only eight-thirty. You wouldn't have been there.'

The lights turned green and I brought my foot off the clutch so sharply the car lurched forwards, making me drop the phone.

'Hello? Hello?' came Snotty-Nosed Nicola's voice tinnily from the floor by my feet. 'Ally? Are you there?'

No. I've jumped out of the car window on to the motorway, you silly cow.

'Yes, but I've dropped the phone!' I bellowed through my knees, swerving to change lanes at the last minute.

'Hello? Hello? Are you there?'

'Oh, shut up,' I muttered, kicking the phone under the seat.

★ ★ ★

Things were fighting for space in the part of my brain reserved for worrying. I had to keep a space for worrying so that the things building up in there didn't spill over into the part that was supposed to deal with holding down a job and keeping myself and various other people alive. The things squirming and wriggling in the worrying part were growing large and fat in a grotesque and obscene manner because they wanted to burst out and take over my whole brain, but I wouldn't allow it.

'I have to concentrate on the traffic,' I told the Worrying Things now as I pulled up at another red light. 'Lie down and go to sleep.'

But they wouldn't. For a start I kept seeing Apple Pie lying in his basket with his eyes full of pain and his tail flicking in desperation. And I kept seeing the bill, or rather, imagining what it was going to look like. Tests, drugs, X-rays, putting on a drip. We were talking Serious Money now, Serious Money that I didn't have. Not that I didn't think Apple Pie was worth it, but where was the Serious Money going to be found when it was needed? Victoria had blown any money, even half-serious, that she'd ever had on the love of her life (her car), and Lucy, of course, being a Poor Student, never had anything to do with money that was remotely serious, the amusing little amounts that came her way being swiftly and gratefully exchanged for nights of drunken revelry, shoes, or lipstick.

The really Worrying Thing about it all was that I might have to ask Paul for money. Again.

The last time I'd asked him for money had been for my car. To bring it back to life after it died suddenly and gracefully on the M25 in a January snow storm, it had needed what seemed to amount to a new heart, lungs and complete digestive system. Apparently I'd been cheerfully and ignorantly driving around in a death trap. The mechanic at the garage had shaken his head sadly in that irritating way they have of pretending not to want to impart bad news, whilst trying to hide the gleam in their eyes behind their oily rags.

'Big end's gone, love, drive shaft's knack-ered, sump's got a hole in it, tyres are bald, wipers aren't wiping, indicators aren't indi-cating, lights aren't lighting . . . '

And the ashtray's fallen out.

I went to Paul with a heavy heart. It wasn't that he objected to helping me out, in fact since we split up he'd been so generous financially that I was tempted to think he was rewarding me for the privilege of being allowed to leave me. It was the asking that I hated. It felt demeaning. It felt as if I was saying I couldn't cope without him. I couldn't, of course, cope without his salary, and that was what I hated. How do other women manage? I suppose they have decent jobs, careers, high-flying executive positions, or they go on the game. I'd considered that, but I was always too tired to go out at night. Anyway, Paul had coughed up the money for my car's life-saving operation without a murmur. And let's face it, the cat was his responsibility as much as mine. He'd even chosen him, the only black and white kitten out of a litter of black ones, when we were shopping for the Christmas present pet all those years ago.

'Let's have that one,' he'd said, smiling as Apple Pie had clambered over his brothers and sisters to get a closer look at us. 'He looks special. I like him already.'

But he'd still left him, hadn't he, ten years later, along with his two daughters, his home, his fish-pond, and me.

★ ★ ★

I was going to be late for work. OK, even later for work than I'd already told Snotty-Nosed Nicola. I was caught up, now, in the Return of the School Run Mothers. There were three schools on my route to work — a comprehensive, where half the kids drove themselves to school and most of the others didn't bother to go anyway; a primary, where

12

the mums drove up in mini Metros or Fiestas crammed with three dozen or more tots with school bags bigger than themselves, who took half an hour each to clamber over each other out of the back seat; and a private school. This one caused the most trouble. Mothers (or nannies) arrived in competing models of Range Rovers, one child per car, and wouldn't consider dropping off their precious cargo anywhere further than two yards from the school gate, regardless of inconvenience or downright danger to anyone else, in case the kid got rained on, suffered sunstroke, got carried off by an unexpected tornado or abducted by aliens. The result was a queue of Range Rovers circling St Nicholas' Academy in much the same way as jets circle Gatwick waiting to land. Once the child had been deposited at the gate, of course, the Range Rover had to filter its way back into the line of traffic so that mum/nanny could head off home/to the hairdresser/golf course/gym. Not that I'm envious, not in the least, lucky cows. But now I was seriously late for work and I was stuck behind two Range Rovers whose drivers were graciously letting every other Range Rover into the line in front of them rather than putting their foot down and sticking like glue to the rear bumper of the one in front, in the time-honoured way.

'Come on, come ON!' I muttered through my teeth at the back of a blonde head in the car in front. 'For Christ's SAKE! Are you going to sit here all day?'

And then I got hit from behind by a taxi.

'Where the fuck were you trying to go?' I demanded melodramatically of the taxi-driver. 'Up my exhaust? On to my roof?'

'Sorry, love.'

He slouched against his taxi door, looking anything but repentant, feeling in his jacket pockets for his insurance details.

'Here you are, love. Insurance'll sort it out. Don't worry.'

Worry? Worry — me? About a crumpled bumper and a registration plate hanging off? About a smashed rear light and a dented boot? Come on, now, I had far better things to worry about. My head was beginning to ache and I could feel that sneaky sort of tickly dry throat coming on that usually means you're going down with the flu or some rare tropical disease. It was now half past nine and my job was probably on the line. You think I'm joking?

I got back in my car, pulled off the road on to the pavement, upsetting three pre-teenage-looking mothers with pushchairs but allowing the five-mile traffic jam from behind me to start crawling forwards, staring at my damage as they passed, and fished around under the seat for my mobile phone. No signal. Bloody thing sulking because I'd dropped it. Tried to start the car again to pull back on to the road. Wouldn't start. Fucking thing sulking because of a little bump from behind. Resisting the urge to get out of the car, jump up and down and kick it after the style of John Cleese, I counted to ten, counted backwards to one again, then calmly and sensibly, without any visible sign of panic, got out, locked the car, and walked through a timely shower of icy rain to the nearest phone box.

'We'd almost given you up,' said Snotty-Nosed Nicola.

'Yes, well. I'm just waiting for the AA and then I'll be on my way again. Hopefully. If it isn't anything too serious with the car.'

It had better not be. Bloody hell, it had really better not be.

'So would you pass on my apologies, please, Nicola? To Simon?'

'Of course,' she sighed, as if it was going to be a strain but she'd manage it somehow.

I spent the whole of the walk back to the car imagining the sheer pleasure of putting her in a black bin bag and dropping her in the Thames. Snotty-Nosed Nicola was the whole problem, the whole reason my job might be on the line. You might wonder how it was possible for a receptionist (and not only that but a useless receptionist whose manner of asking 'Can I help you?' made most people fairly sure that she had no intention of even trying), to have so much power. You might however stop wondering and begin to see the scale of the problem when I explain that S.N. Nicola was having it off with Simon, the Managing Director. Simon's power was absolute, as the only person in the whole world he had to answer to was his father, who owned the joint but lived in Portugal, where he played a lot of golf under the guise of looking into other business ventures. So if Nicola didn't like you, Simon tended also not to like you. Nicola liked people like Jason, Carl and Daniel, who wore designer clothes and dark glasses in the winter, called her 'babe' and offered to screw her if ever Simon got fed up. She liked people like Roxanne and Melissa, who copied her hairstyle and asked to borrow her nail varnish. She didn't like me. I probably reminded her of her mother. I didn't call her 'Nic' and we didn't giggle together. So I was on dangerous ground, and being late for work gave her ammunition to complain about me to Simon. Trouble was, you see, before you start getting all indignant and politically correct on my behalf, trouble was that I'd been late for work quite a few times.

There'd been the previous Tuesday when I'd had to wait in for the man to fix the washing machine, and the Wednesday when I'd had to wait in for him again because he didn't turn up on the Tuesday. Then there'd been the Friday, two weeks before then, that I'd been woken up at four in the morning by the phone call from Lucy who was stranded in Brighton because she'd finished with the boyfriend who drove her down there for the evening, and who now needed me to pick her up and get her to college. Then, of course, I was always having to take my mother to the hospital.

My mother was one of the other Worrying Things that I kept trying to shove back into that special compartment of my brain. She was eighty and quite sharp mentally, but bits of her were starting to go wrong in a sort of rota system. One week it would be her ears, then it would be her eyes. Then her teeth would play up, then there'd be something wrong with her chest. Next it would be her stomach, then her urinary system, and then her legs would give way. As soon as we'd sorted out her feet, it would be back up to the top of her head again. It felt like a constant battle, with doctors of every speciality trying to hold back her rapidly advancing tide of ailments. It would have been bad enough if she'd been a dear, sweet little old thing who never complained, but she'd become a bad-tempered, cantankerous old crab with a wicked tongue whose only pleasure left in life seemed to derive from hurling insults and abuse like knives at the throats of those who were trying to help her. Including me. Especially me.

'Don't rush me!' she'd shout, pushing away the arm I provided for her to lean on as we made our way back to the car after the latest check-up with the ophthalmologist or the rheumatologist or the geriatrician. 'That's your trouble, you young people! Always want to rush everywhere . . . '

And so we'd spend a leisurely twenty minutes walking from the hospital entrance to the hospital car park (where I practically had my own personalised parking space), whilst I sweated and fretted and put up my blood pressure with worrying about my job and its fate in the hands of Simon and Snotty-Nosed Nicola. I didn't even like my job. I didn't (I know, I know how awful this sounds but I'll say it sooner or later so it might as well be now) — I didn't even like my mother. I didn't dare think too much about how many hours of my life I spent with people I didn't even like.

The AA man arrived at a quarter to eleven and started the car at the first attempt, trying without success to make me feel better by assuring me that there certainly could be a problem with the plugs or the distributor which could quite possibly strike again at any time so it'd be best to get it looked at. Perhaps at the same time as the damage to the rear bumper and light? I wouldn't talk to the car all the rest of the way to work. It had made me look bloody stupid in front of the AA man, and if it thought I was going to spend out a whole lot of money on it for a new bumper now, it could bloody well think again. I slammed its door when I got out, to show it who was boss, and the number plate fell off into a puddle.

'So there you are,' said Nicola as I walked into reception. She was leaning back in her chair, holding out one hand as if she was waiting for her nails to dry. Bet she bloody was waiting for her nails to dry.

'So here I am,' I agreed tersely.

'I explained to Simon,' she said loftily. 'He wants to see you. In his office.'

The smile was truly horrible. Drowning in a black sack would be too good for her. I redesigned the fantasy with a stronger leaning towards objects of torture.

19

Simon barely looked up as I walked into his office.

'I was in an accident,' I blurted out. 'Hit from behind by a taxi . . . '

'Much damage?' he asked, still without looking up.

I wanted to shake the miserable little bastard. Couldn't even ask, couldn't even look up to see if I was all right. Much damage? As if he cared!

'Not really. Two broken legs, a dislocated shoulder, an amputated hand and concussion.'

He looked up now, slowly, puzzled.

'I meant the car.'

Yes, quite.

'Nothing I can't forgive eventually,' I said.

He still looked puzzled. Isn't it exasperating? Where's the fairness in life, when the Simons of this world sit at big empty polished desks feeling important and knowing fuck-all about anything, and they can't even understand sarcasm or irony? He drummed his pen on his desk as if to give the impression he was thinking.

'Sit down, Alison,' he said eventually, not looking at me. Here we go.

'I . . . er . . . it's not that there's anything wrong with your work.'

Yes, here we go. I held my breath and

squeezed my fingers up into fists.

'It's your time-keeping.'

'I know. I know, I'm sorry . . . ' I began, desperately, hating myself for the desperation and hating him for not giving me any choice. 'I've had a few problems, but hopefully, now . . . '

'The thing is,' he drawled, finally looking up and meeting my eyes with a cold disinterested stare. 'The thing is that the company really can't afford all these lost hours. Look at it from the company's point of view, Alison.'

On yes, silly me. And there was I worrying about my mortgage and my phone bill.

'But I always try to make up for any hours I miss,' I said, trying to sound less like grovelling appeasement and more like righteous indignation. 'I worked late last Tuesday because of the washing machine man, and I worked through my lunch hour the other week because of my mother's cataracts.'

'No substitute for reliability,' said Simon, leaning back in his chair and repeating it slowly to himself as if it was a prayer. 'No . . . substitute . . . for . . . reliability.'

We looked at each other across the polished empty desk. He with the Pierre Cardin shirt and the father in Portugal and all the balls in his court. Me with a mortgage and a red phone bill to pay, a cat in hospital on a drip and a car with things hanging off it, and despair in my heart.

'Please,' I said. My voice came out wobbly. 'Please give me another chance. I'll be reliable. I'll think about the company. I'll . . . I'll tell my car not to break down . . . '

I considered offering him a quick shag but I didn't think he'd realise I was joking.

'Well.'

He got up and walked to the window. My fate hung limply, anxiously, in his hands.

'I'm not an unreasonable person,' he told the potted plant on the window-sill. 'Let's call this a Serious Warning, shall we, Alison?'

The plant didn't respond.

'That's very reasonable,' I heard a pathetic, obsequious voice saying. 'Thank you, Simon. I appreciate . . . '

'But this Serious Warning is going into your Personal File.' The pathetic obsequious person nodded agreement. Of course, the Personal File. No more than I deserve. A public flogging would be more appropriate but please, the Personal File, by all means, absolutely.

'And if there's any repetition, Alison, any repetition whatsoever, and I will make NO exceptions . . . '

'Of course. I understand.'

'Nobody likes to have to let an employee go.'

The ultimate threat. It vibrated in the air between us, making me shudder.

'Thank you,' I said again, as I got up and scurried out, mouse-like, trailing my shame behind me.

'How did it go?' smirked Snotty-Nosed Nicola as I passed the reception desk on my way to my office.

'Lovely, thanks,' I smiled at her. 'He's a terrific lay, isn't he?'

*   *   *

'The vet phoned,' said Lucy when I got home late after working two hours of detention to make up for Missing Time. 'Apple Pie's got to stay in for at least two nights to stabilise him and then he's got to be on drugs for ever.'

'For ever?' I stared at her, dazed. 'Stabilise? What's wrong with him?'

'Renal something or other. He said it was touch and go but he hopes to stabilise him.'

I phoned the surgery.

'I can't afford . . . ', I tried to whisper into the phone without Lucy hearing me. 'I haven't got Pet Save Insurance.' I felt like the sad case in a TV advert for Pet Save. THIS family didn't take out insurance. THIS family did (camera switches to glowing, smarmy-smiling mother and father fondly watching perfectly groomed children playing with Happily Recovered pet). GUESS which parents wish they'd never been born?

'There really isn't any option,' said the vet in his serious, professional, I'm-getting-your-money-voice. 'Apple Pie will need these drugs to stay alive. Quite simply, if he doesn't have them you'll have to have him put down.'

'Is Apple Pie going to be all right?' Lucy asked me, studying my face anxiously as I hung up the phone.

I changed my face from worried sick to calm and reassuring as only a mother can, and gave her a hug.

'Yes, he'll be fine.'

It's only money, isn't it.

⋆ ⋆ ⋆

'Is Paul there, please?'

Shit. As if it wasn't bad enough having to phone Paul to beg for money, bloody Lynnette had to answer the phone. If I didn't need the money so much, I'd have hung up. I'd have done almost anything rather than have to speak to Lynnette. I'd definitely rather have walked through fire, and it would have been a near thing whether I'd have preferred to boil my head.

'Oh, HELLO, Ally!' she trilled gaily like a budgie having an orgasm. 'How ARE you? How are the GIRLS?'

As if you gave a shit.

'Wonderful, thanks,' I said sourly.

'I'll get Paul for you. PAUL DARLING!'

I felt my teeth clenching together with irritation. Paul Darling? Give me a break. This is my husband, remember. I've known him for longer than you've been out of nappies, and I know just how much he hates that sort of pretentious rubbish.

'Ally, darling!' said Paul when he picked up the phone. She's changing him. The bitch.

The thing about Lynnette, apart from the fact that she stole my husband and she was twenty years younger than me, the thing I really disliked about her was her snobbiness. I mean, who the hell did she think she was? She was nothing special. I had serious doubts that her name was even Lynnette really. I suspected it was Lynn, and she added the 'ette' to make herself sound little and cute. She was a nurse, working in a private hospital, and she never missed the chance to get that bit into the conversation, as if it somehow set her apart from the rest of us poor miserable NHS patients. You'd have thought from the way she spoke that she funded all the operations herself.

'You poor thing!' she said whenever she heard about my frequent and varied trips to Westerham General with my mother, in the tone of voice that implied disbelief that anyone could endure such conditions. 'If only you could afford to go PRIVATE!'

Well, I couldn't. Not even for the cat.

'It's the cat,' I said now to Paul, not wanting to beat about the bush. 'He's ill.'

'Is it serious?'

Ridiculously, annoyingly, I felt my eyes welling up with tears. It was the same whenever I spoke to Paul about something like this. When Lucy broke her wrist falling down the steps of a nightclub. When Victoria got rushed into hospital with appendicitis. When the pipe in the bathroom burst and the lounge ceiling fell in. I was fine, I coped, I didn't even consider going to pieces — not until I heard his voice. Calm, strong, reassuring as ever, sounding like he still cared. If you still care, I wanted to cry, I wanted to pummel his chest and yell — if you still care, why did you go? Why, why, why won't you come back?

But of course, it wasn't me he cared about. It was Lucy's broken wrist, it was Victoria's operation, it was the lounge ceiling, it was the cat being ill. Nothing to do with me.

'It sounds pretty serious,' I said now, swallowing back the tears. 'Something to do with his kidneys. The vet's kept him in, put him on a drip . . .'

'Poor Apple Pie. Poor old boy. The girls must be upset.'

So am I! So am I bloody upset! Comfort me! Care about me! Come back to me!

'Yes. He's getting old, of course, but still . . .'

'Is the vet hopeful? Can they get him better?'

'He's talking about stabilising him. But it means drugs-for-the-rest-of-his-life.'

I said it quickly so it didn't sound so bad.

'Well, whatever it takes. For God's sake. We can't just let him die. Poor old boy.'

'I know. I wish I'd taken out Pet Save.'

The TV advert family with their smarmy smiling children drew together in my mind, arms around their grinning healthy Labrador, and put up two fingers at me.

'You'll be needing some help with the vet bills,' said Paul matter-of-factly.

I hated it. Hated the fact that he knew that was why I was phoning. Not to ask for sympathy about the worry of the cat's illness, not to let him know the cat was ill because I felt it was only fair he should know, but

27

because I needed money.

'Yes. Sorry, I know it's a bit soon after the money for the car.'

'Can't be helped.'

'And I had a prang today. Taxi went into the back of me.' I wasn't going to tell him that. Why the hell did I tell him that? It wasn't as if I knew yet whether I'd need more money for the car.

'Jesus, Ally! Were you all right?'

This time my eyes overflowed completely. I couldn't answer. I sniffed and gasped as the tears ran down my nose and into my mouth.

'Ally? What is it? Were you hurt?'

'No,' I managed to get out eventually with a lot of sniffing. 'No, I was fine. It wasn't anything much. Just . . . annoying . . . '

'God, you've had some bad luck lately. You poor thing. Listen, get the vet to send the bills to me, all right? And let me know if the car's going to cost any more. And you take care, eh? Take care of yourself.'

Take care. Oh, you bastard, you absolute shit-bag, why do you say it? Why sound as if you care about me when you don't, when you walked out on me for a girl of twenty-eight and ruined my life? And I want to hate you but I can't. I put down the phone, blew my nose, hard, and looked round to find Lucy and Victoria watching me.

'Cup of tea, Mum?' asked Victoria, putting an arm around me.

'I'll do the dinner,' said Lucy, giving me a quick kiss. 'Sit down and put your feet up, Mum.'

Made me bloody cry again! Who needs men, anyway? I had my daughters to care about me, didn't I. With their help I'd survive another crisis and live to tell the tale . . . wouldn't I?

With their help, and Paul's money.

2

At this stage in the proceedings, I didn't know anything about the party. The party was, with the best of intentions, being kept a secret from me. It was a surprise party for my fiftieth birthday and was being planned with great and elaborate subterfuge and plot by my daughters, aided and abetted by my mother. I suppose I should sound more grateful, but actually I don't like surprises very much, on account of the fact that I tend to react all wrong. I knew a woman once who went away for a week, and when she came home her husband had had two walls knocked down and a conservatory built on the house. She apparently wept with joy. Me? I'd have been furious at not being consulted, missing out on all the planning, all the decision-making, all the choosing of window-frames. I'd have ruined the whole thing.

There were strange things going on at home; things that I only understood the strangeness of in retrospect. The phone would ring and one of the daughters would dive on it, knocking me out of the way, and slam a door shut between me and the conversation. I put it down to romantic liaisons and didn't take too much notice, but there were other things. Furtive talk involving pieces of paper would stop instantly when I entered a room, with the papers being shuffled out of sight. The date of the Saturday after my birthday was marked with a red ring on the calendar, and when I asked why, there were Strange Looks passed between the daughters before they explained that I was being taken out to a restaurant for a celebratory meal, and that I must keep the evening free. Keeping an evening free had never been a problem since about 1969, so I was able to reassure them that I wouldn't be getting any other offers and I'd look forward to the night out with them.

'Nan's coming too,' said Lucy with a smile that seemed to be saying more than it was giving away.

Oh well. Can't have everything.

My mother's behaviour was the other Strange Thing. She'd look at me and smile this nasty, sneering, secretive smile.

'What?' I'd ask her. 'What are you smiling at?'

You can understand me being nervous. For one thing, she rarely smiled in the normal course of events, and for another, I didn't like the thought that she might be plotting

31

something. Suppose it was something that might need me to take more time off work, like another illness or a pain somewhere unusual? If I had to get the sack, surely it wasn't going to be on account of her bunions or her piles?

'Nothing,' she'd smirk. 'Just thinking. A person can have their own thoughts, can't they?'

'That depends', I muttered, 'what the person is thinking about.'

'Nothing for you to concern your head about,' she'd say airily, still smiling as if at some private joke.

I don't like private jokes. Someone always feels left out. In this case, it was me, and it was making me feel very uneasy.

'What do you want for your birthday, Mum?' asked Victoria, perhaps to throw me off the scent, not that I'd even had a sniff of the scent anyway.

'Drugs for the cat,' I said. 'And a bumper for the car.'

'Dad's doing that,' she replied briskly. 'I'll get you some flowers.'

★ ★ ★

We picked Apple Pie up from the vet on the Saturday morning. He was huddled in the corner of his basket looking lonely and miserable. Half of one paw had been shaved where the drip had gone in.

'Poor baby!' cooed Victoria, opening the basket and scooping him up into her arms.

He looked up at her in bewilderment, yowling faintly.

'He doesn't recognise us!' she said, alarmed, inspecting him for further damage.

'That'll be the drugs,' said Lucy authoritively. 'The drugs might be doing his head in. Might have made him go senile.'

'I'm sure he'll be fine when you get him home,' smiled the veterinary nurse condescendingly. 'Just a bit traumatised by the whole thing. Aren't you, boy?'

Apple Pie turned his head to the sound of her voice and blinked lovingly at her. Lucy gave her a look of pure hatred.

'That'll be one-hundred-and-thirty-nine-pounds seventy-five-pence,' she rattled off with a beaming smile. Most of it going into her pocket by the look on her face.

'Could you send the bill to my husband, please?' I beamed back. Ex-husband. Separated husband. Husband who isn't really a husband any more. 'Mr Paul Bridgeman, 32a Tilehouse Mews . . . '

The beam had vanished abruptly from the condescending face. She put her hand over the cat basket as if to stop it leaving the premises.

'We insist on payment at the time of completion of treatment,' she said stiffly, pointing to a notice on the wall behind her, which obediently stated: 'We insist on payment at the time of completion of treatment.'

'His treatment isn't complete,' pointed out Victoria. 'You said he'll need the drugs for the rest of his life.'

'Each repeat prescription will be billed as a separate treatment,' chanted the white-coat wonder, pointing to another sign behind her stating — guess what? I wondered idly how many more signs she'd learned off by heart. I resisted the urge to test her on the 'Correct Weight For Your Pet' chart and the adverts for Pet Save (complete with smarmy family and healthy Labrador).

'So that's one-hundred-and-thirty-nine-pounds-seventy-five,' she repeated with slightly less of a beam. 'Please.'

'I haven't got it,' I whispered.

I looked round the waiting room, not wanting there to be anyone witnessing my shame. An elderly lady was sitting by the door with an elderly poodle on a lead, and two children were waiting with something small and scampery in a cardboard box.

'Pardon?' said the nurse.

'I said, I haven't got it. I haven't got any money.'

In my mind, the waiting room became a scene from a musical. The elderly lady and the two children leaped to their feet and struck poses of horrified indignation.

'She hasn't got the money! She hasn't
  got the money?
She hasn't got the money for the cat!
She hasn't got the money! She hasn't
  ANY money?
What d'you think, oh what d'you think
  of THAT?'

The nurse danced into the middle of the floor clutching Apple Pie's basket and singing in the slow, growly voice of the villain:

'People say They Can't Pay!
I won't give them time of day.
I insist on PAYMENT ON COMPLE-
  TION!'

The hairs on the poodle's neck stood on end and he began to bark, the little scrabbling thing rattled its box angrily as the whole staff of the veterinary practice joined in the chorus:

'Mum!' whispered Lucy urgently, shaking my arm, drowning out the music in my mind. 'Mum! What are we going to do?'

'If I had any money,' said Victoria sorrowfully, 'I'd pay for him . . . '

'So would I,' said Lucy bravely, opening her purse and showing me a two-pound coin and a few coppers.

'What are we going to do?' I repeated. 'We're going to phone your dad again, of course.'

And the hero comes striding on to the stage, sweeping aside the villain with a single sweeping aside of his velvet cloak, throwing the bags of gold on to the table with a contemptuous gesture. Money? Is that all you want? Here — take the lot. It means nothing to me. All I care about is that my Apple Pie should be set free . . . And the music reaches a crescendo as he takes the heroine into his arms . . .

'Paul? Yes, it's me. Listen, we've got a bit of a problem. I hate to ask, but could you possibly . . . Are you sure you don't mind? See you in a while, then.'

We sat down to wait, whilst Apple Pie was put back in his basket and out of our reach in case of escape attempts, and whilst the elderly lady took the elderly poodle in to have his boils lanced, and whilst the two children took the cardboard box in to have its occupant checked for lice and fleas.

'Hi, Ally DARLING! Sorry, I got here as quickly as I could!'

He'd sent Lynnette. How could he? I hated him. I'd never forgive him. How could he humiliate me like this? I looked at the floor. The girls coughed and stood up and tried to be polite.

'Paul forgot,' she trilled sweetly. 'He had to go to a meeting.'

On a Saturday? What, a race meeting, a dog meeting? A meeting of minds?

'So he asked me to come over with the cheque book. A little rescue mission!'

She giggled happily at this most insulting thing that had ever been said to me in my entire life. THE cheque book? His and hers? To rescue ME? From financial embarrassment? SHE, who'd inherited, without lifting a finger, the serious majority of the financial standing of the man I'd helped to create, whose career I'd helped to shape from the day he took his O-levels? Whose cheque book she'd effectively stolen from me?

'Thank you, but I'll manage without it. Without the rescue mission,' I retorted coldly, still looking at the floor.

37

There were drops of blood on the floor. A bitch on heat? A dog with an open wound? A cat who'd been in a fight? The elderly poodle's boils discharging? Or my heart bleeding?

'Mum!' hissed Victoria, sitting down next to me. 'Come on, we have to. Apple Pie needs . . . '

'I'll get the money somehow,' I told her fiercely, looking up at her young, anxious face. 'I'll borrow it. I'll go to the bank. I'll . . . '

'I know how you must feel,' said Lynnette, a little shakily.

'No, you don't,' I snapped.

'But I'm more than happy to help.'

I finally looked up at her face, her so-much-younger-than-me face, with its absence of worry lines and wrinkles, with its perfect make-up even on a Saturday morning, with its frame of cascading wavy red hair, its oh-so-sincere grey-green eyes with their perfect long lashes. And I wanted to smack that smug smile off her face so badly I had to sit on my hands.

'I don't need your help,' I said, firmly, loudly. So loudly that Miss White Coat came out of the consulting room at an anxious trot like a skittish pony.

'Everything all right?' she asked nervously.

38

What would she do if I went berserk right there in the waiting room? If I pulled the fire extinguisher off the wall and hurled it at Lynnette's head? If I ripped down the Pet Save poster and stamped all over the smarmy family's heads? If I smashed the glass door of the dispensary counter and threw the bottles of dog shampoo and flea treatment all round the room, all over the signs about Payment on Completion and Repeat Prescriptions, all over the display of brushes and squeaky toys and cat ticklers?

'I want to see the vet,' I said, in my new firm and loud voice. 'Now. Please.'

The vet came out of the consulting room wiping his hands on a paper towel.

'Mrs Bridgeman!' he said reasonably cheerfully, having no doubt just checked the records for my name. 'How can I help you?'

'You can help me,' I told him in my no-nonsense, don't mess with me voice, 'By NOT insisting on payment on completion.'

'Sorry?' He looked around the room for enlightenment. 'I don't think I understand . . . ?'

'I haven't got any money,' I said, in my not beating about the bush voice. 'But my husband will settle your bill. I'd just like you to send him the bill. Please.'

'Or you can give me the bill, and I'll settle

it right now,' smiled Lynnette.

'No you can't. She can't settle it.'

'Mum!' whispered Lucy. 'Don't be embarrassing.'

'Take her bloody cheque,' whispered Victoria. 'Who bloody cares?'

'I care!' I returned. 'She's not paying for our cat, and that's that.'

I forced my mind to stay on track. It was wanting badly to go off into the musical again.

'Be reasonable, Ally, darling,' said Lynnette through her teeth. 'It's the same cheque book that Paul would use if the bill was sent to us.'

'But I don't want you signing the cheque.'

'It's Dad's money,' said Victoria. 'You know it is. It's not HER money.'

No. She probably spent all hers getting her eyelashes to look like that.

'If you can't pay now,' said the vet, looking exasperated, 'I'm afraid I can't allow the cat to leave the premises.'

'Oh, Mum!' howled Lucy. 'That's not fair on Apple Pie, is it!'

'It's immoral,' I told the vet coldly. 'You can't keep him here, if he's better.'

'But you can't take him home without his drugs.'

Trump card. Ace of spades. The drugs. There they were, on the counter. I could see them. As I watched, Miss White Coat picked them up and put them in her pocket. Thanks, bitch.

'If we pay for the drugs now,' I said, my voice having somehow slipped back to its normal Quiet and Timid, 'Will you agree to bill my husband for the rest of the fees? Please?' The vet stared at me, stared at Lynnette with her perfect smile and her perfect lipstick, holding the pen poised over the cheque book, looked at White Coat, shook his head and shrugged.

'I don't see why . . . I don't understand the difference . . . '

'Nor do I,' muttered Lucy.

So perhaps I was deranged. Perhaps I was teetering on the edge of a nervous breakdown. Perhaps they ought to watch out in case I went berserk and wrecked their waiting room. But Victoria suddenly spoke up in a new firm and loud voice which she must have mysteriously inherited from me:

'It matters to my mum. It matters more than the actual money. My dad will send you the cheque straight away. So please just let us take the drugs and take our cat home.'

It was dignified. It was calm and impressive. I was impressed, anyway, and as nobody else spoke, I can only assume that they were all too choked with emotion. Lynnette wrote the cheque for the drugs, handed it over, and the package reappeared from the pocket of the white coat. Apple Pie was released into our custody. The balance of power had been retained.

'Just be careful,' warned the vet as we turned to go, 'About letting him out. Watch where he goes.'

What was this? A kidnap threat? He won't be safe till we get the money?

'Didn't my nurse explain to you?'

His nurse looked suitably shamefaced, studying her nails.

'This type of kidney failure is often caused by poisoning.'

'POISONING?'

Four loud, dramatic piano chords sounded in my head.

'DA DA DA DAH!'

The villain appeared, clutching a bottled labelled 'POISON', with a skull and cross-bones on it.

'Probably slug pellets. They're the worst. Gardeners don't realise cats pick them up. They're lethal, quite literally. He's lucky he didn't succumb.'

Succumb. Such a deceptive word. It sounds soft and sleepy, like suckle and snuggle and slumber, and it lures you unsuspectingly to a dark and dreadful death, courtesy of a slug pellet.

'I wish I knew where I could get some,' I said viciously, looking meaningfully at Lynnette as she put her cheque book — Paul's cheque book — carefully away in her handbag. Even Apple Pie shrank away from the tone of my voice.

Well, you SAY things like that, don't you. You don't necessarily mean them.

'There was no need for that, Ally,' Lynnette reproached me in a hurt After-All-I've-Done-For-You whine as we left the premises and headed for our separate cars.

'Joke,' I said, sourly.

She opened the door of her perfectly polished gleaming red Peugeot. It matched her nail varnish and lipstick exactly. What would she do when she wanted to wear a different colour nail varnish? Get a new car? She regarded me solemnly for a moment, one leg in the car, one leg out, poised like something out of a Peugeot advert. Then she shook her head as if it was all too much trouble. Not worth wasting her breath arguing. Too silly for words. After all, she'd always hold all the winning cards in this game, wouldn't she. She had the cheque book. She had Paul.

'See you, then, Ally. Bye, girls. See you on

7th June, then, if not before!'

And she was off into the distance, a whirr of red Peugeot overtaking everything in sight, whilst I stood fumbling with my car keys and fumbling with my confusion.

The silence in the car going home was punctuated only by anxious twitchings and exchanges of raised eyebrows and nudges in the back, culminating eventually in a highly obvious change of subject along the lines of:

'Well then, so anyway, what are we having for lunch?'

'What's happening on 7th June?' I snapped immediately.

'Nothing,' said Lucy.

'Don't know what she was on about,' said Victoria.

'Yes, you do. I can't believe it. Tell me it isn't true. Tell me you haven't done it. You haven't, have you? You surely to God haven't invited that . . . that . . . woman to my meal? For my birthday? My fiftieth birthday? You wouldn't, would you?'

'She must have got the wrong idea,' said Victoria desperately. 'She must have heard us talking and thought she was invited.'

'Well, you'd better relieve her of any wrong ideas she's harbouring, and pretty quickly. You'd better make it plain she's not invited anywhere, any time, to anything to do with

44

me and certainly not to my bloody birthday, because if she's going to be there, I'm not.'

I looked in the mirror at the two stricken faces behind me and softened slightly.

'Is that OK?'

'Yes,' said Victoria quietly.

'Yes,' said Lucy in a whisper.

'Fucking hell,' I heard Victoria add to Lucy under her breath.

* * *

I had a couple of good friends at work. They weren't all like Snotty-Nosed Nicola and her admiring posse of hangers-on, thank God. Liz, who worked in the same office as me, was only a couple of years younger than me, and Mary, who worked in accounts and usually had lunch with us, had celebrated her own half-century a few years previously. So it was inevitable that conversation occasionally turned towards the ageing process and its effect on our physical and emotional health. Whether we were on the verge of collapse or not. Whether we'd survive to see our pensions and whether they'd be worth anything by the time we did. The usual cheerful, life-enhancing sort of discussions you have to cheer you up during a depressing day at work.

'When I had my fiftieth,' said Mary over lasagne and chips a few days later, 'Derek took me to New York.'

Liz and I regarded each other dismally over the vinegar bottle. Like I say, she was a nice person, was Mary. It wasn't her fault her Derek got on our bloody nerves without us even having met him.

'We flew Concorde,' she added, her eyes lighting up at the memory of it.

'Lovely.'

'And we saw Michael Bolton in concert.'

Ah well. Can't win 'em all.

'I'd like that,' I mused, toying with my chips. 'I'd like to jet off somewhere . . . with someone . . . '

'Well, you never know . . . ' tried Liz gently.

Oh, I do, I do. Unfortunately I know all too well.

' . . . and never come back!' I said, smiling triumphantly as if I'd just made a serious decision. 'I'd jet off somewhere, if I could, and never come back!'

'What about your kids?' asked Liz.

She looked anxious. Her kids were still at the age where leaving them would make you feel anxious.

'Mine are grown-up,' I sighed. 'They wouldn't miss me.'

'Not till the money ran out!' laughed Mary.

'Then they'd have to cope.'

Was this really me talking? Being so harsh and uncaring? But it was true, wasn't it! At their age, I was Fending For Myself. Standing On My Own Two Feet. My home was obviously too comfortable for them, with its stereo CD-players and volumising hair-dryers and no ice on the insides of the windows. Why would they want to go and stand on their own two feet somewhere less comfortable? Why would they want to learn to cook, or load a dishwasher? No, the obvious solution would be for me to leave them where they were, and jet off somewhere myself.

'What are you grinning about?' asked Liz, still sounding anxious.

'The more I think about it, the better it sounds,' I said, sauce dripping off the chip which hung, forgotten, from my fork. 'I could come back and see them whenever I wanted. By private jet.'

'Or helicopter,' smiled Mary, getting into the game.

'And I'd invite them out there occasionally. Whenever I had a big party.'

'Banquet,' Mary corrected me.

'Ball,' I said firmly. 'I always fancied a ball. A ball with a banquet.'

'Never mind, Ally,' said Liz in her usual

gentle way. 'I'm sure your party will be just as nice.'

There was a silence that lasted probably only about ten seconds. For about as long as it takes for a chip to fall off a fork. About as long as it takes for a splodge of sauce to land on the table. Roughly about as long as it takes for two people to gasp and look at each other in a way that very definitely says 'Oh shit!' without actually saying it.

'I'm not having a party,' I said.

'No. But if you did. If you did, it would be nice.'

'But I don't even want a party.'

'No, no, but if you did want one, it would be a nice one.'

'It wouldn't, though. It wouldn't be nice, because I wouldn't want it, so I wouldn't enjoy it.'

'Well, then!' said Mary in a very hearty tone. 'Good job you're not having one, isn't it!'

'Yes,' I said, looking at her suspiciously, resentfully. I had this unhappy, niggly feeling that I was being taken the piss out of.

'So what ARE you doing, for your fiftieth, then, Ally?' soothed Liz. 'Something nice?'

With all this niceness around, I was beginning to feel a little sick. I thought about the 'nice' birthday meal the girls were supposedly organising for me, with my mother apparently taking pride of place and gloating about it already, and my husband's mistress presuming she was invited and expecting me to welcome her with open arms and a prawn cocktail, and something suddenly came over me. Whose bloody birthday was this, after all?

'Nothing,' I said, firmly and cheerfully. 'I'm not doing anything.'

'Oh, really?' said Liz. 'Why? Why nothing at all?'

'Because,' I said, suddenly finding an interest in my chips again, 'I'm not going to be fifty. Not till next year. I'm only forty-nine this birthday!'

And that was the first lie.

★ ★ ★

I read somewhere once that the first lie is the hardest; after that it gets easier and easier. I didn't murder that man. I didn't pull the trigger and I didn't put the gun against his head. I didn't put his body in a black sack and I didn't drop it in the Thames. I didn't steal his passport and take on his identity, forge his signature, use his credit card to buy up all the ammunition in the world and I didn't start World War Three. One lie leads to another. Once you start, you have to go on and on. I didn't mean to fall in love with another woman. I didn't mean to keep seeing her when I knew I should have stopped. I didn't want it to happen. I didn't intend to have sex with her, even though she was twenty years younger than you and had beautiful red wavy hair and grey-green eyes and was offering herself to me on a plate like a cheap tart. I tried to stop it. I tried to say no. I tried to think of you and the children, the cat, the fish-pond. I didn't want to leave you. I didn't mean . . . I didn't want . . . I loved you . . .

Lies, lies, lies. So easy. I didn't find the first lie hard at all, because I just said it without thinking about it. It didn't seem such a terrible thing to say. It didn't really matter at all. Who cared? Who really cared whether I was fifty, or forty-nine, or a hundred and one that birthday, that June the fifth?

It just made the next lie a little bit easier, that was all.

★   ★   ★

In the backstage of my life, people were tearing around like blue-arsed flies, making phone calls, exchanging gasps and exclamations, cancelling things. Cancelling parties.

50

Me, I sailed on blissfully unaware, well perhaps not blissfully but you get the picture. Giving the cat his drugs and trying to watch where he went in case he picked up slug pellets from some inconsiderate gardener's vegetable patch, feeding people and listening to their problems, tying the number plate on to the rear bumper of the car and tying it back again when it fell off, and so on, and so on. And it was getting warmer again, and there was less wearing of double layers of dressing gowns and more opening of windows, and April drifted into May with sunshine and short sleeves and diets in the house in order to get into bikinis for the summer, and it was at least a couple of weeks before I got the phone call from Paul.

'Ally, what the bloody hell's going on?'

You tell me.

'About what, in particular?'

'Your birthday. What are you playing at? You're fifty this year.'

'I know. I can't help it.' Well, he made it sound like an accusation. 'YOU were fifty, three years ago.'

'We're not disputing MY age, here. What is it? Are you afraid of admitting it, or something? Have you got a problem with it?'

'Of course I haven't. What do you take me

51

for? I don't have to try and compete with your young . . . '

'Don't start that.'

I didn't. I didn't start it, actually. You did, when you went off with her. When you shagged her. When you loved her, and stopped loving me.

'You've been telling people. I've just heard about it. You've been saying you're not fifty till next year.'

Oh. The Lie had caught up with me. But how?

'How? How did you hear that?'

'Never mind. The fact is . . . '

'No, I do mind. I don't understand. It was only two girls at work, going on and on about fiftieth birthdays, and I decided to shut them up by telling them I wasn't going to be fifty. I was bored with the conversation. Who the hell told you?'

'Victoria did. She's worried about you.'

Could have fooled me. She'd been out in her car with her latest boyfriend every night for the past week. I'd only seen her in passing when she ate two lettuce leaves from the fridge on her way to the bathroom to weigh herself.

'How did SHE know?'

'Doesn't matter. The fact is . . . '

'Don't keep saying what the fact is! It

DOES matter how she knows! What's all this snooping and spying and whispering and nudging going on?'

I'd only just remembered about the whispering and nudging. Now I suddenly felt frightened and isolated and talked-about. What were they hiding from me? Was I going to die?

'Am I going to die, or something?' I burst out with a touch of drama for Paul's benefit.

If I was going to die, he could bloody well suffer. He'd have to come round and help look after me, and he'd cry and beg my forgiveness and promise never to look at Lynn (ette) again, and feel guilty for the rest of his life because it was his fault that I got ill, and . . .

'Ally! Ally, are you listening to me?'

'What have I got? Tell me straight, I can take it.'

'Ally, people turn fifty every day. It's no big deal. It's not old, nowadays, in fact it's the beginning of a whole new era. It's not a decline into old age, or . . . '

'Who do you think you're talking to, you patronising git?!'

Well, honestly! Well! Fucking cheek!

'The girls and I are worried about you. Seriously. You seem to be in denial.'

'No I'm not!'

'See what I mean? Now, listen. We've cancelled the party. Fine, if you didn't want the party, in the frame of mind you're in, it's better if it's cancelled, but . . . '

'Party?' I said in a small voice.

'But you do really need to face up to this. This birthday. You can't spend the rest of your life running away, pretending . . . '

'I wasn't. I didn't know . . . '

'And while I'm at it: I know you're under a bit of a strain, but there was no need to speak to Lynnette the way you did.'

'Sorry?'

'The other weekend. At the vet's. She very generously offered to come and help you out with the cat . . . '

With your cheque book.

'And you caused a terrible scene in the waiting room, apparently. Embarrassed everyone. And threatened to get some slug pellets to poison her.'

'It was a joke,' I said, still in my little, dazed voice. Like a child being unexpectedly told off despite being good all day. I could feel tears pricking at my eyes. Were you supposed to cry when you were told off when you were nearly fifty? Nearly fifty but perhaps in denial (perhaps not)?

'Not funny, Ally. Remember what we used to tell the children? It's only a joke if

54

everybody's laughing. Lynnette wasn't laughing.'

No, well. She's a miserable, boring fucking cow with no sense of humour, but I didn't choose her as a mistress, did I?

He waited for me to say sorry. I could tell that was what he was waiting for. He used to do it when Victoria or Lucy had scribbled on the newspaper, drawing moustaches on the prime minister's face and blobs of poo dropping from the backsides of anyone whose backsides were in the photographs. He never used to ASK them to say sorry. He just sat there with the paper open on his lap, with the felt-tip moustaches and poos in front of him, and looked at them with that 'Well?' look until they said sorry. Sorry for making the prime minister look a prat and the Queen look as if she's got diarrhoea. Bringing down the tone of the nation. Sorry, sorry, sorry. Sorry for scaring your precious little tender flower of a mistress with talk of slug pellets.

'I'm not going to apologise,' I said, suddenly shaking myself out of my role of the naughty child and stamping my foot to match. 'It's about time she bloody grew up and learned to take a joke. And stopped using your cheque book.'

'It's OUR cheque book,' he said, coldly. I didn't like it. I didn't like that cold.

I'd apologise if necessary, to get rid of the sound of that cold.

'And it's about time YOU stopped being so jealous and spiteful, and tried to accept Lynnette as a friend,' he went on. 'I really think you need some counselling! Or something! You're fifty, Ally! Face it!'

And he hung up.

He hung up!

I stared at the phone, trembling just a little bit in the foot I'd just stamped.

It was such a surprise.

We never argued, normally, not even since we'd separated. We'd been Amicable. Reasonable. Sensible. We'd agreed it was Better Like That. But was it? Who was I trying to fool? What hidden anger and hatred lurked beneath the surface of that reasonableness, that sensibleness? Perhaps I really did need some counselling. Perhaps I really was cracking up.

And anyway. What was all that about a party?

3

'What's all this about a party?' I asked Lucy when she sloped downstairs later to refuel with more crisps and Coke for some serious exam revision.

'It was supposed to be a surprise,' she shrugged.

'Sorry,' I said. 'I didn't realise . . . you must have gone to a lot of trouble . . . '

'Doesn't matter, Mum,' she shrugged again, looking in the fridge as if for inspiration. Then she turned to look at me with sudden renewed interest. 'But are you all right?'

'All right, how?'

'Dad thinks you're in denial and you need counselling.'

'Oh. Nice of him to tell you. I suppose the whole world thinks I've flipped my lid, just because I didn't want everyone going on and on and on about being fifty?'

'Well, women are suppose to start getting a bit strange at your age, aren't they?' she replied affably, turning her attention back to the fridge with the lack of concern it's only possible to display about such a statement at the age of nineteen.

* ★ *

I looked at myself from all angles in the mirror. Put the light on and did it again. Held in my stomach and bum and tried a final twirl. That made my boobs stick out unnaturally and also made me go red in the face from holding my breath, so I let it all flop again and tried it with my hands on my hips like I'd seen the daughters doing. Nothing wrong with me, nothing that a good diet, a course of strenuous aerobics and a complete new wardrobe couldn't cure. Did I LOOK fifty? How was fifty supposed to look, nowadays? Not like my mother looked at fifty, long tired dresses, matronly coats and cardis, sensible shoes and no life outside the kitchen. An apron over everything. So should I throw caution to the wind, my skirts over my head and go out clubbing, wearing little bra tops like Lucy? People said you could do what you liked nowadays at fifty. But what did I want to do? What did I want out of the rest of my life? And why was I standing here on my own in my bedroom staring at myself in the mirror?

Fifty hadn't been an issue in my life. I hadn't given it any thought, hadn't lost any sleep over it, hadn't considered it any different from forty-eight or forty-nine — until Paul accused me of being in denial.

Now I'd suddenly started obsessing about it. If I wasn't careful, I'd be booking my own counselling.

★ ★ ★

'Selfish, I call it,' declared my mother, filling up my kettle from my sink to make herself a cup of my tea. Without offering me one.

'I'm sorry that's how you see it,' I sighed. It really wasn't worth arguing with her. I'd learned that much, if nothing else in my life since I left school.

'Everyone was looking forward to it,' she said, slamming down the kettle and plugging it in with vicious energy. Amazing how a bit of temper improved the arthritis in her hands.

'You could have gone ahead with it. I didn't ask anyone to cancel it. I didn't even know about it,' I pointed out reasonably.

'All that fuss about Lynnette coming,' she sniffed.

'Have a party for HER, then,' I retorted, 'if you want a party so much. It must be her eighteenth birthday coming up any day now.'

'Jealousy,' she pronounced, wagging a finger at me, 'will get you nowhere.'

Oh, God. If only I'd realised that, it would have made all the difference. I'd have been this wonderfully un-jealous person, beaming with pleasure at my husband's new young mistress, kissing her on the cheek and wishing her all the best in her future life with him, hoping the sex was better than I remembered it and that he didn't leave the toilet too bad too often.

'I'll have a cup of tea, too, please, while you're at it,' I said instead, trying to balance the washing basket on one hip whilst putting the Sunday joint in the oven on the way to the washing machine, pushing a dropped potato out of the cat's reach with one foot, performing a tap-dance and singing a solo.

'Expect me to do it all!' tutted my mother irritably, slamming another mug on to the table and manhandling the kettle again. 'At my age!'

Perhaps I'd rather be nearly eighty than nearly fifty (in denial)?

★ ★ ★

It was over Sunday dinner that she announced she was going away. It was done at the moment of everyone's first mouthful, for maximum effect. Well, get stuck in everybody; mmm, looks lovely doesn't it; got enough mint sauce, Nan? What's that you say? You're going where?

'Majorca.'

'You have to get a plane, Nan. Or a boat,' pointed out Victoria. 'It's an island.'

'Don't try to be clever, Miss. I do know what I'm doing. I wasn't born yesterday.'

Not by a long shot, no.

MAJORCA? She'd never been further than the Isle of Wight as far as I could remember.

'Have you got a passport?' I asked, genuinely interested. She looked at me as if I was no better than Victoria but then again she'd expected nothing more from me.

'I got one for France,' she said. 'Didn't I.'

Oh, yes. I remembered now. How could I forget? We'd taken her to Calais once because she wanted to buy cheap wine like she'd heard her cronies at the retirement club talking about. It had been eventful. She'd felt ill on the ferry, complained about Paul's driving ('Don't let these foreigners overtake you, boy! What's the matter with you? Can't you go any faster? You've got your GB plates on, haven't you? They can see you're British! They should give way to you!'), and then embarrassed us so much in the hypermarket by talking to the shop assistants in very loud, very slow English and telling them off if they replied in French that we ended up buying nothing for ourselves and rushing her away as fast as we could with her trolley-load of

GERMAN wine ('Can't stand that French muck'). 'Never again,' said Paul about five thousand times on the way home. I shuddered now to think of the fate awaiting the poor Majorcans.

'Who are you going with, Nan?' asked Lucy brightly.

'A friend,' said my mother enigmatically.

She stuffed a huge piece of roast lamb into her mouth and chewed quickly, concentrating on her plate.

'What friend?' persisted Lucy.

'Never you mind.'

The girls and I looked at each other across the table. My mother continued to chew her lamb, looking at her plate. Lucy raised her eyebrows and Victoria stifled a giggle. I threw down my knife and fork. I couldn't help it. It was such a shock.

'It's a man, isn't it!'

'So? So why shouldn't it be? So what's wrong with a person having a holiday with a friend?' she gabbled, spitting gravy all over the tablecloth. 'Unless of course you want to deprive me of every last little pleasure I'm likely to get in this life . . . '

Lucy and Victoria were by now convulsed.

'Of course there's nothing wrong with it,' I soothed. 'Nobody's trying to spoil your . . . pleasure . . . '

I hadn't even realised I was going to start laughing. It was the girls, falling off their chairs giggling like that, setting me off. It was the word 'pleasure'. It suddenly reminded me of giving Victoria The Lecture, the first time she went away with a boyfriend. Should I be talking to my mother about Safe Sex? Should I ask her whether she'd booked single rooms, the way she used to ask me when I went away with Paul? Ha! What goes around, comes around!

'Well, I'm sure I don't know what's so funny!' she snapped, a bit red in the face, a bit flustered.

Lucy was almost crying, holding her sides, gasping for breath.

'Nan's getting more nooky than I am!' she said eventually. 'Where's the fairness . . . ?'

'Lucy!' I hissed at her nervously, trying not to start laughing again myself. 'Nobody's talking about nooky . . . '

'His names's NOT Nicky,' declared my mother, laying down her knife and fork and sitting up straight, looking at us all severely over her glasses. 'It's Ted.'

Lucy pretended to need the toilet, but didn't manage to get there before the scream of manic laughter burst out of her every orifice. Victoria calmly collected the dinner plates (not finished) and made it into the

63

kitchen before giving into spluttering noises which she tried to drown by running the taps.

'So how long have you known this . . . Ted?' I asked Mother in the dignified silence that followed.

'A year or so,' she replied defensively.

'And how old is he?'

And what are his prospects? And what do his parents do?

'He's sixty-six, if it's got anything to do with you.'

A toy-boy! Christ, the lucky old bitch. Let's hope he managed to put a smile on that sour old face.

'Well, good for you,' I said eventually, meaning it, really meaning it. Good for her. Why the hell not? 'When are you going?'

'Friday. And we'll be needing a lift to the airport. Ted can't drive. He's got cataracts.'

I nearly found myself thinking that that explained a lot. But I couldn't be so nasty as to think that, could I.

★ ★ ★

On the Tuesday night, Apple Pie went missing.

'He hasn't had his evening tablet,' said Victoria, staring dismally out of the back door.

64

There comes a time in your life when you really, really wish you hadn't given your cat a silly name.

'Apple Pie!' I shouted in the middle of the garden at midnight, prowling around the shrubbery with a torch. 'Apple Pie! Come on, Apple Pie, where are you?'

'Good boy, Appley! Come on, Apples, good boy!' echoed Lucy plaintively.

'Mum, how COULD you?' accused Victoria, close to tears, when two o'clock struck with no sign of the cat and I announced that I was calling off the search until first light and going to get some sleep. 'He could be ANYwhere . . . '

'He's probably asleep,' I yawned. 'Asleep somewhere nice and snug and warm, and can't even hear us shouting. When we get up in the morning he'll be lying in his bed large as life . . . '

'And going into kidney failure!' moaned Lucy. 'He hasn't had his tablet!'

'Missing one dose isn't going to hurt him,' I said with more confidence than I felt. 'Now come on, we'll all be better able to help him when we're not so tired . . . '

Still moaning and sniffing back tears, the girls allowed themselves to be shepherded up to bed as if they were still eight and ten years old. I tucked them in and kissed them goodnight as if they were still eight and ten years old. They protested that they'd never be able to sleep a wink, they were so upset and worried about Apple Pie, and then they both fell immediately into a deep and untroubled sleep — as if they were still eight and ten years old. I, meanwhile, lay on top of my bed in my clothes (just in case I should hear him miaowing or crying in the garden), and tossed, and turned, and turned, and tossed, and put on the light, and turned it off again, and drifted once or twice into a fitful doze, waking in a cold sweat wondering what Paul would say if the cat was dead, or whether we could buy another kitten the same as Apple Pie and whether the girls would ever accept it, and eventually, at five o'clock, I got up and went back downstairs to reassure myself that he was indeed curled up in his bed looking at me with one eye open, so that I could get an hour of real, anxiety-free sleep before the alarm went off. But he wasn't. No cat, curled up or otherwise, one eye open or otherwise. No cat at all.

Five o'clock in the morning is not a good time to be out in the garden whispering 'Apple Pie' as loudly as you can whisper. I'm sure there are people who advocate early rising, who would extol the virtue of a stroll in the garden on a fresh May morning, the dew glistening on the grass, the sun slowly warming the air and the birds tweeting their irritating little songs at each other. Me, I bloody hated it. Dawn is a time for turning over and going back to sleep, for looking with relief at the clock and sighing as you realise you've got another hour in bed yet. It's not a time for being out and about unless you're some sort of pervert or unless you're still on your way home from the night before, in which case you're likely to be too pissed to notice it at all.

'Apples!' I hissed, nearly stumbling into the fish-pond in my semi-stupor. 'Stop sodding about, you stupid cat! Where are you?'

Fish-pond. I stared into its gloomy depths, suddenly filled with a dread that woke me almost right up. A large orange fish stared back at me, wondering about its breakfast.

'Have you seen the cat?' I whispered to it. 'Big, furry, black and white thing?'

The fish blew a raspberry at me and swum off.

★   ★   ★

'Perhaps we should search the pond,' I said at breakfast (a gloomy affair of not much cornflakes and more than normal coffee). I tried to say it gently. But it had to be said.

67

Once that fish had looked at me like that, I felt it had to be said.

'Oh, Mum!' howled Lucy. 'How could you? What are you saying?'

'I'm not SAYing anything,' I tried to pacify her. She shook off my pacifying arm. 'I just think we should reassure ourselves . . . '

'Mum's right,' said Victoria stoutly. 'We shouldn't leave any stone unturned, Lucy. Come on, Luce!' She tried a bit of pacifying herself. 'We'll find him!'

'What, at the bottom of the pond?' shuddered Lucy.

I shuddered myself. I swallowed a lump of tears down quickly with my coffee. I loved the damned cat too, you know.

★　★　★

By the time we'd got all of the water out of the pond, we'd blamed everyone. It was Paul's fault for having a fish-pond. It was my fault for not filling it in after he moved out. It was the fishes' fault for living so long, for needing a pond to carry on their lives in. It was my mother's fault for always saying how nice it was to see a pond in a garden, in that tone of voice that implied that Paul had more taste, more sophistication, more savoir-faire and interest in fish-ponds than I'd ever have.

It was Lucy's fault for not calling Apple Pie in for his evening tablet earlier, before it got dark. It was Victoria's fault for going out for the evening when it was supposed to be her turn to call him in for his evening tablet.

'Turn?' I asked in amazement, emptying another bucket of slimy water and wiping the sweat off my face. 'You have TURNS at calling in the cat?'

I tell you, you don't even know what goes on in your own house. The hierarchy, the politics, the administrative organisation. The rotas for putting out the rubbish, the sanctions applied for failure to apply new toilet rolls, the distribution of Tampax purchase responsibility, the rostering of cat-calling.

'I think,' said Victoria, stepping gingerly down into the murky, weedy shallows remaining sadly at the bottom of the pond, 'we can see now, can't we.'

We all followed her gaze as she stirred the water uneasily from side to side with a net.

'Nothing,' she said, and her voice came out squeakily with relief. And none of us could talk for a few minutes as our ghastly, unspoken fears retreated to the nightmare zones of our minds. 'Empty,' she said more firmly, smiling now. 'Apart from this.'

She fished out a Rubik's Cube, thrown in

there during a fit of temper by Lucy during the Rubik's Cube craze days, and swiftly forgotten. Lucy blushed and laughed. Then we all fell silent again as we contemplated the fish (flicking their tails angrily in the kitchen sink full of water) and the empty pond (now needing a fast refill), and more to the point, we contemplated, without any of us wanting to voice it to the others, the fact that it was now mid-morning and if Apple Pie wasn't in the pond then where was he?

And then the phone rang, and we all became aware that mid-morning on a Wednesday, we were supposed to be else-where.

'That'll be my work!' exclaimed Victoria as I went to answer it. 'Tell them I'm sick!'

But, of course, it wasn't her work. It was mine. It was Snotty-Nosed Simon, Simon who controlled my life, who had entered my Serious Warning on to my Personal Record, who would never understand about draining a pond to look for a cat, never in a million years.

'I'm sorry, Simon,' I said. 'I'm sick.'

That was the second lie. It was amazing how easy it was. Like I'd been born to it, like I was lying every day of my life. I didn't even feel any shame, any regret. Oh, I don't doubt Victoria did it, probably every time she fancied a lie-in she had the flu or an upset stomach. But let me tell you, she hadn't been brought up to it, and no, neither had I. Much less had I! I'd been to Sunday School in my time, you know, and there had sat in a pew at the back of a cold church on a Sunday afternoon (which was where I met Paul, you might be surprised to know, and disliked him intensely at the time on account of his too-long short trousers), and learned by heart the perils of lying, of stealing, of cheating in exams and using dirty words. I didn't even know any dirty words until I moved up to Senior Sunday School and had them pointed out to me in the Bible by a fat boy called Graham who also asked to look inside my knickers. I've often wondered what became of him. But this is all by the way. The fact is, I seemed almost overnight to have become an accomplished liar.

'Oh, dear,' said Simon, sounding unconvinced and not a little bored. 'What seems to be the trouble?'

'Sickness,' I said, vaguely. 'Bad, really bad sickness. I'd better go, I think I'm going to be sick again.'

'Well, I hope you feel better . . . '

I hung up, doing a good impression of someone just about to be sick again.

We all went sick that day. Victoria invented

a sore throat and Lucy, who was only supposed to be in college for the morning anyway, said she'd think of her excuse when she went back the next day. We searched the shed. We searched the house, opening cupboard doors and throwing out their contents on the floor. We crawled under beds, we peered up chimneys, we even climbed halfway up the apple-tree. Well, Lucy did. I held the tree for her. We walked the streets, calling out 'Apple Pie' dismally and gloomily and ignoring the looks we got from passers-by, who probably thought we were homeless and hungry.

Finally Victoria said she'd drive around in her car with the windows down and Lucy said she'd go with her and lean out of the windows looking. They went to the car and discovered the windows to be already open. And Apple Pie asleep on the back seat.

'You must have left the windows open when you got home last night!' Lucy shouted at her sister, inexplicably bursting into tears as she lunged at the surprised cat and grasped him fiercely to her chest. He hung awkwardly in her arms, blinking in the sunlight, half-strangled by the tightness of her embrace. 'Poor baby!' she moaned, burying her face in his fur.

'Poor baby, nothing!' I retorted, suddenly

tired and exasperated by the whole episode now that he'd turned up safe. 'He hasn't been shut in there against his will! He probably crept in there during the night when it was cold and he's been lying there ever since, all the time we've been calling and hollering for him! He's just bloody ignored us! All that work draining the pond . . . '

'Mum!' rebuked Victoria. 'Suppose he HAD been in there!'

I'd been supposing it all the time we were emptying it, thanks very much. To say nothing of supposing him lying in a ditch somewhere, or having been hit by a car, or having swallowed some more slug pellets.

'Yes. Well. He wasn't, was he,' I snapped.

It was late in the afternoon and not worth going back to work. I cleaned the oven.

★   ★   ★

The car didn't want to start the next morning. I reminded it, firmly but kindly, of all I'd done for it recently. All Paul had spent on it. How it had embarrassed me in front of the AA man and I'd still loved it. I promised it faithfully that if it would stop sulking, I'd get its bumper fixed as soon as I had time, and money, and furthermore I would get its rear number plate fitted on properly. I did understand how an old bit of string could make a car feel less than its best. I just needed it to start today. Please. Please! When it still wouldn't start, I got out, slammed its door and swore at it. It could wear its number plate tied on with bits of string for the rest of its life for all I cared! Bloody thing!

'What's up, Mum?' asked Victoria sweetly, tottering out to her own car in high heels that it was impossible to imagine her driving in. How could you put your foot down on a pedal when your foot was six inches above the floor?

'Bloody car won't start. Again,' I muttered. 'And if I call out the AA it'll make a fool of me. I just know it. And it'll probably be the same guy.'

'What was he like? Nice?' she asked, hesitating. You could see the antennae coming out. Man alert! Was it worth her hanging around to do some chatting up?

'Old. At least fifty!' I smiled.

She pulled a face and opened the car door.

'Give me a lift to work?' I asked.

'All right. Hurry up.'

I grabbed my jacket and rushed to get into the car before she changed her mind.

'Although . . .'

Here we go. I've got to go the other way. I've got to pick up five friends . . .

74

'. . . Why don't you stay off work and get it sorted out, while you've got the chance?'

'Stay off work?! You must be joking?' I tried to keep the hysteria out of my voice. 'I might as well phone up Simon and ask him to sack me. I might as well say I've decided I don't need a job any more . . .'

'But he thinks you're sick.'

So he did.

'You could still be sick.'

So I could.

I paused, halfway to sitting down in Victoria's car.

'Make up your mind, Mum. I've got to get to work.'

I got out and waved her goodbye. And in a way, that was the third lie, although I didn't actually say anything. I just pretended, inside my head, that I was still sick. And I called AA Home Start (it was a different guy, and he was actually about twenty-five and very good-looking. Eat your heart out, Victoria!) — and he jump-started the bastard and we got it to a garage. And they said Leave It With Us and we'll put the number plate on for nothing. We'll See What We Can Do (with much head-scratching and wiping of hands on oily rags) about having it ready for tomorrow morning — can't promise, love, depends what we find when we get under the bonnet, know what I mean love? And I walked home from the garage and thought about everyone at work, managing without me, and I felt as if I was on holiday. I swung my arms, I held my head back to feel the sunshine on my face, and I laughed out loud. A boy on a bike stared at me and nearly fell off, and an elderly woman tutted and shook her head and said something about drug addicts, which made me laugh even more. Her scowl reminded me of my mum.

My mum.

Shit, shit and thrice shit. She needed a lift to the airport tomorrow. She and her half-blind toy-boy and their baggage for Majorca. I stopped dead in the street, upsetting a few more pedestrians, and wondered about going back to the garage and telling them I had to have the bastard car back for the morning, working or not. Then I told myself to calm down and talk sense. What good would it be if it wasn't working? There was only one thing for it.

'Victoria? Yes, it's Mum. No, nothing's wrong. Yes, the AA man came. No, he wasn't fifty, he was young and gorgeous and I've got a date with him for tomorrow night. I don't know why, he must just like older women. Yeh, we snogged in the back of the car. Mmm, lovely. Listen, Victoria, darling

. . . What do you mean, what am I after? Look, can you get the day off work tomorrow?'

Oh, typical. I see. Just bloody typical. Tomorrow is the day she happens to have booked a day off anyway, to go out for the day with the new Darren in her life.

'Why tomorrow?' I pleaded. 'Can't you do that another day? I need you tomorrow . . . '

It had to be tomorrow, apparently, because it was the second anniversary of Victoria and the new Darren going out together. Second anniversary as in two weeks.

'Can't you go for a nice drive together to Gatwick Airport? With Nan and her boy-friend?'

'I LIKE Darren,' said Victoria pointedly.

'Can't you go out in his car?' (and I can borrow yours).

'He hasn't got one.'

'Don't you ever wonder whether some of these boys are only after you for your car?'

'Why do you think I love my car so much?'

Can't argue with that one, can you.

★   ★   ★

I phoned Paul in the evening, after I'd checked with the garage about the state of my car.

'They say it MIGHT be ready,' I explained to him after we'd got over the initial slight coldness in the conversation caused by him hanging up on me last time we talked. We got over it by me being very pathetic and creepy and apologetic. Blaming it all on hormones, which I hate to do. But the thing was, I was after something, wasn't I. 'But I have to leave at nine-thirty to get Mum to the airport. And if it's NOT ready . . .'

'She'll kill you.'

'You know her well.'

'Ally, I don't know. I don't know if I can take the time off work at such short notice.'

Work? Work! Bloody hell, I'd forgotten about that. Two days off, two unofficial, LYING days off, and I was acting as if I'd retired. What was the matter with me? Did I WANT to get the sack? I felt weak and jittery at the thought of it. Perhaps I really WAS ill.

'I'm ill!' I told Paul, interrupting him in the middle of his long spiel about why it was difficult for him to take time off work at short notice in May, particularly near the end of May, and most particularly on a Friday, even more particularly when there was a Bank Holiday coming up soon . . .

'What?' He sounded alarmed, to be fair to him. I was quite pleased to think he would sound alarmed about me being ill.

'It's not anything serious,' I added quickly. I was going to go on to add that it was so NOT serious, it was non-existent. It was a non-illness, a made-up illness, an illness of the fictitious degree. But something came over me. Something to do with the gratification it gave me to hear him sounding alarmed. Something that invented a little scenario in my head of me lying in bed, thin and ill, pale and weak, with the covers pulled up to my chin and lots of bottles of medicine on the bedside table, and Paul sitting next to me holding my hand and looking alarmed as the doctor warned him not to tire me . . .

'It's probably just . . . some virus or other . . . ' I said vaguely, trying to make my voice sound weak without the deterioration into weakness sounding too sudden and obvious.

'Have you been to the doctor?'

'No . . . no need for that. I don't want to make a fuss.' Oh, it sounded weak now all right. I knew it did. I was getting into the part. And well into the Fourth Lie, of course, although I hadn't even stopped to think about it.

'Well, I think you should. I really do think . . . '

OK, enough was enough.

'I'll see how it goes,' I said.

'Well, you should have said. You should have said you were ill. You can't possibly drive your mother to the airport, car or no car!' Bit difficult without the car, actually.

'You're not to even consider it.'

Yes! Result! He'd take the day off, even if it was a Friday near the end of May.

'I'll ask Lynnette. She won't mind. She's only part-time.'

Lynnette? Lynnette, driving my mother and her heart-throb to the airport? Could I inflict that on her? Could I, come to think of it, inflict them on each other? Could I?! By Christ, I was going to enjoy it!!

'Well . . . ' I said in my little weak, ill voice. 'Only if you're absolutely sure she really won't mind . . . '

'Mind? Of course she won't mind,' said Paul firmly. 'If only you'd give her a chance, Ally, you'd realise what a very generous, kind person Lynnette is.'

Which, of course, is why you shagged her, nothing to do with her being twenty years younger than you and slim and pretty with those eyes and that hair . . .

'And how much she wants the two of you to be friends.'

Come into my parlour, said the spider to the fly.

The spider's mother was about to eat the pretty little fly alive, chew her up and spit her out again. I almost wished I was going with them to watch. But I was ill, wasn't I.

★ ★ ★

'I don't think it's anything serious,' I told Snotty-Nosed Nicola, who was answering Simon's calls as he was probably too busy practising his golf swings in his office. 'Probably some sort of virus.'

Not really Lie Number Five. Just a repetition of Lie Number Four, to a different person. Actually it was beginning to feel as if it was true. I was beginning to sort-of grow into it, like putting on a coat that belongs to someone else and gradually getting used to it, feeling like you own it, and wanting to keep it.

'Perhaps it's your hormones,' said Snotty Bloody Cow Nicola, with a sneer in her voice.

'I don't think so,' I returned coldly.

'But that's what happens, isn't it,' she persisted. 'Women of your age . . . when you get to FIFTY . . . start having problems . . .'

'I'm NOT getting to be fifty,' I said, wanting to smack her one. 'I'm getting to be forty-nine, actually.'

Not really another lie. This one was just a

81

repetition of Lie Number One, and necessary if I wasn't to lose face amongst my colleagues. If you're going to lie, you have to be consistent. Ask me, I was beginning to be an expert.

'Well, whatever,' said Nicola, sounding flustered, or perhaps she just had another call waiting, 'Whatever, you need to get a certificate.'

'Sorry?'

A certificate proving my age? My BIRTH certificate?

'Sickness! Sickness certificate! You've had three days off!'

So I had. Bloody hell, I must really be ill.

'Get your certificate, send it in, or you won't get paid.'

End of conversation. End of joke. This wasn't funny any more. I'd have to lie to the doctor now.

★　★　★

'Paul says you MUST go to the doctor. Today.'

'I know, I know. I'm going.'

I'd made an appointment for five o'clock. Only because of the wretched certificate. And I'd only invited wretched Lynnette into my house because I wanted to hear how it went with my mother. Come into my parlour . . .

'Sit down, Ally. You're not well.'

'It's all right. I'll make you a coffee,' I said ungraciously. 'How did it go with my mother?'

She sat down at the kitchen table. I was pleased to say she looked worn out. Ha! The old girl must have given her a bad time.

'Fine,' she said. 'She's a dear, isn't she?'

A dear? That wasn't exactly the first word that sprang to mind when I came to describe her, no.

'And Ted!' she smiled. 'Such a sweetie! So funny! They're so cute together! All the way to Gatwick they were snuggled up together in the back of my car, holding hands, laughing at little jokes together . . .'

Now I really did feel sick.

'Laughing?' I echoed bleakly. 'My mother, laughing?'

'It must be love,' she smiled knowingly, taking the mug of coffee I passed her and stirring it thoughtfully. 'They looked . . . just the way Paul and I look at each other.'

I watched her stirring the coffee and took great comfort from imagining I'd dropped a couple of slug pellets into it.

'I've put poison in that,' I said viciously, turning away. 'So perhaps you'd better go now. Before you start throwing up. I've just washed the floor.'

'Ally!' she spluttered, spraying coffee over the table. And some specks on her little-girl-pink blouse. What a shame. 'Ally, I wish you wouldn't BE like this. It isn't funny.'

Wasn't meant to be.

'It's hurtful.'

Don't talk to me about hurtful. I KNOW hurtful. I LIVE hurtful. Hurtful is when someone who regularly screws your husband sits opposite you in your own kitchen, looks at you with big cow-like eyes and talks about love. Being threatened with a poisoned coffee is a mere little headache, a little graze on the skin of life compared with my hurt.

'I never mind helping you out . . . doing you little favours like this . . . and all I get in return . . . '

Her eyes were sparkling with tears. Why didn't she look a mess? If I so much as thought about crying, I became a red-faced, swollen, dribbling wreck, like someone on a geriatric ward having a sneezing fit.

'It has to be said, Ally,' she went on in a whimpering voice, wiping her nose prettily on a pretty pink tissue that matched her blouse. 'I think YOU're the one with the problem.'

'Of course I am!' I replied. Was that my voice? Was I shouting? How did that happen without me knowing? 'I've got ALL the bloody problems! I'm the one whose husband

84

walked out, remember? I'm the one with the house, the bills, the girls, the cat, the crappy car and the crabby mother! You . . . YOU, you smug cow! All you've got to worry about is . . . is your lipstick!'

Which she was, unbelievably, studying in her little handbag mirror even now whilst I was yelling at her like a madwoman. She patted her eyes dry with her pink tissue, snapped the mirror shut and got to her feet.

'I'm not staying to listen to any more of this,' she said, flicking her hair and her perfume at me. 'I'll put it down to your being ill, Ally. That, and your age.'

Thank you and goodnight. She shut the door quietly and I threw my shoe at it. I considered, just for a moment, going after her and showing her up in public by having a shouting match out in the street. Then I suddenly decided I couldn't be bothered. I was too tired. I had some ironing to do. And anyway; I needed some quiet time to get my head together to work out my next lie. I'd had no trouble with the lies up till now, but I had a slightly nervous feeling that Lying To The Doctor was going to be a whole new ball-game. It was taking lying up a stage, up to the next level. I was going into the realms of Premeditated Lying and Lying to Authority.

But what must be, must be.

4

Dr Lewis had known me since we were both young and enthusiastic about life. He was enthusiastic about being the new and vibrant young doctor at the new and vibrant general practice which had just opened at the local health centre. I was enthusiastic about being newly pregnant with Victoria. We'd both calmed down somewhat over the years, of course, what with putting up with ungrateful patients and NHS constraints in his case, morning sickness and nappy rash in my case, and newness and vibrancy wearing off generally. But I'd been one of his first pregnant mothers and he saw me through two pregnancies, in every shape and from every angle, going on to offer comfort and antibiotics in times of the usual childhood horrors that followed. It had been nice, over the years, to be able to consult a trusted family friend when there were problems like Paul's embarrassing rash and Victoria's sudden urgent need for the Pill. However, it wasn't quite so nice now, sitting in the waiting room outside the familiar door marked 'Dr S Lewis, MD', and practising in my head the lies I was going to tell him. I had the most illogical feeling that however convincing my story was going to sound, he'd look at me with a hurt but pitying look and ask why I didn't feel able to be honest with him.

'Because I'm skiving off work,' probably wouldn't be the best response in the circumstances.

Would he be able to tell from my eyes that I was lying? There's no knowing what doctors can tell just from looking at you. Apparently just from looking at the backs of your hands they can tell if you're constipated, if you like foreign holidays or shellfish and whether you're likely to commit suicide. They stare into your eyes to find out about your liver, whether you're anaemic and how much sleep you get. Or is it how much sex you get? Of course, I might be mixing some of that up with what they check for when they feel around your ears and ask you to stick out your tongue. It's all very mysterious, and I can understand why they need so long at university. Then there's the blood pressure thing. That gives a lot away about a person, too, doesn't it — blood pressure. I'm sure they can tell from your blood pressure and heart rate if you're lying. My heart was going faster and faster just thinking about it.

Suppose I had a heart attack, collapsed right here, right now in the waiting room? He'd know then, for sure, wouldn't he. But of course, it wouldn't matter any more because I wouldn't have to lie. I'd need a certificate anyway.

'Mrs Bridgeman?' called the receptionist, making me jump so sharply I dropped the magazine I'd been pretending to read. That one paragraph had been quite interesting, anyway, up till the fifth time.

'Yes!' I squeaked, breathless from my impending heart attack as I jumped guiltily to my feet.

'Dr Holcombe will see you now, Mrs Bridgeman.'

Dr Holcombe? Who the hell was Dr HOLCOMBE?

'Where's Dr Lewis?' I asked the receptionist in a slightly trembly voice, knowing even as I asked that he must have seen me through the waiting-room window on his way into his surgery, noticed from my eyes and the backs of my hands that I was skiving off work and had absolutely nothing the matter with me, and had refused to see me. Dr Holcombe was probably the psychiatrist, brought in to treat people with Skiving Off Work disorders and Lying problems.

'Dr Lewis is on holiday,' smiled the

receptionist. 'Dr Holcombe is his locum.'

New vet, new doctor, what next? With a bit of luck when I went back to work I'd find Simon gone and a locum boss in his place. I pushed open the door of the consulting room and found, to my surprise, that there was nobody sitting in the green leather chair behind Dr Lewis's desk. Locum doctor on strike? Locum doctor cleared off home because too many patients are skiving malingerers?

'Hello, Mrs Bridgeman. Come in and sit down.'

A girl who looked considerably younger than Lucy and couldn't have been more than four foot six tall appeared from behind the filing cabinet, slinging my medical notes on to the desk before leaping into the chair in a way that I'd only ever seen cats and very agile small dogs doing. I sat down, wondering nervously and with the last vestiges of hope whether she might be the doctor's young and exuberant daughter who was playing off-ground-touch in the surgery whilst he went for a pee.

'I'm Dr Holcombe. How are you?' she beamed at me. Hope died a nasty, heart-attack type of death. How could a sweet young doctor of about fifteen years of age be expected to listen to a pack of lies from an old malingerer so early in her career? It was more than anyone could expect of her. It just wasn't right or fair.

'I'm fine, actually,' I said, looking at my watch. 'Actually, I feel much better and I don't think I'll take up any more of your . . . '

'Wait!' she said in a surprisingly commanding tone as I stood up and turned towards the door. 'Let's just have a quick chat about why you came. Since you're here now. Even if you do feel better.'

'Oh, well . . . ' I hesitated, hand on the doorknob. 'I was thinking of asking you for a certificate. A certificate for work. Sickness certificate.' What the hell. It was easier lying to a stranger. It wouldn't feel like lying to a priest in quite the way it would if it were Dr Lewis. I looked her straight in the eyes, which wasn't easy as I could only just see her over the top of the desk. 'I've been feeling ill for the past few days.'

'Have you?' She sounded so sympathetic, I let go of the doorknob and returned to her side of the room. 'Please, do sit back down. Just tell me a little about how you've been feeling.'

'Sick. Really badly sick. Not vomiting, just . . . '

'Nauseous?'

'Yes! And headaches. And . . . just generally

90

. . . yeuk. You know.'

'Feverish? Aches and pains?'

'Yes!' I looked at her with a new respect. She was even better at inventing symptoms than I was. 'Sort of shaky. Sweaty. I suppose it's a virus?' I added hopefully.

'Off your food?'

'Definitely.'

'Not sleeping?'

'Not a wink.'

I was beginning to forget I was lying. I watched as she jotted something indecipherable on my notes and then suddenly she was on her feet (not that it made much difference to her height) and advancing towards me with a thermometer, a digital thing, which she stuck in my ear. My EAR! I flinched and stared at her in amazement.

'You think it's an ear infection?'

'No,' she laughed. 'This is the way we do it now.'

Before I'd had time to express surprise, she'd taken my pulse, done the feeling around the throat and behind the ears bit, looked into my eyes and had the blood pressure gadget round my arm.

'Everything seems fine there,' she smiled.

So that was that. No sick note, just a ticking off for wasting time and malingering. I hung my head, waiting for the lecture. Back at school again, in the headmistress's office having skived off detention. ('And what excuse have you got THIS time, Alison?' — 'Sorry, Miss, but I had to get to the bank before it closed, to deposit the five million pounds I've just won at Bingo.')

'Are you worried about anything?' asked the very young, very small doctor in a very soft voice.

I looked up at her in amazement.

'Worried?' I repeated stupidly.

'Any family problems? Relationship problems? Money problems?'

What was this, a survey? Did I choose one, or tick all three? She ran her finger over the details at the top of my file, and then stopped abruptly, tapping the page thoughtfully before looking up at me again.

'Worried about turning fifty?'

'My husband's been talking to you!' I gasped. 'He has, hasn't he! Or my children! For God's sake!'

'They haven't. Should they have?'

'No!'

I felt angry. Tricked, in some way, into getting back on to the subject of this bloody fiftieth birthday lark, when all I wanted was a sick note for a few days off work.

'It's just that they all seem to think I'm in denial about it!' I scowled at her.

'Are you?'

I was beginning to dislike her. The way she threw things back at me with her soft, calm voice — do you?, should you?, are you?

'No, I'm not! It was just — I didn't want a party, so they cancelled it. Then everyone at work kept going on about being fifty, and it got on my nerves so I pretended to be forty-nine, and then . . . '

'Are you having problems at work?'

'No!'

I felt myself flush. I was cross, and I'd been caught off guard. I knew, knew all the way through me, that she could tell that I was lying now.

'Well,' I amended, shrugging awkwardly. 'Not really. It's just that this Nicola doesn't like me, and she's going out with this Simon, the Managing Director, and he's given me a Serious Warning.'

'Do you like your job?'

What the fuck did that have to do with it?

'It pays the bills,' I muttered.

Apart from the cat's drugs and the car's operation.

Dr Holcombe was scribbling frantically in my notes. She looked as if she was really interested and really enjoying herself. Glad somebody was.

'Well,' she said at last, putting down her

pen and leaning back in the chair. She looked up at me and gave me that sweet angelic smile again. 'I don't think you've got a virus at all.'

Shit. Not such a good liar after all. I picked up my handbag ready to leave in shame, but out of the corner of my eye I noticed she'd picked up her pen again and was filling out a sick certificate. Yes!! She felt sorry for me! She wanted to give me a few days off even though I was a liar! Who said the NHS was going down the drain? I for one would vote for upping the doctors' salaries.

'You're suffering from stress,' she said, still smiling. Stress? STRESS? I was the least stressed person I knew!

'I've never felt stressed in my life!' I protested.

'You're internalising it — bottling it up.'

'I am?'

'That's what's causing all your symptoms. I want you to read this leaflet. And this one.' She pushed them into my hands. 'Coping with Stress in Middle Age' and 'Psychiatric Problems of the Menopausal Woman'. Oh, great. Thanks a bundle. I came in feeling like a young lying troublemaker and I'm going out feeling like an old stressed-out nutter.

'And here's your certificate,' she added.

Oh well, whatever it takes. I grabbed it

ungraciously and made for the door.

'Rest!' she called after me. 'And I want to see you again before you attempt to go back to work.'

Attempt? Was it going to be that difficult? Was I going to lose the use of my legs or go completely barmy and forget the way? Was there something she hadn't told me? I'd worked myself up into a panic by the time I got home. I fished the certificate out of my handbag and smoothed it out on the table. What was that she'd written? Why couldn't doctors ever manage to write properly? Then the words suddenly leaped out at me, becoming horribly, sickeningly clear:

'Suffering from work-related stress'.

Work-related stress!

WORK-related stress!

The silly cow! Why the hell did she go and put THAT down? How was I supposed to send THAT into work? How the bloody hell could I turn up back at work on Monday and hand it over to Simon? — 'Here you are, here's my certificate explaining how I had to stay off work last week because, quite frankly, working for you has made me ill.' Oh yes, go down a bundle, that would!

And then I saw the next line.

'Should refrain from work for a period of . . . not less than . . . three weeks.'

★ ★ ★

I was lying on the sofa when Lucy came in from college. It was the shock.

'What's wrong, Mum?' she asked from inside the fridge, mouth already full of Jaffa cakes.

'Stress, apparently,' I said in the weak little voice of one suffering but trying to be brave.

'Stress?!' she echoed in tones of hysteria, almost dropping the Jaffa cake box. 'You?!?'

'Apparently,' I repeated, huffily. Could be if I bloody wanted to be! 'Here! Look!' I pushed the doctor's certificate under her nose.

'Work-related stress,' she read, obediently. She sat down next to me and gulped loudly. 'Christ, Mum! I never realised you were stressed!'

She looked quite shaken. I felt a bit bad.

'Nor did I,' I admitted.

Lucy studied the certificate for a while, nodding her head, then shaking it, looking at me sideways and then shaking her head again.

'Would you like me to cook the dinner?,' she asked solemnly. There was a rushing in my head like I was going to faint. Partly from shock at Lucy offering to cook, partly from fear at what she might kill, dig up, or chop up and what might end up on our plates.

'Hello! What's up?' called Victoria from the front door, seeing us both on the sofa looking solemn.

'Mum's ill,' said Lucy, jumping up at once and rushing to lead her sister out of earshot into the kitchen. I could, however, hear 'whisper whisper whisper' from Lucy, and then 'STRESS?! You sure? Fucking hell!' from Victoria. After which they both approached me again, cautiously, as if unsure how I was going to behave, and Victoria announced gravely:

'We're taking over. Me and Lucy. We'll cook the tea and we'll wash up.'

'Yeh. You're not to worry, Mum, we'll do it all,' agreed Lucy. 'Till you're better.'

'Well, till tomorrow, at least,' amended Victoria, giving Lucy a filthy look and a nudge that nearly sent her flying. 'I'm seeing Darren tomorrow.'

'We're going to make a curry tonight,' went on Lucy, ignoring her. 'So you just . . . lie there.' It's a despicable thing to lie to your own children. It's probably the worst kind of lie of all. In self-defence, all I can say is that I didn't actually INTEND to lie. I was on the point of telling them — laughing, jumping up from the sofa and shrieking at them:

'Ha! Not really! The doctor's a fucking idiot! There's nothing the matter with me!'

97

But then something came over me. Something that had a little bit to do with how nice it felt to lie on the sofa and be told to stay there. Something about a curry being cooked that didn't need any input from me, not even the chopping of an onion, not even the warming of a plate or the turning on of the gas. It wouldn't hurt, I persuaded my protesting conscience, just to go along with it for a very short while, an hour or so, just as long as it took to cook the curry and wash up. They'd probably both kill me afterwards but it'd be worth it. They'd understand one day, when they were running a household and a family themselves and feeling worn out and wanting to close their eyes . . . just for a few minutes . . .

I dreamed I was on the back seat of my car with the young AA man, talking to him about the symptoms of stress in middle-aged women. Just my bloody luck. Anyone else, ANYone, if they dreamed about being on the back seat of a car with a good-looking young man, would at least get to snog him in the dream even if that was their only pleasure left in life. Me, I have to dream I'm not only admitting to being menopausal but boring him to tears at the same time. Quite honestly it was a relief to be woken up by the smell of burned curry.

'Eat it all up, Mum,' said Lucy earnestly. 'We scraped the worst of the black off, and the saucepan's in soak.'

She'd make some man such a lovely wife one day.

★ ★ ★

I waited till the worst of the indigestion had worn off before I broached the subject of the Lie.

'I was only joking,' I said, putting my arms round both the daughters' shoulders simultaneously and giving them a hug. 'Ha, ha!'

'Mum! We're watching *EastEnders*!' said Victoria crossly, pushing me off.

'Joking about what?' asked Lucy without the faintest vestige of interest.

And then the phone rang. Explanations would have to wait, as no one else was going to answer the phone whilst *EastEnders* was on.

'Ally!' Paul's voice was deep with concern. 'How are you feeling?'

Feeling? Feeling? What was this? Suddenly realised he might have caused a ripple of emotion when he walked out of my life two years ago? Suddenly found out I was a human being who bled when she was knifed in the heart? Or been reading 'Psychological Problems of the Menopausal Woman'?

'Fine,' I muttered vaguely. 'Why would I not be?'

'Ally, you must have realised the girls would tell me straight away. Obviously, they're worried about you. Well, we all are . . . we're all worried, Ally.'

The next most despicable lie, after lying to your children, must be lying to the husband who used to be the closest person to you in the whole world, before he walked out of your life into the bed of a young tart. Again, in my defence, I can only plead that I didn't MEAN to do it. It was on the tip of my tongue, almost falling off the tip in fact, to say that (ha! ha!) the whole thing was just a joke, ask the kids, I'd just been on the point of explaining to them how it was all a joke to get them to cook the curry, never mind the burning, and I'd have admitted it by now if it wasn't for *EastEnders*, and we could all have a good laugh about the silly doctor making ridiculous diagnoses and signing me off work for three weeks with a book about the menopause . . .

But it was something about the way he said that bit about being worried. 'We're ALL worried about you, Ally.' It sounded so caring, so sincere, I could almost believe he meant it. I could almost believe he still thought of me as a person, as Ally, his wife, the girl he'd loved from the age of fourteen when we first kissed in the sports equipment cupboard, and not just some whingeing, annoying nuisance who asked for money for the cat and threatened his girlfriend with slug pellets.

'You mustn't worry about me,' I said, softly, gently. Do, do. Worry, worry like hell. I want you to, I like it. Say it again.

'But you're obviously very poorly. We had no idea, any of us. Of course, we knew you weren't quite RIGHT . . . '

'What do you mean? Not quite right in what way?' I snapped, my softness and gentleness having dropped away like snot from a sneeze.

'Well. One thing and another. The retreating from reality . . . '

'WHAT?' I almost shrieked. 'What reality?'

'You see?' he continued sadly. 'You're beginning not to even recognise it.'

'Is this all about the fiftieth birthday business? Because if it is . . . '

'Not just that. Not JUST.'

Silence ballooned out into the room like a giant tumour. The girls turned their faces towards me, looking at me pitifully as the final chords of the *EastEnders* theme tune

101

died away . . . da daaa da da DAH DAH DAH . . .

'What, then?' I managed to whisper eventually.

'You haven't . . . been acting . . . altogether . . . rationally,' said Paul slowly, picking his words carefully, weighing each one judiciously before he threw it at me. 'What with Lynnette . . . the party . . . the cat . . . '

'You think I've flipped my lid, don't you,' I said stonily.

I stared at Victoria and Lucy, watching me with a sort of fascinated horror as if I was going to suddenly tear off all my clothes and beat myself around the breasts with the broom handle. I thought about Paul, sitting in his new home with Lynnette, telling her how worried he was about me, how out of touch I was with reality, how he'd suspected I hadn't been quite right in the head since I'd threatened to feed her slug pellets.

'You think I'm fucking mad, don't you,' I said.

And then I screamed.

★　★　★

As screams go, it wasn't all that dramatic. I hadn't screamed for a long time, you know, probably not since I'd got hysterical at a

Beatles concert in about 1964. Even in childbirth I'd groaned rather than screamed, moaned a bit, made a lot of fuss, but never really screamed. I suppose we're mostly too well brought-up to utter such a primeval thing as a scream more than once or twice in our lives. And then, when we really want to, it lets us down by coming out as a sort of watered-down version, a tame scream, a polite scream, a scream not really worth getting a sore throat for. But it was a gesture, and as such, I felt it made its mark.

'Mum!' yelled Victoria and Lucy together, jumping up from their post-*EastEnder* sprawl and rushing to grab my arms. No ripping off of clothes allowed, no beating of bodies with broom handles. No sudden violent movements. We've got you now, we're holding your arms by your sides for your own protection. Bring in the medication, nurse.

'Yeeow!' yelled Apple Pie, backing away from me, hissing. Fur standing on end all round his neck. They say cats react to insanity, don't they? Witches, nutters, middle-aged women with stress disorders — cats can smell them a mile off. He bolted out of the room with his tail pointing at the ceiling.

'Ally!' shouted Paul into the phone. 'Calm down! Can you hear me? CAN YOU HEAR ME?'

103

'I'm crazy, not bloody deaf,' I pointed out calmly, the scream having relieved the tension and leaving me strangely composed.

'Right. Listen. Has the doctor prescribed you anything?'

I burst out laughing.

'Yes. Three weeks off work.'

'Good. Let me talk to the girls again, OK?'

'No. There's nothing you need to discuss with the girls, Paul. I'm perfectly all right. I'm not on any drugs, I'm not cracking up, I've just been given a certificate for three weeks off work because I pretended to have a virus.'

'Right.'

'Paul, I'm serious. I'm perfectly fine, I'm not suffering from stress, or anything else. It's all just a . . . misunderstanding.'

'If you say so.'

And I knew then how it must feel to be buried alive. I was communicating but I wasn't being heard. I was speaking English but being translated into Swahili. Nobody was going to take any notice of a single bloody word I said. And it was all my own fault for ever uttering the very first lie.

★ ★ ★

By that Monday, I'd discovered the infuriating truth of the concept of having too much

104

of a good thing. All weekend, one or other of the daughters had ushered me back to the sofa every time I'd shown any signs of movement beyond lifting a cup to my lips or the remote control in the direction of the TV.

'Just lie there and relax, Mum. We'll take care of everything,' had been my idea of the unattainable dream for most of my adult life. Now it just felt ridiculous and increasingly irritating. Especially the way they kept looking at me, warily, as if I might burst into song or speak in tongues at any moment.

'I'm absolutely fine,' I kept trying to explain.

'Yes, Mum,' they soothed. 'Tea or coffee?'

Buried alive.

★ ★ ★

On the Monday morning, Victoria insisted on taking my sick certificate in to Snotty-Nosed Nicola for me on her way to work.

'I can post it. Or I could deliver it myself!' I protested from my sofa, pushing up the lid of my coffin, glimpsing the movement of life beyond the grave.

'No. I'll take it straight there now. Or you won't get paid.'

Who was this strange girl, so thoughtful and caring, so kind and considerate? She looked like Victoria, she was wearing Victoria's clothes and playing her Prodigy CD, but it must be an alien inhabiting her body. Or was she just nervous of the prospect of no maternal pay cheque?

'Now, don't you move!' ordered the alien Victoria as she left the house. 'Lucy will get you breakfast before she goes to college. You should have stayed in bed!'

Is that what people do when they suffer from stress? Lie in bed all day and feel like they're losing touch with reality, like their children are aliens and their sofas are coffins? I felt a hot panic steal over me. Perhaps I really was going loopy. The alien Lucy brought me fruit juice and toast and made a great thing about me putting up my feet on cushions to rest my legs.

'I've got stress,' I snapped, 'Not varicose veins!'

Then I remembered. I didn't have stress! I was suffocating in the grave of my own fabrications!

After they'd both gone, in the sudden and unaccustomed silence, I got up from the sofa and sneaked around the house like a disobedient child, tidying things up at random, picking up a towel here and a book there, until it suddenly struck me that I didn't know what to do. I'd never had free time

106

before, and now I'd got it I didn't know what to do with it. The ironing was up to date. The dishwasher was stacked, nothing even looked dirty enough to clean. With a sinking heart I realised my life was so sad, I lost all sense of purpose after the washing bin was emptied. I might as well go back to work. Except that I couldn't, because by now S.N. Nicola would have showed my three-week certificate to Simon and Simon would, in all probability, have Got In A Temp.

The Getting In of A Temp was standard procedure for absences of more than about a week. I'd lived through many a Getting In of Temps in my time, and few of them had been pleasant experiences. Some temps were as timid as mice, some couldn't type, some refused to make the tea or answer the phone, some never got OFF the bloody phone to their boyfriends, mothers, best mates, hairdressers, bank managers and personal beauty advisers. But the worst were the ones who wanted to run the joint the minute they set foot in the door, changing the absentee's log-in, the height of her chair and clearing out her desk drawers as if she hadn't just gone off sick but left the country or died. By the time the poor sick colleague had returned from her dose of the flu, slipped disc or work-related stress, the temp had completely reorganised the work station, put a photo of her children on the desk, entered her own personal data into the computer, and everyone was inviting her to their hen-nights. The returnee felt like an interloper in her own office. She answered her own phone and people said 'Where's Julie?' Colleagues who'd worked with her for eighteen years made her black coffee instead of white tea and said 'Sorry, I wasn't thinking, that was what Julie used to have.'

I sat in my kitchen and brooded. Was I to be replaced by a Julie? Would anyone miss me? Would anyone care if I never went back? I might, on many occasions, have wished never to go back, but I did at least want to be missed. The phone rang, jolting me out of my fantasy of never going back and Simon telling everyone he never realised how much he'd miss me.

'Ally!' Liz sounded distraught. 'Christ, Ally, I never realised you were stressed!'

'Nor did I,' I admitted cheerfully, and then amended quickly, 'I mean, I never realised that was what was wrong. Till the doctor explained everything.'

'You poor thing! Are you all right?'

Well, obviously not. I'm stressed, aren't I.

'Not bad,' I said bravely. 'Bearing up.'

'Well, I mustn't keep you talking, and tire you out . . . '

'But I'm bored,' I admitted.

'Are you?'

She sounded surprised. Perhaps stressed people didn't normally get bored. I'd better read up on the symptoms if I was going to keep this up for three weeks. Three weeks! It stretched ahead of me like an endless desert, a silent, colourless desert of sofa-lying with feet up.

'I suppose it's part of the illness,' I guessed hopefully. 'The boredom.'

'Perhaps. Would you like some magazines?'

'Why? Have you got some?' I asked, surprised. People didn't normally keep a stack of *Woman's Own* in their desks.

'I'll bring a few round tonight, if you like.'

'Oh. Yes! That'd be nice. It'd be nice to see you.' It felt as if I'd been away for months already. There must be some gossip or scandal to catch up on. I wasn't missing them all already, was I? Come on, now, surely not?!

I must be even sicker than I was pretending.

Liz and Mary both turned up at about eight that evening, bearing gifts of chocolates and magazines. We sat in the kitchen so we didn't interrupt *EastEnders*, and ate the chocolates together and reminisced about when I used to be at work with them.

'Is there a temp?' I asked. 'A Julie or a Jackie sitting at my desk, going through my files? Is she better at spreadsheets than me?'

'Simon's TALKING about Getting In a Temp,' said Mary. 'But he hasn't done it yet.'

'Don't let her use my mug for her coffee. My blue one with the cow on it. Hide it in the filing cabinet. And don't let her access my e-mail.'

'She's not even there yet,' soothed Liz.

'And watch out for her getting too friendly with Snotty-Nosed Nicola. And another thing . . . '

'Ally,' said Liz, looking at me with big worried eyes, 'You shouldn't be thinking about these things. That's why you've been signed off work. Because it's been causing you stress.'

'But that's the funny thing,' I admitted, shoving four squares of Dairy Milk in my mouth at once. 'When I was there, I didn't feel it stressing me out. Only when I was being interrogated by Simon about my timekeeping, but not otherwise. Now I'm away from it, I keep thinking how I might be replaced. Someone might be better than me. You know, they might be younger or . . . '

'That's the thing! You see! It's this AGE thing. I knew that was behind all this stress

110

business!' cried Mary triumphantly.

'No, it's not,' I returned forcefully, spitting chocolate everywhere. 'It's not age, it's everything else. It's the bills, and the car bumper, and the cat needing drugs for the rest of his life. It's my mother and her illnesses and her jetting off to Majorca with her boyfriend. It's Victoria spending her whole salary on her car so she can pull the lads, and Lucy doing her exams while she's worried about me being off work. It's Paul thinking I'm cracking up just because I joked about giving his girlfriend poison.'

'Poison?' queried Mary and Liz together, their mouths both dropping open wide, teeth glinting horribly with undigested Dairy Milk.

'It was a joke,' I sighed, feeling suddenly tired and depressed.

Nobody laughed.

'I think you ought to get away,' said Liz suddenly.

'Oh, very funny. The private yacht's in for repair at the moment,' I said sourly.

'No, really, I mean it. Remember what you were saying that day at work? That lunchtime when I . . . when we let slip about your surprise party?' She smiled a guilty little smile. 'How you were saying you'd like to swan off somewhere and leave everyone to get on with it?'

'Well, of course I SAY that. Everybody SAYS that.'

'It'd do you good,' agreed Mary. 'Take your mind off work. As long as you sit around here, fretting, you're not going to get better.'

Especially as there's nothing wrong with me in the first place. Or is there?

'If I win the lottery,' I tried to smile, 'I'll remember that.'

'There must be a way you can manage just a few days away,' persisted Mary. 'A mini-break of some sort. A late booking, or . . . '

'Phone for you, Mum!' shouted Lucy, backing into the kitchen with her eyes still on the TV screen, where someone in Albert Square was having hysterics over someone else having an affair. 'It's Auntie Bev!'

'Beverly!' I exclaimed with genuine pleasure. My older sister and I were very fond of each other but didn't get round to communicating terribly often. 'How are you?'

'More to the point,' cried my sister across the miles from Cornwall, 'How are YOU, and what the bloody hell is all this nonsense about being stressed? What do you expect if you will insist on being cooped up there in London all summer? For Christ's sake, get yourself down here and get some sea air into your lungs, girl, and get some colour back in your pasty cheeks! When are you coming? I'll get Thomas out of the spare room and wash the duvet!'

So I had to go, didn't I. If only to find out who Thomas was, and what he'd been doing on the duvet.

5

How do people manage to pack everything they need for a couple of weeks into one little suitcase? Victoria had been on a back-packing holiday the previous year. I remember looking at that one bag on her back and thinking: 'What about the hair-dryer? What about the four different pairs of shoes and the nail varnish collection?' How she managed without so many of the little luxuries that usually make up her life I will never know, but she seemed to enjoy herself, and seemed to slide effortlessly back into the taking for granted of the little luxuries (to say nothing of the big ones like the house, the shower and the TV) when she returned. Now here I was, contemplating not a back-pack around Southern Asia but a swift jaunt down to Cornwall, and I couldn't do up my suitcase for sleeves and plugs hanging out of the edge of it.

'You don't need THAT, for a start,' said Lucy firmly, removing my curling tongs from the case. 'Bev will have some if you REALLY can't do without.'

'It's hopeless!' I retorted, sitting back on

my heels and staring at the pile of stuff still needing to be packed. 'I need a bigger case.'

'Then you'd never be able to carry it,' pointed out Victoria.

'Take the car,' said Lucy. 'I don't know why you want to go on the train.'

'I don't WANT to, Lucy. I just don't want to spend most of my holiday on the motorway waiting for the AA man.'

Even if it was the young good-looking one. You can only go so far on the motorway.

'Take MY car, then,' said Victoria.

The silence was so startled and so electric with shock, I thought she'd immediately retract —

'No, no, I didn't mean it! I was thinking about someone else's car, someone else's mother, not you!'

But she looked from me to Lucy and back again, returning our stares, and merely said:

'What?'

'Well!' I swallowed my amazement and tried again. 'Well, I mean, Victoria, you can't be serious. Your car is your life, your baby, your most treasured possession. If I take it away from you, you'll cease to exist in the eyes of everyone you care about.'

'Darren thinks that, too. He thinks I'm selfish and uncaring and all I think about is my car.'

The bastard!

'So I've got to show him, haven't I.'

Aha. The ulterior motive rears its ugly head. Thank God for that. I was beginning to worry that she was settling down into a nice mature person.

'And you think it'll impress him if you tell him you've offered your car to your poor ageing mother to drive down to Cornwall?'

'Something like that,' she admitted.

'And after he's been suitably impressed, I suppose you'll expect me to pretend I don't really want to take it. That no matter how much you beg and plead, I'll say 'No, Really, I'd much rather drive my own heap of rusting decay, or heave my suitcase around British Rail platforms . . . ''

'Well, I . . . '

'Well, forget it. Thanks, Victoria!' I planted a big kiss full on her cheek, which she wiped off with a look of grave anxiety. 'I'd LOVE to accept your kind offer, and I'll tell Darren myself what a thoughtful, caring person you are!'

'Oh.'

She looked at the carpet intently for a few minutes before leaving the room very silently. Lucy looked at me expectantly. I knew that expectant look. She was waiting for me to call Victoria back, laugh and hug her and say of course I wouldn't dream of taking her car. Victoria's slow progress towards her bedroom told me that she was waiting for the same call, laugh and hug. So perhaps I should have felt a bit guilty, carrying on with my packing, putting back the curling tongs and the extra pair of jeans now that I knew anything spilling out of the suitcase could go in a black bin-bag in the boot of the car. Victoria's car. Victoria's car, paid for out of her own earnings, taxed and insured and MOT'd out of her own earnings, run on petrol she bought from her own earnings. Her own earnings of which she'd agreed to give me twenty per cent as housekeeping, of which I rarely saw a penny. She lived with me virtually rent-free and board-free in order to run her car, and I let her get away with it because she was my daughter and I loved her — but I shouldn't have done. It wasn't right for her, and it certainly wasn't right for me. I juggled with the bills for the gas and the electricity and the cat's drugs, so that she could enjoy that car — and if she was offering it to me for a week, even if it was only to make Darren fall in love with her, then I was bloody well going to take it. Without any guilt. Or hardly any.

'Look after it,' she said in a sorrowful voice, stroking its roof gently as I packed my things into the boot the next morning. FIVE pairs of shoes. Well, why not? And two jackets, just in case it was cold in the evenings . . .

'Sure you've got enough stuff?' asked Lucy sarcastically.

'The weather's unpredictable in Cornwall.'

'Don't forget to use fifth gear,' said Victoria, still caressing her car. 'Only I know you're not used to it.'

Used to it? They hadn't invented it when my car was made.

'I'll drive perfectly,' I reassured her, getting in and starting the car. First time! That would take some getting used to.

'No need to give it any throttle!!' warned Victoria too late as I hurtled out of the driveway. I pulled up sharply and nearly flew through the windscreen. No need to stamp on the brake, either, apparently.

'It'll only take a minute to adjust to the controls,' I smiled at her. 'And anyway, YOU be careful with MINE!'

'Huh!' was all she could manage to say. I don't think she was planning to go out on the pull much in that old wreck. Wouldn't do much for her street cred.

'See you in a couple of weeks, Mum!' called Lucy from her bedroom window. 'Have an excellent time!'

'I will!' I waved back to her, and drove off — very smoothly, I thought — to start my holiday. I was two miles down the road before I remembered it wasn't supposed to be a holiday. I was supposed to be ill. I was supposed to be recuperating. THEN I did start to feel a little bit guilty. But only a little bit.

★ ★ ★

There's something very pretentious about driving a sports car, I don't care who you are. Victoria carried it off because of her youth, her sunglasses and her short shiny skirts. The first few looks I got from other drivers passing me on the motorway, I felt slightly ridiculous, imagining their disappointment on seeing a middle-aged woman in a cardigan at the wheel. But after a while I got into the game. Why not? We all knew it was the car and not my hairstyle they were admiring but it sure as hell beat the looks I normally got when anyone overtook me in the Metro. They were usually trying to attract my attention to point out the bumper hanging off or the lights not working, and I'd be pretending not to notice because I already knew. It was harder to ignore the glances of sheer envy from these young men driving similar, but older or less powerful models. Less impressive. Less sexy. It was true — it made you feel good driving this thing. I was beginning to understand my daughter a little better and wonder if she'd lend me the car on a more regular basis, perhaps to do the Tesco run on a Friday night. See if I could pick up more than a bag of potatoes. I smiled a mixture of pity and pure white-hot lech at a lovely young man driving a red Fiesta in the middle lane, and laughed out loud to myself at the fun of being able to behave outrageously, safe in the knowledge that I'd never see him again. Then I pulled into the motorway services, and within five minutes I was seeing him again.

I was queuing to pay for my tea and buttered bun. Tea and buttered bun, for God's sake! I mean, it couldn't have shouted 'Middle-aged! !' more loudly if it had come with carpet slippers. As soon as I looked up and recognised him, I wanted to abandon my tray, pretend it was someone else's that I'd picked up by mistake, and choose something else. I don't know what — champagne and strawberries, perhaps, except that they tend not to have them in the M5 services.

'It's the MG lady!' said Fiesta Man with a smile.

He might have been smiling, but I knew he was really sniggering inside at the tea and bun. I sneaked a look at his tray. A bottle of Coke and a hamburger. Youth food. He was about thirty, at a guess, with those sort of eyes that smile along with the mouth.

'Hello,' I managed, and flushed at the memory of the lustful look I'd given him out on the road. Shit. That's what you get for playing silly buggers.

'Smoking or non?' he asked as I started to walk away with my tray and what was left of my dignity.

'Sorry?'

'Can I sit with you? Or do you prefer to be alone with your thoughts?'

Completely flustered now, I indicated a table in the non-smoking area and almost ran to it. He joined me, sitting astride the fixed grey and red tubular metal seat with an easy comfortable grace. I fidgeted with the bun, worried about crumbs and butter and their combined effect on my lips and chin.

'Nice car you've got,' he said, untroubled by half a hamburger in his mouth.

'It's my daughter's.'

There. Truth's out. Now take your half-eaten hamburger and your Coke and your smile and go find a real sports car driver to chat up.

'You don't look old enough to have a daughter who can drive.'

Oh, please! I almost snorted a mouthful of tea out through my nose.

But on the other hand, if he was sad enough (despite the looks) to come out with shit like that, why should I care?

'She's only five,' I returned, grinning back at him and beginning not to worry about the crumbs. 'She's a child genius so they gave her a driving licence when she started school.'

'And is she as lovely as her mother?'

'Not quite. But she's young yet.'

Who the hell did I think I was? I was flirting with him! We laughed at each other as if we were the funniest, wittiest people we'd ever met, and by the time I'd finished the tea and bun we'd told each other everything trivial and nothing of any consequence about ourselves.

'Nice to have met you, Ally,' he said as if he meant it. 'Maybe another time?'

'Maybe when I pass you at a hundred down the road,' I smiled.

And we went our separate ways, and he overtook me once, and I overtook him twice, and after he turned off, somewhere around Bristol, I smiled about him to myself for the rest of the journey. And it felt more like a holiday than ever.

★　★　★

'What are you smiling about?' asked my sister almost as soon as I'd got through the door.

'The pleasure of seeing you,' I said, giving her a hug.

'You look unnaturally happy for someone suffering from depression.'

'Not depression. Stress.'

'Whatever. I was expecting you to look worn-out and sort of anorexic.'

'Sorry to disappoint you. Perhaps I feel better now I've got away from it all.'

'Good. Now, listen.'

Always a bit brusque, was Bev. A bit of the bossy big sister, still.

'I've put you in the back bedroom. Thomas has been warned. If he does come in at night, shout loudly. He's a bit deaf. Anything you need, just let me know. OK?'

'OK,' I agreed meekly. 'Who's Thomas?'

'Oh, sorry. Next-door's rabbit.'

Rabbit? Thomas the RABBIT?!

'Why?!'

'He has the run of the house. It's a long story. He's clean — reasonably — considering his age. But he does like the back bedroom. I've told him you're coming, and I've moved his stuff into the little room, so he shouldn't be a problem. But shut the door at night. Just in case.'

Consider it shut. Nocturnal visits from an

elderly, semi-housetrained rabbit I could do without.

'I've got some marking to do,' said Bev, handing me a mug of coffee and pointing out the biscuit tin on the shelf. 'Can you get yourself settled in?'

Of course, I hadn't expected a fuss. Bev wasn't the type, and anyway it would have been embarrassing in view of the fabricated nature of my illness. I lugged my suitcase, black bin-bag full of shoes, curling tongs and a bag of novels (in case I got bored) up to the back bedroom, opened the window and stared out over the rooftops to the sea. I'd only been here once before. Beverly invited me with the girls when Paul left. She'd just moved here from London and made Newquay sound like the Promised Land. I think she was a bit put out that I didn't immediately start to feel better about the whole business of my life being ruined and my heart being broken. Newquay may be nice, especially in summer, but it doesn't have magical healing qualities. This time, I hadn't come here with any illusions about escaping from my problems. I just wanted time off from them, that's all. A couple of weeks of relaxation. Not thinking about anything in particular. Recharging my batteries. I sighed, smiling to myself in anticipation of the relaxing and recharging I was going to do, and turned back from the window just in time to witness a large white rabbit defecating on my pillow.

'He's been so good recently,' sighed Beverly, stroking Thomas's ears with one hand while she put the pillow-case in the sink to soak. 'I suppose it was the trauma of changing his room.'

'I could have had the little room!' I protested.

Who wants to carry a whole load of guilt on behalf of a traumatised, incontinent rabbit?

'Of course you couldn't! It hasn't even got a proper bed in it! I wouldn't dream of it!'

She stroked Thomas's ears a little more and he snuggled into her chest. Is this what happens to middle-aged women who haven't had children? They get a rabbit substitute?

'Just shout at him, that's the thing. Show him who's boss!'

Thanks. I'll bear that in mind next time he craps on the bed.

'We'll just get a take-away tonight, shall we?' proposed Bev, opening a bottle of white wine and passing it in my direction. 'Indian or Chinese?'

'Either. Lovely.'

I poured the wine and took a gulp while she phoned the take-away.

* * *

Sharing chicken korma and mushroom bhajis at the kitchen table with more wine felt companionable and sisterly. It felt like having a flatmate probably felt.

'Are you seeing anyone at the moment?' I asked as I mopped my plate clean with a chapati, wanting intimacy and secret-sharing. Dare, Command, Truth or Promise? You tell me and I'll tell you. Except I had nothing to tell.

'One or two,' smiled Beverly enigmatically.

'At the same time?' I tried not to sound shocked. Even within the questionable framework of Victoria's moral standards, it was not correct to take on a new lover without first dumping the old one, however cruel and calculated the dumping might be. Well, it wasn't correct to ADMIT to it, anyway.

'Listen, Ally,' retorted Bev, swaying towards me slightly as she poured out more wine. 'I'm fifty-two. I've got no ties, no responsibilities . . . '

'Fine, OK, I know . . . '

'And I'll do whatever I fucking well like.

With whoever I fucking well . . . want to do . . . whatever I want.'

She'd lost the thread somewhat but the gist was clear.

'Absolutely. I didn't mean you shouldn't . . .'

'And they all know the score. Anyone I see . . . they know there's no commitments. No relationships. No one gets hurt.'

'But it sounds . . . sort of lonely,' I said thoughtfully. 'Isn't it? Like screwing a series of strangers?'

'Nothing wrong with that!' she snapped, and then added, 'Anyway, they're not. Not strangers. Friends. My life is full of friends.' She waved her arms somewhat drunkenly around the room as if they were all hiding behind the chairs. 'Life should always be full of friends.'

'Mine isn't,' I said bleakly.

I thought of Paul, supposed to be my best friend, my soulmate and life partner, now defected to Cow Lynnette. I thought of the girls at work, even now probably making plans to go to the pub with the temp. I thought of Victoria and Lucy, rightly engaged in their own lives with their own friends. And I struggled against an onslaught of drunken self-pitying tears.

'All I've got is a sick cat who needs drugs

for life, a sick car with no bumper and dodgy lights, and a boss who puts Serious Warnings in my Personal File. And our mother.'

'No wonder you're stressed,' said Bev without the slightest sign of sympathy.

'But,' I said, brightening with the sudden memory of it, 'I did get chatted up by a young man on the way down here.'

'Good for you!' Beverly smiled encouragingly as if I was a child beginning to master a few phrases of a new language.

'Only because of Victoria's car, of course,' I added quickly.

'So what?' she countered. 'Why waste time looking for reasons, looking for excuses, Ally? Life will have passed you by while you're still shivering on the edge. Jump in! Immerse yourself, girl! Take hold of life! Grab it by the bollocks and squeeze all you can out of it! Squeeze until it screams for bloody mercy!'

The kitchen echoed with the force of her rhetoric. The pots and pans positively rang with it. I expected the plates and cups on the dresser to get up and dance to a clash of saucepan lids.

'That's what I do,' she added unnecessarily. 'You squeeze life.'

'I not only squeeze, I fucking strangle it!' she grinned. 'Anyway, tell me more about the guy on the motorway.'

And we got a little drunker, and a little more sentimental, and we hugged a bit, and said how we didn't see enough of each other and should do, and I cried a bit about Paul and Lynnette, and Beverly said she'd never liked him anyway, in her opinion he was an arrogant, supercilious git and now I'd got rid of him I could start to enjoy life.

Enjoy life? I lay on top of the bed in the back bedroom (checked for rabbits) watching the ceiling spin round in an inexplicable, nauseating fashion and thought about what she'd said — what I could remember of it. Grabbing life by the bollocks. I liked that, liked the aggressive sound of it. That was what I needed now, I decided, a bit of aggression, if I wasn't going to die a sad and bitter miserable old cow. But as I disappeared over the edge of consciousness into a totally pissed oblivion, I was still crying inside. Crying without even knowing why. Always the worst kind, that.

★   ★   ★

I was woken up by a hammering at the door. Or was it a hammering inside my head? Ouch! It was both, one echoing the other like thunderclaps. I rolled off the bed and staggered down the stairs with a pillow folded over my head, protecting my ears, which had suddenly become very delicate. Too late, as I flung open the front door in a desperate mission to stop the knocking before it killed me, too late by a fraction of a second, which was the time it took for my bleary, bloodshot eyes to focus and blink in recognition of the appearance on the doorstep of the most beautiful man I'd ever seen in my entire life — too late I remembered what I was wearing. Or more to the point, what I wasn't wearing. Apart from the pillow over my head, not a lot. A flicker of the most amazing chocolate-brown eyes I was ever likely to have the pleasure of staring into, registered amused acknowledgement of my position, which was standing naked on the doorstep apart from an old pair of pink knickers and (now) a pillow clutched against my boobs, swaying and gasping with the worst hangover it was possible to have without being dead.

'Sorry,' said the beautiful man, and his voice was like dark chocolate truffles dipped in honey, 'I didn't realise you'd be in bed.'

He smiled on the word 'bed' as if it was a wicked secret between the two of us. I felt my whole body go into a hot sweat, and didn't have enough brain cells functioning to decide whether it was the sudden onslaught of the menopause, sexual excitement, or a prelude to serious vomiting. I didn't dare speak, just in case.

'You must be Ally,' he went on.

I nodded thoughtfully, memory slowly returning. Ally, yes, that rang a bell. It probably was my name.

'Is Bev at work?'

'I . . . don't know.'

My voice sounded odd and tinny, and the taste in my mouth was frightening. I clamped one hand over it, suddenly horribly aware of how a waft of my breath could knock Beautiful Man clean off his feet. Then I realised the pillow had slipped so I put the hand back again, but not before I'd noticed the look in his eyes as he watched this manoeuvre with interest. And as, by now, I was pretty sure my body heat had nothing to do with incipient vomiting, I tried my voice out again, this time directing it down at my feet.

'I've only just woken up.'

'I expect she's at work. It's nearly twelve o'clock.'

Nearly twelve . . . ? TWELVE o'clock? How did that happen? I looked around wildly for a clock. Perhaps this guy had flown in from another time zone and hadn't altered his watch yet. I NEVER slept till lunchtime, never, and certainly never since going down with fake stress, the worry of which had

131

added genuine insomnia to my list of invented symptoms.

'Can you give her a message for me?' asked the Beautiful One just as it was beginning to look as if we'd both be standing on the doorstep locked in silent contemplation for the rest of our lives (and I could certainly think of worse punishments.)

'Of course! Of course!' I stammered, flustered, embarrassed that I hadn't made this obvious suggestion. 'Anything else I can do to help?'

Fly to the moon on a paper aeroplane? Fall to your feet and kiss the ground you walk on?

'Just the message,' he smiled, this time a full, face-stretching smile that made his eyes dance and dimples deepen beside his mouth, and which would make most normal red-blooded women want to drop the pillow from their chests, tear off their knickers, fling themselves to the ground and shout 'Now! Take me now or lose me for ever!' Most normal women, I said, not me, of course. I just fantasised about it for a few minutes but it made my hangover feel worse.

'Just let her know I'll be here tonight, could you? I forgot to confirm.' He dropped the smile and looked me up and down before adding, 'That's all — for now. See you later,' and turning away.

Maybe I'd save the fantasy for later. When I was feeling better.

* * *

'I can't believe I was so hungover I never even asked who he was!' I admitted ruefully to Beverly, recounting the incident when she got home from college a few hours later. She laughed.

'That's James. And I'm furious with him for spoiling the surprise.'

'What surprise?'

'I TOLD him it was meant to be a surprise welcome do for you.'

'For ME?' I blushed scarlet, feeling like a child being taken out for a treat I didn't deserve. 'Why?'

'Why not? Do you good, cheer you up, meet some people. Some of my friends.'

'Is James one of your 'friends'?' I asked pointedly.

'If you mean have I screwed him, yes, of course I have, but years ago, and got it all out of my system. Took some doing!' she laughed dirtily. 'As you can probably imagine!'

I tried to shrug a nonchalant little shrug. Could I imagine? Did I even want to? Could I HELP imagining that smile, those eyes, that ripping off of the knickers fantasy . . .

'Well, of course you fancy him — it's

133

written all over your face!' pointed out Bev helpfully. 'He's gorgeous. Thinks he's God's gift to women, of course . . . '

With a certain amount of justification.

' . . . but a terrific shag.'

*   *   *

I didn't think about that at all whilst I got myself ready for Beverly's dinner party. Not once did it cross my mind, whilst I did my eyes with my least clogged mascara, sprayed myself all over with my least old perfume and searched through the suitcase for some underwear that didn't look as if it belonged to an overweight, middle-aged matron with stress incontinence. I might have run through the episode on the doorstep once or twice in my mind, or a couple of dozen or fifty times at the very most, and tried to de-hangover the whole thing and perhaps move it all on just a few steps in my imagination, so that instead of just looking at me with those eyes like sparkling coals, he'd pushed me indoors, tossed the pillow to one side, ripped off all his clothes and . . .

'Phone for you, Ally!' hollered Bev from downstairs. 'Victoria!'

*   *   *

'You haven't called to say you arrived,' said Victoria sulkily.

'Sorry. I've arrived.'

'Car OK?'

Oh, I see. Now I understand the concern.

'No. I crashed it. I was racing this gorgeous young man in a red Fiesta . . . '

'Very funny, Mum.'

' . . . and we had lunch together in the motor-way services and then we raced some more . . . '

'Mum!'

She'd stopped listening. If I'd told her I'd chatted to the most beautiful man in the world on the doorstep in my pink knickers she'd only sigh 'Mum!' in that same tone that implied complete disbelief in the sexuality of anyone over thirty.

'And I was chatting on the doorstep this morning . . . ' I began.

'Mum, please. I didn't phone to hear about your gossips with Beverly's neighbours,' she complained.

See what I mean?

'What's wrong, then?' I asked, suddenly alarmed by the edge of anxiety in her voice. 'Has Apple Pie been sick again? Has the bumper come off my car?'

'No. Nan's phoned from Majorca. She says she's not coming back. Ever.'

6

See how it happens? You can pretend to yourself that you've got away from it all, that you've exchanged, within little more than twenty-four hours, a life of burdens and anxieties for one of cavorting naked on doorsteps with men too handsome for their own good, but the things you were running away from don't just disappear, they're still there, and they come after you. They come running after you, all the way from home, all the way from bloody Majorca.

'She's doing it on purpose, to spite me,' I wailed into my coffee-cup.

'Why?'

Beverly was completely useless. I wanted someone to sympathise, to agree with me that the whole world, and especially my mother, was against me, not to rationalise.

'What's wrong with her staying out in Majorca? I should have thought you'd be glad.'

'Glad? Glad?' I stormed. 'Glad that she's taken leave of her senses? Glad that she's now certifiably insane as well as going into a steady physical decline? Glad that she's shacked up with some . . . some . . . TED, who wants to run a British bar in Palma?'

'At least he's prepared to work,' she pointed out, pouring more coffee.

'There's nothing else for it,' I sighed with resignation, thinking about going back upstairs and repacking the things I'd just started unpacking. 'I'll have to go out there.'

'You'll WHAT?'

This must be how Bev addressed her less amenable students. Hands on hips, glaring at me over her glasses. It made me nervous, and I was only her sister.

'I'll have to go out there,' I repeated, 'And sort it out.'

'Just listen to yourself!' snapped Beverly, sounding so genuinely angry I dropped the spoon in the coffee in surprise. 'You'll have to go out to Majorca and sort it out, will you? What's the matter with you? Can't you bear to let Mum be happy?' The silence reminded me of that 'twang' you get when you stretch an elastic band really tight. Just before it snaps, when it vibrates until the air around it seems to echo with its tension.

'And what would you know about it?' I hissed. 'When have you ever done anything for Mum?'

Twang!

'I send her flowers. I phone her. I care.'

137

Stretch it a bit more. Twang, twang . . .

'Oh, you CARE, do you? You think sending flowers and phoning once a week means caring? Perhaps you should try sitting in hospital waiting rooms for hours on end while she gets her various complaints sorted out? Perhaps you should try having her turn up unannounced at your home at all hours of day and night, expecting to have meals cooked for her while she sits there criticising everything you do!'

SNAP!!

'You're so bitter and resentful!' shouted Beverly.

'And you're so fucking lazy! You never did anything to help . . . '

'She wouldn't let me! She only wanted you, the bloody favourite daughter, and God knows why, when all you do is whinge and complain . . . '

'YOU'd complain if you had MY life . . . '

'And you're so fucking SORRY for yourself!'

'Hello! Am I too early?'

The first guest for the evening, having given up with knocking on the door, had stuck his head in at the kitchen window. Of course, it had to be James.

* * *

'We're making a habit of meeting like this.'

Beverly had bolted for the bathroom, leaving me little option but to let him in, wearing only slightly more than I'd been wearing that morning on the doorstep. OK, I'd got as far as sorting out the underwear, but despite being black and lacy it didn't do anything to disguise the overweight, middle-aged bit and it certainly didn't disguise the absence of any more suitable top garment than a tea-towel wrapped hastily across me at nipple level.

'Sorry. Come in.' I flapped around, panic-stricken, trying to hold on to the towel. 'You wouldn't mind, would you, if I . . . '

I gestured wildly in the direction of my bedroom.

'Sure. Take your time. Sorry if I interrupted anything.'

'No. I mean, it doesn't matter. I'll . . . just be a minute. Sit down. Have a drink.'

Gabbling like an idiot, I ran upstairs two at a time, realising with horror that I shouldn't have offered him Beverly's drink, especially as I hated her and was about to pack my case and leave.

Or was I?

In the three or four minutes it took me to put on jeans and T-shirt and start throwing things into the suitcase, I slowly calmed

down, and debated a few crucial considerations in my mind:

*1. There was chicken chasseur in the oven,
which was my favourite.*
*2. Not much fun driving back to London
now, what with it getting dark soon.*
3. I'd told Victoria not to worry.

This third consideration was the most
crucial of the Crucial Considerations. Don't
worry, I'd told Victoria, as mothers do,
making space in the Worrying Things
compartment of my brain, shifting the other
Worrying Things over so they had to sit on
top of each other. Welcome into my brain,
new Worrying Thing, the Worry about Mum
staying on in Majorca. Leave Victoria alone
now, let her get on with her life, with her
pressing concern of how to keep Darren
keen whilst driving a D-reg Metro. Leave
my child alone, come and bug me instead.
I'm already off work with stress so what the
hell?

Now, if I went bolting back from Cornwall
tonight like a bat out of hell, having fallen out
with Bev after only one and a half days, how
was that going to rate as a no-worry situation
from Victoria and Lucy's point of view? No
good: I'd promised to straighten things out

from this end and that was what I'd have to do.

Also, there was the chicken chasseur.

Also, I'd quite like James to see me with my clothes on just once.

I quickly pulled off the jeans and T-shirt, pulled on my black dress and legged it down to the kitchen to be met by a delicious smell of chicken chasseur and an icy air of hostility, with a shortly clipped 'No thank you' when I offered to help serve up the food.

I took my place at the table and did my own introductions. Jane, a colleague of Bev's from college, was (apparently) thrilled to meet me at last in the flesh. I couldn't quite figure this out unless she'd already been living with a cardboard cut-out of me, which seemed unlikely, but I spent the eternity we waited for Bev to bring in the first course smiling back at her in response to her warm and effusive girl-chat and wondering if she was gay. The other guests were a mature student of Bev's called Michael whose only topic of conversation seemed to be his thesis on the influence of ambient social and sexual attitudes on the writings of the metaphysical poets, and an even more mature post-hippy beatnik called Bo, a bearded and boring nerd whose real name was probably Nigel or Brian, who called everyone 'Man' and droned on about smoking a joint as soon as dinner was over, but actually got drunk so quickly on the wine he never managed it. And there was James.

Over the prawn cocktail he talked to me, his voice dripping sex appeal like syrup into the sauce, about living in Newquay and being divorced, and working in conference management and having holidays in South Africa, and what it was like for me living in London with two daughters and working in insurance and holidaying with Beverly in Newquay, thus building up a mini-profile of each other which excluded only:

1. The fact that I was not on holiday but pretending to be ill;
2. Any suggestion that I might be suffering from delusional stress, menopausal psychosis or any type of behavioural problems associated with being nearly fifty;
3. My husband being shacked up with the tart from hell;
4. The sexy car on the drive outside the house being not mine but my twenty-one-year-old daughter's;
5. The reason for my sister and I not talking to each other being, not because we were such excellent hostesses we preferred to talk to our guests, but because we had

just discovered a new and frightening mutual hatred of each other.

None of these counted as lies, you understand, just avoidance tactics. The lies started with the main course, roughly coinciding with the wine entering my bloodstream and taking it over, and James beginning to look at me across the table with looks that bore into my eyes, through my head, in and out of my brain without pausing to engage it, and straight into my soul. You know those kind of looks? I used to have a dog that did it, a spaniel. Except that when he looked at me like that, with his tail gently wagging, it didn't have the same effect on me. It didn't make my legs tremble and my heart race and it didn't make me keep dropping my knife and fork into my chicken chasseur.

'You don't look old enough to have two grown-up daughters,' he said, his voice caressing me with softness.

'I'm thirty-nine!' I giggled prettily.

Well, it probably wasn't pretty at all. It probably came out as a drunken cackle, but we can only try. We can only lie. I shot Beverly a furtive glance to make sure she wasn't listening, about to shout out: 'Ha! Listen to her, silly old cow, she's nearly fifty, as if you couldn't guess . . . ', but she was

143

deep in debate with Michael about John Donne's use of sexual imagery in his religious poetry. Instead, I waited for James to smile back at me, a slow, easy smile of understanding that said, 'Of course, we both know you're no more thirty-nine than I'm the Queen of Sheba, but we won't discuss it any further.' But he didn't. He reached across the table, lifted my hand in his and pressed my fingers very gently.

'You look much younger,' he said.

Now, you have to remember that I'd lived like a nun since splitting with Paul, and that this was the most beautiful man I'd ever seen in my entire life. If that hadn't been the case, I would of course have thrown back my head, howled with laughter and told him to piss off.

'Thank you,' I smiled back sweetly.

The dessert course, which I could hardly eat for excitement, passed in a blur of burning looks across the table and nudged knees under it. Coffee grew cold in the cups whilst we tickled each other's fingers and stared into each other's eyes. Brandy was licked suggestively off lips. What was happening here? Within the space of a couple of hours I'd turned from nun to nympho. At about half past one, Michael having left early to work on his thesis, with Bo crashed out on the sofa and Jane and Bev having retired to the kitchen to make more coffee, which seemed to be taking for ever and a lot of giggling, James leaned as close to me as our separate armchairs would allow and said:

'I think it's time to go.'

'Don't!' I responded before I had time to be shocked by my own daring. 'I don't want you to go!'

In the moment of hesitancy before he kissed me, I understood that old thing about the world stopping turning. It lurched on its way again with a savage and sudden jolt at the lingering end of the kiss, when I caught my breath painfully, almost choking on our combined saliva and wondering if it was acceptable to wipe one's mouth with the back of one's hand at such moments.

'I meant,' he whispered, pulling me to my feet, 'It's time for us both to go.'

He said goodbye to Beverly. I didn't. In the circumstances of our mutual hatred I didn't see the point. While he was in the kitchen I was panicking with a new and urgent worry, which was: just what was one supposed to take with one when going back to someone's flat for sex? Nightie? Toothbrush? Condoms? Should I pack an overnight bag with clean underwear and my make-up remover? Face cream? I suddenly felt stupid and naive and unready for all this. I hadn't grown up with this sort of stuff, I didn't know how to handle it. He'd know. I'd do it all wrong and mess it all up. He'd laugh at me and kick me out of bed. The effects of the brandy and the kiss started to wear off and I decided to shake hands with him politely, thank him for the offer but decline. I'd congratulate myself in the morning for staying calm in a potentially awkward situation.

'Come on, then,' he smiled, appearing back in the room. He took my hand and propelled me gently towards the front door. 'Let's go,' he said into my ear, making me shiver to the soles of my feet.

'OK,' I said.

★   ★   ★

And so it was that the eve of my fiftieth birthday saw me waking up alongside the (even more beautiful without his clothes on) man in the world, having had wild, uninhibited sex, which I somehow seemed to know how to do after all, during much of the night and finishing off with an encore at dawn. I didn't realise it was the eve of my fiftieth birthday at the time. It wasn't exactly the first thing on my mind. Nor the second, nor the third nor . . . well, let's just say I'd forgotten about it completely. I'd forgotten about a lot of other things, too, but they all came swiftly flooding back with the morning light, like flies round a dog turd. The immediate anxieties were trivial ones, like how one decently takes leave of someone one hardly knows but has just shagged senseless. I mean, 'See you around, then!' sounds rather too casual, 'Thank you very much for having me,' too crudely obvious, but anything more intimate at this stage in the game, this level of inertia and lack of clothing, could be construed presumptuous. And where the hell did my knickers end up? I lay in bed, watching James sleeping quietly next to me, contemplating these issues and wondering whether other, more experienced people worried like this or whether they just leaped naked from the bed, crying 'Terrific fuck! Thanks so much!', found the knickers and left. But before I could spend too long contemplating this, the Other Worries came sneaking back up, intruders slipping into my mind by the back door when it was unguarded, bashing me over the head with their cudgels of panic.

Bash! Take that! That's to remind you about your sister Beverly, who's probably chucked your suitcase and all your clothes out on to the pavement.

Bang! Bash! That's just to make sure you

147

don't forget about your mother who's done a runner to Majorca.

Crash! Wallop! Got you! Thought you could forget about your husband, did you? Yes, your husband, Paul, the man you promised to stay faithful to until the end of your life. One minute you're crying your eyes out over him deserting you, next minute you're cavorting in bed with this . . . this . . .

James turned and sighed in his sleep and the intruding worries vanished out of the window. I touched his face gently and traced the line of his smile as it deepened, and as he opened his eyes I had to stop myself from gasping out loud. He WAS gorgeous. I could hardly believe my luck. Why couldn't I just stop worrying for once and accept this moment of pure pleasure, and be grateful for it?

Dear God, thank you for providing me with a lovely man to have a night of fantastic, uncomplicated sex with. Amen.

'What are you thinking?' he murmured, propping himself up on one elbow and studying me closely.

'Saying my prayers,' I smiled.

'And what were you praying for?'

More of the same, please. As soon as possible. And my knickers, somewhere accessible.

'Oh, you know. The usual stuff. World peace, kindness and love for little fluffy animals, a win on the lottery . . . '

He laughed gently and kissed me, very slowly, until my toes curled in the twists of the sheets.

'And more of the same, please. As soon as possible . . . '

* * *

It was half past nine when I let myself back in at Beverly's house, and the silence told me she'd probably left for work already. Not that easy to be sure, though. These college lecturers seem to work almost as infrequently as their students. I crept up the stairs as stealthily as a thief, and into my own room, where I threw myself on the bed with a sigh of relief, telling myself I'd just have an hour or so to catch up on some of the sleep I'd missed during the night, before getting down to some serious consideration of my new anxieties, to say nothing of brooding on the old ones. If I hadn't thrown myself on to the bed with such abandon, it wouldn't have come as such a shock when something big and furry jumped out from under my legs. I fell off the bed like I'd been shot, shrieking blue murder, trod on the big furry thing and finally tripped over him as he hopped away.

'Thomas! You bastard rabbit!' I shouted after his retreating tail as I lay in a heap on the floor. Beverly's bedroom door opened slowly and Beverly, completely naked, followed by Jane, completely naked, peered around the door at me as I stared back in surprise.

★　★　★

'Don't worry,' said Bev later over breakfast. Worry? Me? 'I'm not actually gay. Jane is, of course, and she's such a good friend, I just sleep with her occasionally, you know how it is.'

'Sure, whatever,' I said, trying to adopt the same casual tone.

The incident with Thomas seemed to have broken the ice on our frozen relationship and we'd been laughing together somewhat nervously over the breakfast preparations, unsure which of us was going to voice an awkward topic first.

'So what about last night?' asked Bev, fixing me with a very knowing look as she spooned vast quantities of Shreddies into her mouth.

'Yeh! Great dinner! Thanks, Bev. Sorry I didn't say . . . '

'Cut the crap, Ally. Not the dinner. How did it go with James?'

Annoying how a smile will insist on taking over your face even when you try to fight it. I tried to think about something sad. Apple Pie in the fish-pond. Or something worrying. A temp sitting at my desk, doing my job, doing it better than me and sucking up to Simon. Mum getting married in Majorca. But it was no good. The smile took over. Before I could help myself it had me grinning like an idiot.

'That good, eh?' Bev smiled back.

Yeh. That good.

★ ★ ★

'Is that the Hotel Picador? Yes? Could I speak to . . . do you have a Mrs Dobson staying there, please? Or they might be booked in under his name . . . Mr . . . er . . . his name's Ted,' I faltered. Didn't know the bugger's surname. 'No, I'm sorry, I don't know the room number. They're English. And elderly,' I added helpfully.

There was a pause during which I could hear a muttering of exasperated Spanish and then a clonking sound followed by the ringing tone.

'No reply,' I mouthed to Beverly.

'Well, at least they didn't say they've checked out.'

'No.' I hung up and stared grimly out of the window. 'Probably out looking at properties.'

'Ally . . . '

'I don't like it, Bev. It's too sudden, it's too rash, she hardly knows him . . . '

'So when are you seeing James again?'

Ouch. I felt myself go a little red. Well, pinkish, anyway.

'Well, all right. But I'm not thinking of going into business with him, am I?'

⋆　⋆　⋆

So what WAS I thinking of getting into, exactly?

'He's not permanent relationship material, you know,' warned Beverly that evening as I was trying on the sixth or seventh outfit in a frenzy of desperation about what to wear for dinner with him.

'Jesus, Bev! What do you take me for? We're both adults here, right?'

'It's just that you seem . . . a little bit stressed out about it all. Taking it a bit seriously, perhaps.'

'Of course I'm stressed out,' I snapped, pulling off a pair of white trousers in disgust.

Why the hell I ever bought them I can't imagine, they made my bum look so huge I might as well have gone out with a sign round my neck saying 'Big Fat Momma'. 'I'm ALLOWED to be stressed out, I'm suffering from stress, remember?'

'Calm down,' she said, a little more kindly. 'The black skirt looked nice. With that red top.'

'You think so?'

'He'll love it.'

'You're sure?'

'For Christ's sake! I thought you said you were an adult, not a thirteen-year-old on her first date!'

Well, now, there's the thing. It WAS my first date, actually, in a kind of way. You see, I'd known Paul virtually all my life so we never went through the same sort of dating stuff that other couples do. We just drifted into going out together as an extension of hanging around together, which was in itself an extension of playing marbles together. I always felt comfortable with Paul because we were mates first and foremost. I never had to beat myself up over what I was going to wear when I went out with him. There was never this angst, this worry, this . . .

Shit. I was just about to say there was never this excitement. I didn't mean that, of course.

I didn't mean, did I, that there hadn't been any excitement in our relationship, not ever, nothing but the comfortable, caring love of a couple of best friends. I couldn't have meant that! It would be unthinkable even to THINK it . . .

Horrified, I sat back on the bed, clutching the red top and staring at myself in the mirror.

'You OK?' asked Beverly, looking at me dubiously.

Fine, fine, never better. Just discovered my whole life up till now has been a complete sham, a framework of self-deception and pretence. A play performed on the stage of matrimony, for the benefit of the audience of the world. Lines learned by heart, smiles and gestures performed on cue. Nothing real. Nothing. Nothing beneath the costume and the greasepaint. Bring on the fucking clowns.

'I don't think I was ever really in love with Paul,' I whispered at the mirror.

My reflection looked back at me, white with shock.

'Come on, now,' said Beverly, looking very anxious now. 'This thing with James . . . '

'No, no, it's nothing to do with James,' I shook my head impatiently. 'Of course it's not. I've just . . . realised. I loved Paul, but I wasn't in LOVE with him.' I just assumed I was. Because I was supposed to be. We were married, for Christ's sake, we had sex, we had babies together. It's absolutely obscene to suddenly start thinking about never having been in love with him. Like you've been having sex all your life with your brother or something.

'Perhaps I really AM losing my mind,' I conceded softly, still staring at my reflection, still holding on to the red top as if my life depended on it.

'Not losing your mind. Finding it, perhaps,' Beverly said, surprisingly gently. To my surprise, she held out her arms to me, and even more to my surprise, in fact to my total and complete amazement, I slid into her arms and sort of collapsed against her, whilst she rocked me like a baby, like I'd seen her doing the other day with the rabbit, stroking my hair and shushing me as if I was crying. Come to think of it, perhaps I was crying. I wondered what the noise was.

*　*　*

'So when are you going to be forty?'

I frowned at James across the table of the restaurant. So far, the evening had gone well. I'd managed not to get too pissed too soon, and not to spill anything down the red top, so

155

as first dates go, it was looking good. HE was looking good. I was having trouble keeping my mind on the conversation and off the question of how soon we were going back to his place.

'Forty?' I smiled politely.

'You're thirty-nine now . . . I just wondered when your birthday was, that's all? Does it bother you, the Big Four-O?'

'Oh . . . er . . . not at all, really.'

Well, it wouldn't, would it. It was so long ago I'd forgotten how it felt. Shit, change the subject, quick, quick, quick . . .

'Only as old as you feel, eh?' he smiled.

'Absolutely.'

What a bloody stupid lie to tell. Why did I do that? Perhaps I should just tell him the truth now, quickly, while I had the opportunity. Oh, by the way, that thing about the Big Four-O, actually it's a few years out — well a whole decade out, in fact, but hey! what's a little decade or two between friends, ha ha? No, sod it, I couldn't do it.

I'd made my bed now, I'd have to lie in it . . . in a manner of speaking.

'Forty's nothing to worry about, nowadays,' I smiled cheerfully, with complete honesty. 'It's merely the beginning of maturity.'

'You're right, of course. Fifty worries me a

little more, though.'

I choked on my chocolate gâteau.

'Still,' he added with a meaningful smile at me, 'We've got a while before we have to face that one, haven't we.'

'Yes, thank Christ,' I nodded, spitting chocolate crumbs discreetly into my napkin.

Coffee came as a welcome respite from any further discussion of age. I breathed a sigh of relief. All I had to do was keep the conversation on safer ground. Not a problem.

'So how long have you got?' James asked me as he stirred his cappuccino.

'Well . . . ' I looked at my watch. 'I expect Bev will be home about midnight, so I suppose . . . '

'I didn't mean that!' he laughed, and the look he fixed me with as he added 'We've got all night if we go back to my place,' was like having all my birthday and Christmas presents wrapped up in one. 'I meant, how long is your holiday?'

I must have stared a stare of total blank lack of comprehension, because he laughed again and persisted:

'Your holiday! With your sister! How long?'

'Oh!'

Holiday. As in sick leave. As in pretended sickness, invented sickness, sickness that was supposed to have me confined to the house in a state of nervous exhaustion, not hopping in and out of bed with Beautiful Men with Beautiful Smiles . . . not a HOLIDAY at all, for God's sake! I felt myself flush crimson with guilt.

'Well . . . probably just a couple of weeks,' I said, vaguely.

'Depends if they can manage without you at work?' he asked sympathetically.

'Something like that.'

Something like whether they got a temp in who was better than me. Whether my Serious Warning in my Personal File had become any more Serious. Whether there was still a job for me when I got back.

He covered my hand with his as he called a waiter for the bill.

'Don't let the job stress you out,' he told me, gently. 'Take a tip from me. I know how it can be. Take your holiday. You deserve it.'

'Yes,' I squeaked miserably.

Deserve it? I wasn't even supposed to be having it. I was SUPPOSED to be stressed out! He didn't know the half of it!

'Coming back for a nightcap?' he asked meaningfully, taking my hand as we left the restaurant.

Funny how quickly you can forget all about work-related stress.

I should have told him the truth, of course. It had to come out sooner or later, and I couldn't have known it was going to be sooner. Do you ever wonder how you might have done things differently if you'd only known what sneaky little tricks Fate had lined up for you, just out of sight round the corner of time? Well, you shouldn't. You shouldn't waste time wondering about it, because you probably wouldn't have done anything differently, would you? No, be honest! You wouldn't. We all do what we want to do, at the time, and it's too easy to say afterwards 'If only I'd known . . . ' If only I'd known my mum was going to piss off to Majorca with Ted with the intention of staying there, would I have tried to get on with her a little better? Would I hell. If only I'd known Paul was going to leave me for some bimbo tart, would I have tried to love him a bit more, a bit better, a bit more often? Livened things up with suspenders and crotchless knickers? Sod that for a game of cowboys. Well, if I'd known my daughters were going to be lying in wait for me back at Beverly's house when James and I let ourselves in the next morning, would I NOT have spent the night having sex with him? Well what do you think?

Perhaps I would have made a bit more effort with the look on my face, which was probably still glazed with post-coital satisfaction. Or perhaps James and I would have entered the house a bit less entwined, a bit less smoochily, a bit less caressingly . . .

'Hi, Mum! Happy Birthday!'
'Happy Fiftieth, Mum! Oh . . . '
Oh.

They'd done well, really, bless them. The room was bedecked with flowers and 'Happy Birthday Nifty Fifty' balloons, and apparently they'd only been there a very short time because Beverly had been in the kitchen trying to get hold of me on the phone to pre-warn me. The look on her face told me that. It also told me she was terribly sorry but what could she do? She could hardly refuse her nieces entry to the house when they'd come all the way from London by train to see their mum on her birthday.

'This is James,' I said to their united stance of stony disapproval.
'A friend of mine,' explained Bev helpfully.
'My daughters,' I told James automatically. 'Victoria and Lucy.'
'Pleased to meet you,' he said quietly.
They nodded.

'I'll . . . be going, then,' he said, turning back to me. The twinkle had gone out of his eyes. The dimple had gone out of his cheeks. He didn't look impressed.

'OK.'

'Have a . . . happy birthday,' he added, raising his eyebrows at the balloons.

'Have we interrupted anything?' demanded Victoria aggressively, misinterpreting the embarrassed silence.

'Yeh,' joined in Lucy. 'Don't mind us! We'll wait outside if you want . . . '

You know how sometimes people say things with the best of intentions, which turn out to be the worst possible thing they can say? 'You look marvellous, you've lost such a lot of weight' to an anorexic, or 'Give my regards to your husband' to someone who's just been widowed. They usually feel worse than the person they were talking to, don't they. So I didn't blame Beverly. She was only trying to help.

'James is just a friend of mine,' she repeated patiently to Victoria and Lucy as if they were slightly thick students who needed extra tuition. 'He's just been helping me look after your mum, that's all. You know. While she's not been well.'

It wasn't enough. I wasn't completely dead yet. I was still twitching with the occasional spasm of rigor mortis. Stick the knife in again, Beverly, go on, right up to the hilt.

'While she's suffering from this stress syndrome thing. This menopausal . . . '

Enough! Enough! I'm dying, can't you see I'm dying for Christ's sake!!

'Thank you, Beverly,' I said very quietly as James turned to go.

'What?' she asked the shocked and silent room as the door closed after him. 'Was it something I said?'

7

'We're not STUPID,' declared Victoria, taking the tone of an understanding but concerned parent. 'We did REALISE you were having a thing with him.'

'Were' being the crux of the matter. The past tense of the matter. Judging by the speed of his exit, it looked pretty unlikely that James was going to be reappearing in my present or future tenses, and who could blame the guy? Being propelled through a woman's life from the age of thirty-nine to fifty overnight could perhaps be a little disorientating, to say nothing of taking on board her menopausal neuroses.

'I didn't realise you had boyfriends,' admitted Lucy thoughtfully.

'I don't! I mean, I haven't, up till now.'

Why did I feel the need to answer to my own children? I should have said I'd have fifteen men every day if I wanted to. Why could I feel Paul's eyes looking back at me through Lucy's, challenging me, accusing me? Boyfriends, eh? Thought you were supposed to be suffering from a broken heart?

'So is this part of your syndrome, then? Needing to get a man? Part of your, you know, your condition?'

Even Victoria stared at Lucy as if she'd just stepped out of the spacecraft.

'Don't talk bollocks, Luce. It's nothing to do with Mum's illness. It's probably just her age.'

Well, thanks. That's reassuring.

'Or perhaps it's because of, well, you know. Because of not getting it, since Dad left.'

They nodded wisely together. Two beautiful young heads nodding together in sage contemplation of the possibility of sexual frustration in the older generation.

'Have you quite finished?' I snapped. 'Discussing me as if I'm not here? I'm sorry if I embarrassed you by coming home with my LOVER . . . '

'Embarrassed? Us?!'

'Get real, Mum! Embarrassed! Huh!'

' . . . but the fact of the matter is, I'm not old, I'm not ill, and I'm not frustrated. I just met someone I liked, and he liked me, so we went to bed together. OK?'

Shocked silence.

'So now we've cleared THAT up . . . ' I got up and went over to where they were sitting together on Beverly's sofa, scooped them both into my arms and gave them a group

164

hug. 'It's lovely to see you both! Thank you for all this . . . ' I waved at the room full of floral tributes and balloons. 'And thank you for coming all this way . . . '

'Couldn't miss seeing you on your FIFTIETH!' smiled Lucy.

'Don't keep on about it, Luce!' hissed Victoria. 'It's just a birthday, isn't it, Mum, same as any other, but, you know, older.'

'It's all right,' I laughed. 'I haven't really got a problem with being fifty, honestly. It was just all the fuss I didn't want. The surprise party, and everything. Although I do appreciate all the trouble you must have gone to, organising it,' I added, feeling guilty. 'And cancelling it.'

'Never mind,' said Victoria stoutly.

'How did you get time off work to come down here?'

'I'd already booked a couple of days off. The party was going to be on Saturday . . . '

'Oh yes.' More guilt. Heap it on, go on, don't spare me.

' . . . so I would have been doing stuff, today and tomorrow. You know, catering stuff.'

'Catering?!' Now I REALLY felt bad.

'Making sandwiches and all that.'

God. No wonder she needed two days off. And thank God they'd cancelled the bloody party.

'Who's looking after the cat?' I asked. The words were hardly out of my mouth when I was aware of a sort of chill, a little *frisson* of wariness passing between the girls and wafting over to me on a current of cold, tense air. They exchanged looks and coughed.

'Well, we couldn't ask Nan,' began Lucy diplomatically.

'On account of her legging it to Majorca with Ted,' added Victoria unnecessarily.

Also on account of her never having looked after the cat in her life and being absolutely one hundred per cent certain to refuse.

'So?' I prompted in the ensuing silence.

'So Dad said he'd do it.'

'Oh. Good.'

'In a manner of speaking.'

I looked at Victoria sideways.

'What manner of speaking?'

'Well, as in: Dad's in charge of the situation, but . . . '

'Lynnette's doing it, isn't she!' I exclaimed. 'You've left that cow looking after my cat?'

'OUR cat, Mum!'

'Dad's cat too, remember!'

'And she's coming into the house? MY HOUSE? When I'm not there? Touching my things?'

'Only the cat's dishes and the tin-opener,' said Lucy miserably. 'Oh, Mum, we had to ask her! Dad works too late. Apple Pie would get hungry . . . '

'We couldn't have come to see you, otherwise,' pointed out Victoria. 'Sometimes, you just have to do what you have to do.'

I pictured Lynnette, letting herself into the house with my key. Going into my kitchen, opening my cupboards. Calling my cat, picking him up and cuddling him. I could feel my mouth turning down at the corners. The post-coital glow had gone cold.

'Don't worry, Mum,' said Lucy gently, slipping an arm through mine. 'Apple Pie hates her. He miaows at her and digs in his claws when she picks him up. And she doesn't like getting his hairs all over her skirts.'

Perhaps there's a God up there after all.

★ ★ ★

We went shopping in Truro. The three of us, just like the old days when they were little and I used to take them out to buy their new outfits from Top Kids. Except this time it was MY treat.

'I haven't got much money,' I admitted as we parked the MG in the multi-storey and headed for the shopping centre.

'It's all right,' said Victoria, to my

astonishment. 'I have. I've just got paid.'

'But you've never got any money!'

'I've been staying in.'

Of course. Difficult to get out and about in London without a sports car.

'Darren doesn't like the Metro?'

'Darren who?' she retorted pointedly.

The bastard! How dare he? How DARE he dump my daughter just because she didn't have her car to take him out in! How dare he dump her when she'd only lent me the car to impress him with her kindness and generosity! How dare he, the snivelling little shit, the despicable, miserable rat's turd . . .

'I dumped him,' she went on, swinging her bag cheerfully on to her shoulder.

Good. He deserved it, the pig, the little git, the nasty little sore on the arse of humanity . . .

'Because of Reece.'

'Reece?'

Hang on, I'd lost the plot here. I was several pages short of a chapter. Where did Reece come into it?

'Who's Reece?' I asked, looking at Lucy for inspiration. She raised her eyes to the sky, obviously knowing what was coming.

'He's gorgeous!' mouthed Lucy silently, doing an impression of her sister looking soppy over Reece.

'He's gorgeous!' sighed Victoria, looking soppy.

'I think I love him!' mouthed Lucy, putting two fingers to her mouth and pretending to puke.

'I think I love him,' smiled Victoria happily with no sign of puking.

'Oh. Well. That's nice, then,' I said, trying hard to sound impressed, more impressed than I'd sounded a few short weeks ago about Darren, and a little while before that about Adam, which was only a mere flicker of time after Nathan and definitely pretty quick on the rebound after Ben and Liam.

'Reece is definitely The One,' she said dreamily.

'She's looking at *Brides Magazine* again,' Lucy warned me ominously.

'Lovely,' I muttered.

I wasn't too worried, though. Even if Victoria ever got as far as booking a wedding, by the time the banns had been called, Reece would have been unceremoniously dumped in favour of someone who was even more definitely The One.

* * *

'Did you know about Dad as soon as you met him?' asked Lucy whilst we were trying on trousers in New Look.

'What about him?'

'Well, that he was . . . you know . . . The One.'

'Like Reece,' put in Victoria, with the soppy smile back on her face.

I sat down on the little stool in the changing room, with a pair of green combat trousers half on and half off.

'I don't know what I thought,' I said, feeling suddenly tired and sad, remembering the fright I'd given myself the previous night when I started thinking about not being in love with him. It wasn't the sort of thing you said to your daughters about their father, though. 'We knew each other when we were just kids, remember.'

'Yeh. Childhood sweethearts,' said Lucy happily.

'Sweethearts, meat-hearts,' said a sneaky, uninvited little voice in my head. 'You only went out with him because you didn't meet anyone else you particularly liked. You only married him because everyone expected it. You only stayed together because it was safe, it was secure, it was normal and nice and tidy and . . . '

'Did you never have any doubts, Mum?' persisted Victoria. 'Did you never fancy anyone else? Didn't you ever look at other men and think: cor, I wouldn't mind giving HIM one . . . '

'No,' I said, speaking to the floor, looking at my bare feet where they stuck out of the too-tight combat trousers like little sausages bursting out of their skins. 'Not really, no. I never really looked.'

'No, but if you HAD done . . . ' pointed out the uninvited little voice with irritating determination, 'If you HAD ever looked at anyone else, say you'd looked at someone like James, eh? Hmm? Someone with those eyes, that smile, that line of chat that had you eating out of his hands, almost tearing off your clothes as soon as he touched you? Are you trying to tell me you'd have stayed faithful to good old Paul then? You'd have ignored that raging torrent of hormones, looked the other way, concentrated on your marriage . . . your good, stable, nice, secure . . . DULL marriage? Answer me that now, if you can, if you dare, with the feel of HIM still warm inside you . . . and tell me you still don't understand how it happened with Paul and Lynnette?'

I jumped up off the stool again, nearly falling over the trouser legs in my haste to get out of them.

On the whole, I think, uninvited little

171

voices in one's head are best told to shut the fuck up.

★ ★ ★

'Nothing fits,' I told the girls crossly when I'd tried on most of the trousers in Truro. 'What's going on here? Have the sizes been changed recently?'

There was an awkward silence. Lucy clutched her Miss Selfridge bag with its contents of assorted skimpy pastel-coloured summer tops and hummed a little tune to herself. Victoria pretended to be looking at shoes in a shop window.

'What?' I demanded of my own reflection in the glass.

I watched Victoria's reflection turn towards mine, look at me for a minute as if considering saying something, and then look back at the shoes again. In that instant, I recognised the awful truth of it. It was no good hiding, no good pretending. No good everyone trying to be kind because it was my birthday, my FIFTIETH birthday, my Big Fat Half-Century. The facts spoke for themselves. The mirror never lied.

'I've put on weight, haven't I.'

'Maybe just a little bit,' conceded Victoria.

172

'Not that much,' amended Lucy.

I was huge. I was a great, massive, blob of a woman, with fat hanging out everywhere. My arms and legs were so heavy I could hardly lift them. My face was bulging out in all directions. My neck was flabby, my stomach was blubbery and my bum wobbled like two giant mounds of jelly. How could I not have noticed this before? Oh, the shame of it! How could I have got naked into bed with the most gorgeous man in the universe; how could he have stood the sight of all this disgusting flesh? How could he have touched it without flinching? What was he? Some sort of a pervert? A fat fetishist?

'I'm going on a diet!' I shouted, much to the amusement of a group of teenagers passing by. Hysteria wasn't far off. Well, can you blame me? This just wasn't fair. Anyone else, ANYone, who got a dose of work-related stress, would LOSE weight, wouldn't they? They'd become pale and thin and fade away to within an inch of their lives. They'd have people fussing around them, telling them to drink up their nourishing soup and try, please try, to eat just one mouthful of lovely steamed fish and spinach. They'd lie weak and still on their couch, trying to conserve their energy and their calories for the fight to keep body and soul together. They wouldn't be pigging out on Jaffa cakes and Walnut Whips every night, you can bet your sweet arse. They wouldn't be going out to posh restaurants with gorgeous men and being bought four-course dinners with those little truffle things in paper cases to go with the coffee, nor would they be guzzling a bottle of Hungarian Rioja with the main course and tipping two French brandies down their throats after the dessert. This, then, is where life is so cruel. You try to be cheerful, try to keep going for the sake of everyone around you, despite everything, despite the crap life throws at you from every direction (including Majorca). You don't give in and mope. You don't lie around feeling sorry for yourself. You get on with your life and try to make the best of it. And what happens? You get fucking fat.

Fat and fifty.

Fat and fucking fifty.

'I am!' I shouted after the retreating group of teenagers. 'I'm going on a diet, and I'm going on it now! Right now!'

'Try some more clothes on, Mum,' soothed Victoria, taking my arm.

'Yes, come on, try a different shop. Some of these shops have such SKIMPY sizes, NOBODY can get into them' said Lucy encouragingly.

Lucy with her bag of size ten Miss Selfridge tops.

They steered me into Size Out.

To be fair, I did try on some quite nice clothes in Size Out. But there was no way I was going to admit it. I tried them on quickly and took them off again in case anyone was looking, in case anyone I knew from London happened to be sneaking around the changing rooms in the Truro branch of Size Out. I didn't really NEED to try them on, you see, because I was going to start this diet tonight so I'd soon be so much slimmer, it would be a waste of money getting any clothes in this gigantic size.

'Try a sarong, Mum,' suggested Victoria brightly.

'Why?' I asked suspiciously.

'They're One Size Fits All. They don't come in sizes. You can get into any. They're really fashionable this summer. And when you lose weight, it will still fit you.'

'All right, all right, point taken. I'll get one from Marks & Spencer's.'

So I went home happy with my sarong, and the girls went home ecstatic with their several carrier bags full of mix and match outfits, bikinis and things that looked small enough to be dolls' clothes. We spent the afternoon giving each other a fashion show, the girls modelling their dolls' clothes, and me wearing my sarong with a fixed smile on my face that was beginning to hurt. It wasn't so much that I was thinking about James. It was just that I was making a determined effort NOT to think about him.

'Perhaps he'll come round. When he's had a chance to get over it,' said Bev when she got home from work and noticed the look on my face.

'I'm not bothered one way or the other,' I lied.

'Don't lie to me.'

'No. That's the problem, isn't it. I shouldn't have lied to HIM. I seem to keep doing it. I never used to tell lies, and now I can't seem to stop.'

'Don't beat yourself up over it, Ally. It's not really the end of the world that you're older than he thought. Or that you're sicker than he thought!'

'Very funny.'

Not sick at all, actually. Lying again.

'I'm not really sick at all,' I told her, wanting to stop all the lies once and for all before they caused any more trouble. 'I only went to the doctor for a certificate because I needed a couple of days off work.'

'Doctors aren't stupid,' Bev told me sternly.

'This one was.'

'No. You just didn't like what she had to tell you. If you ask me, Ally, it was a bloody good thing you did go to the doctor, otherwise who knows how long this might have gone undiagnosed?'

'What? My malingering? My lying?'

'Your stress. You didn't even realise you had it!'

'I haven't! I'm trying to tell you . . . '

'And you're still in denial! You see?'

I gave up. People never seemed to believe me when I told the truth.

★   ★   ★

We had a birthday party in the evening, just the four of us, with sausage rolls, pizza cut into funny shapes, trifle and double chocolate gâteau. I nibbled on bits of cheese and celery and felt sorry for myself.

'This is silly,' said Victoria eventually, shoving a piece of gateau in front of me and putting a fork in my hand. 'It's your birthday, and you're making yourself and everyone else feel miserable. Eat something, Mother, for God's sake, and think about the diet tomorrow if you must.'

I hate when they call me Mother. It sounds so exasperated.

'Sorry,' I said in a small voice, picking up the fork.

'Unless, of course, it's that MAN you're pining over!' she added in an even more exasperated tone.

'Don't be ridiculous!' I snapped.

I wasn't.

I wasn't, actually, whatever you might be thinking, I wasn't pining in the least. I'd known perfectly well it wasn't going to last with James. I just felt sorry that it had to end like that, before I was ready, after so few days. And so few nights. With such an air of disapproval. In such an unfriendly way. While I still wanted him. I knew one day I'd probably laugh about it, about the look on his face when he saw the 'Nifty Fifty' balloons, about the way he turned heel and scarpered at the mention of my stress syndrome. It just could take a little time to reach that point, that's all.

I put a big forkful of chocolate gâteau into my mouth, to a smile of satisfaction from Victoria, and nearly choked it all out again when the phone began to ring.

'You get it,' smiled Beverly. 'Told you he'd come round!'

'Hello, Alison, dear,' crackled my mother's voice over the line from Majorca. 'Just calling to wish you a Happy Fiftieth!'

'Mum!' I spat, spraying chocolate gâteau into the phone. 'We've been trying to get you! What's all this nonsense? All this stuff about staying out there . . . '

'It isn't nonsense,' she said stiffly. I could picture her face setting itself into hard, angry lines. 'We're going into business. We're taking over a little bar in the main square, by the seafront.'

'You haven't! For God's sake, Mum, please tell me you haven't signed anything yet . . . '

'Oh yes, we have! We'll be home for a couple of weeks at the end of the month, to sort out all our stuff there, get everything packed . . . '

'Mum!'

' . . . and we're having the bar redecorated and refurbished in cockney style.'

'MUM!'

' . . . and we'll be ready to open next month. Catch the best part of the season. There's living accommodation over the . . . '

'MUM, LISTEN TO ME!'

Silence. I could hear myself breathing, heavily, into the phone. In, out, in, out. Calm down, calm down.

'No need to shout,' she said, sulkily.

'I can't believe you're doing this,' I breathed. In, out, in, out. 'You don't know ANYthing about running a bar . . . '

179

'Oh yes we do. Ted used to have a pub. The White Hart in Tottenham. You know where the bus pulls in around the back of Woolworths . . . '

'It's not the same as a bloody cockney bar in Majorca!' Breathe. In, one, two, three, out, one, two, three. Think calm thoughts . . .

'What's she say?' hissed Bev from across the room.

'They open for business next month,' I said, passing her the phone. 'YOU talk to her.'

'Mum?' Beverly was trying to sound bright and encouraging. 'How's it going? You've found yourself a little place, then?' Not a good idea to patronise my mother. I could hear the indignant mouthful Beverly was getting, as she ruefully lifted the phone away from her ear.

'Yes, of course we want it to go well for you, Mum. No, we're not being negative. We're just concerned. You must expect us to be a little bit concerned about you . . . Yes, I know you've got Ted to look after you but we don't really know anything about him, do we, Mum? . . . Yes, I'm sure he IS a lovely man . . . Yes, I expect he IS a lot more caring and more interested in you than I've ever been . . . Oh, for Christ's sake!!'

She threw the phone back at me, red in the

face and beginning to shake slightly.

'I need a drink!'

I breathed steadily into the phone for a few more minutes before beginning again.

'Your health,' I said slowly, 'isn't good.'

'I'm much better out here. The sunshine. It agrees with me. I feel twenty years younger.'

Twenty years younger. Christ, that was something, wasn't it. And it had to be said, she sounded different. Animated, excited. She had an interest in life, something to plan for. A hope. It's what we all need, isn't it, when it comes down to it. We need to wake up in the morning and think: 'Today could be good. It could be fun, it could be exciting!' — even if it turns out to be dull and boring. Even if every day of our entire life turns out to be just as dull and boring as the day before, we need to have that little defiant spark in us that tells us it MIGHT, just this once, be different. Otherwise, what the fuck is the point of it all? We might as well stay in bed every day.

* * *

My mother probably felt like staying in bed every day, up till now. What did she have to get up for, when you think about it? She was fed up, bored and miserable. Every day she found another problem, another ache or pain or malfunction somewhere in her body. Something to complain about, something to make everyone else's life miserable about. Now she was out there in the sun with a man who loved her, excited about her life, feeling twenty years younger. What was the matter with me? Was I JEALOUS or something?

'I'm sorry, Mum,' I said quite gently.

'Sorry? What for?' she asked, obviously taken aback.

I felt a sudden and amazing warmth for her. There's a first time for everything.

'Sorry I've been . . . yes, a bit negative about all this. As long as you've got good legal advice . . . yes, I'm sure Ted knows what he's doing but . . . yes, and good financial advice . . . I'm sure he does, yes, he sounds like an absolute Superman . . . well, I hope it all goes well for you. So does Beverly. Yes, she's nodding at me across the room, she hopes it does, too.' Beverly was lifting her wineglass at me with a glazed look of insouciance. 'And the girls are here, Mum! Victoria and Lucy — they're both saying they hope it goes well, too! Now, listen, this phone call's costing you a lot of money, so . . . Yes, I'm having a lovely birthday, thank you. And we'll see you . . . well. Whenever.'

Whenever it all goes wrong. Whenever you fall out of love with Ted. Whenever the holiday atmosphere wears off, the reality kicks in and the dream goes sour. When you start arguing and you suddenly wish you were back in England, with the old familiar worries and the old familiar miseries. When that happens, if that happens, we'll see you then, Mum, because that's what families are all about, aren't they.

I hung up and looked around the room, at my daughters in their new clothes with the remains of my birthday tea spread out on the table in front of them and my sister slouched in the armchair with her glass of wine and her apron on, to make the point that she'd worked in the kitchen to prepare the pizza shapes and the crisps. And the flowers and the birthday cards, and the balloons hanging from the curtain rail. And I felt so emotional about it all, I had to swallow a couple of times and pour myself out another drink.

'What else did she say?' asked Beverly with a slight slurring of the consonants.

'That she missed us all.'

'Bollocks she does!'

'And she'll see us in a few weeks when they come back to pack up their stuff.'

'If they haven't changed their minds by then!'

'I thought YOU were the one in favour of letting them get on with it . . . '

'Sure, yes, absolutely. I'm just a bit cynical

about their long-term prospects.'

'So what?'

We all looked at each other for a minute. Victoria scraped the last of the trifle out of the bowl and licked her lips.

'Mum's right,' she declared. 'So what if it doesn't last? As long as they're happy for now. For a week, for a month, for a year. It's all a bonus, at their age, isn't it.'

'Being happy is a bonus at any age,' I reminded her. 'It's not an automatic state of affairs.'

'Then Nan's lucky, isn't she,' said Lucy earnestly. 'Because up till now she's never seemed all that happy, if you ask me.'

'Better late than never!' laughed Victoria.

'Yeh. And at least I won't have to take her for any hospital appointments for a while,' I said, feeling a huge black cloud suddenly lift off my shoulders. 'And if you want a holiday,' I added with a smile, 'She said any of us would be welcome out there any time.'

It was like I'd lit the touch-paper of a volcano. Victoria leaped out of her chair shouting with excitement, Lucy whooped and danced around the room, Beverly tried to shout them both down with information about flights to Majorca and Did They Realise How Much It Cost? and the phone started ringing again, and . . .

184

'The phone's ringing!' I called.

'Hello?' yelled Beverly, trying to make herself heard above the mayhem. 'James? Yes, she's here, James, hang on . . . '

I grabbed the phone out of her hand so quickly, she claimed later to have blisters in her palm.

'I didn't wish you a happy birthday properly,' he said.

I'd taken the phone into my bedroom to get some peace. And shut the door. And laid on my bed.

'Well, in the circumstances I could hardly expect you to.'

'I just wish you'd been honest with me. Did you really think I'd care whether you were thirty-nine or fifty?'

'Not really. I said it as a joke, but it got more difficult to explain as we went on.'

'So you're not really on holiday. You're recuperating from . . . what? A nervous breakdown?'

I laughed out loud.

'No! I'm not really ill at all. But no one believes me, even the doctor . . . '

'Ally, have you heard about the boy who cried Wolf?'

'I'm not ill. I tried to skive off work, and I somehow got myself into this situation where everyone thinks I'm suffering from stress. Even my family. I've given up trying to convince them . . . '

I didn't like the silence.

'What?' I asked.

'There's nothing to be ashamed of. You shouldn't be embarrassed about suffering from a psychological illness, any more than you would be about suffering from a physical one.'

'But I'm not . . . '

'I mean, if someone's got the flu, or tonsillitis, or something, people feel sorry for them, but if they have a nervous break-down . . . '

'I HAVEN'T . . . '

' . . . nobody wants to talk about it, not even the person with the problem. We all pretend it isn't happening, like it's a disgrace to admit to it . . . '

'James!'

He was beginning to seriously get on my nerves. I could feel myself getting close to the brink of telling him to shut up.

'Suffering from stress is a consequence of our modern lifestyle. We all try to live our lives in the fast lane, taking on too much pressure, and never pausing to watch the flowers grow or . . . '

'James?'

'Yes?'

'Can I tell you something?'

'Of course.'

'You're the best-looking man I've ever met, but you already know that, don't you. I had a fantastic time in bed with you, and I'm really glad you made me realise it was still possible.' I could almost hear him smirking. 'But you don't half talk some crap,' I added calmly.

'What . . . ?!'

'Thanks for phoning, James. I'm glad we could finish up as friends.'

'Yes, but . . . '

' 'Bye!'

Funny thing was, it felt SO GOOD.

★   ★   ★

'Is it all over, Mum?' asked Victoria anxiously, looking at my face.

'Yep!'

'Oh, well,' she shrugged. 'Plenty more fish in the sea, plenty more pebbles on the beach, plenty more . . . '

'Victoria!' Lucy told her sharply, 'Mum's not like you! She's not going to be rushing straight from one relationship to the next! Are you, Mum?' she added, giving me a warning look.

'Hardly likely,' I smiled, 'Considering how

long it took me to move on from your father . . . '

I faltered, realising this was perhaps not the correct thing to say to my daughters, but they hadn't batted an eyelid. No, it was me that was shocked. What a thing to say! Moving ON from Paul? How could I even think such a thing? He was my husband, not just some casual affair like . . . well, like my fling with James. There was no comparison! I couldn't believe I'd THOUGHT such a thing. Far from talking about moving on, I should be fighting to get him back from that bitch from hell Lynnette, shouldn't I.

Shouldn't I?

Strange how I didn't feel very much like fighting.

'Nice birthday, Mum?' asked Lucy, topping up my wineglass. 'You do look better, I think. Cornwall seems to have done you some good.'

In more ways than one, perhaps.

8

Victoria and Lucy slept in Beverly's lounge and stayed for another two days. We went to the beach and watched the surfers, and Lucy chatted up a bronzed, blond young god of the surf called Neil, who snogged her in full view of the rest of the family (to say nothing of the whole of Newquay) and took her out to the pictures that evening.

'What was he like?' I asked her in the morning.

'Horny,' she said, with a smile of appreciation. 'And his friend Martin's got the hots for you, Victoria . . . '

'I wouldn't even look at him!' declared Victoria stoutly. 'My life is in limbo till I get back to Reece.'

I did notice her giving Martin a few flirtatious glances over her magazine on the beach the next day, but I thought it best not to mention it.

The sun shone, the sea sparkled and our skin turned slowly golden brown as we basked on the sand with our personal CD-players and our Ambre Solaire Factor Twelve. We might as well have been in the

South of France. Or Majorca, with Mum and Ted, helping to clean up the cockney bar.

On the Sunday morning we woke up to grey skies and the threat of rain. More than two days of sunshine in England and we start to get over-excited, don't we. Victoria moped around the house for an hour or so after breakfast and then announced that she was missing Reece and that as she had to go to work the next day, they might as well start heading for home. Lucy said she couldn't go without saying goodbye to Neil, so they had to wait for him to be contacted on his mobile phone and turn up at the house on his motorbike. He and Lucy then spent nearly an hour saying goodbye outside the front door. He was too shy to come inside until we bribed him in with a Coke and half a packet of Jaffa cakes, and he then spent another half hour saying goodbye to Lucy a little more thoroughly on the sofa, whilst Victoria, Beverly and I talked amongst ourselves in the kitchen. Eventually Victoria couldn't stand it any more.

'Lucy! I'm going! Right now, whether you're coming or not!' she shouted at her sister, who gave Lover Boy a last lingering kiss, exchanged addresses, phone numbers and souvenirs of each other and waved goodbye to him until his motorbike was a speck in the distance.

'Bloody hell!' commented Victoria as she looked at Lucy's slightly glazed expression. 'You only met him yesterday!'

It happens, girl. It happens.

'I suppose you want to take the car back,' I said with a certain amount of resignation.

'Oh, Mum! We couldn't deprive you . . . ' began Lucy.

'Are you sure you don't mind?' cut in Victoria quickly. 'Only it WOULD be easier, you know, to get home fast so I can get ready for work tomorrow . . . '

'And see Reece for a bit longer,' muttered Lucy under her breath.

'No, I don't mind,' I laughed. 'It's the least I can do, since you came all this way to see me for my birthday. But you'll have to take my black sack of clothes back with you. Just leave me with my suitcase to bring back on the train next week.'

I'd hardly worn any of the clothes, anyway. Most of the time so far I'd either been in my swimming costume on the beach, or naked in bed with James.

* * *

'Got any plans for your second week?' asked Bev as we chilled out with a microwave supper and wine-box that evening.

'Not really. Got any suggestions for me?'

'Well. I daren't introduce you to any more of my male friends. You seem to want to tear their trousers off them the minute my back's turned . . .'

'Not ALL of them,' I smiled. 'Didn't fancy Bo very much.' She laughed.

'No. I think he's an acquired taste. I haven't acquired it myself yet!'

We studied our plates thoughtfully.

'Actually,' I said, 'I wouldn't mind not doing very much at all. It's all been quite . . . unsettling . . . James, and everything. I could do with some time to think about things.'

'Paul?'

'Those sort of things, yes.'

'Well, it has been two years, Ally.'

What was that supposed to mean? It's been two years, so it's about time you got over it? It's about time you found someone else? Moved on? Made a new life for yourself?

'It's about time you accepted her. Lynnette.'

Oh, great! I have to accept HER, do I? Perhaps she should have accepted ME, when she decided to steal my husband — accepted that I was his wife, that he was married, spoken for, not available for general consumption.

'I have no reason,' I said, frostily, 'To accept her. No reason, and no need.'

'But what would you say if they wanted to get married?'

★   ★   ★

Now, there's an interesting thought.

I thought about it that night in bed, tossing and turning and furious with Beverly for bringing it up, spoiling my night's sleep. I thought about it the next day, sitting indoors with a book because it rained again, but unable to read the book because my mind kept straying to the Paul and Lynnette Getting Married Thing. I was still thinking about it the day after THAT, when it stopped raining and I went back to the beach again. Paul and Lynnette getting married. They couldn't. They wouldn't, would they? It had never even crossed my mind before.

So am I stupid, or what? Why hadn't it crossed my mind? I always consoled myself, whenever I thought about Lynnette (which I mostly tried not to do), with the fact that she might have him NOW, but I was still Paul's wife. Official. Certified. Legal. In Church. So however long it took for him to come to his senses and dump her, I would always have the upper hand and he would come back to me

193

eventually. Divorce had never been mentioned. He'd never asked, never even suggested it, and it hadn't even occurred to me because of the temporary nature I'd always ascribed to our separation.

Temporary, but well, you know. I was kind of getting used to it. Over the course of two years, you have to, don't you. You have to get used to it. Not that I didn't still want him back, of course.

Of course I did. That was obvious.

Wasn't it?

I lay on the beach, with my eyes closed, and pictured a very strange scene in my head. There was Paul, dressed up to the nines in his best grey suit (the one he keeps for interviews and christenings), with a white carnation in his buttonhole, and there was Lynnette, in a flowing white bridal gown, veil and all, tripping down the aisle towards him, and behind her, two bridesmaids in pale pink dresses holding on to her train and . . . Hang on! Run back that video just a minute! Who WERE those bridesmaids with their sweet angelic smiles and their satin shiny shoes and their posies of pretty pink rosebuds . . . Victoria and Lucy?! My eyes shot open in shock and horror. Surely not! Surely my own daughters wouldn't turn against me, would they? They wouldn't be bridesmaids to the

Bride From Hell, the husband-stealer, the Wicked Stepmother . . .

Stepmother! I recoiled in terror from this new, even more scary thought.

How dare she! How dare that trollop even CONSIDER becoming any KIND of relation, step or otherwise, to MY daughters! My daughters, my babies, my little girls, that I brought into this world with agony and much moaning and cursing and calling out to God to kill me off and be done with it. SHE didn't go through that, did she? SHE didn't watch her body getting slowly fatter and fatter for nine months and then be torn apart like a worm in a sparrow-fight. SHE didn't have her boobs shrivel up from feeding them, and her bank balance shrivel up from providing for them, and worry lines sprouting on her forehead from worrying about them. She would NOT become their stepmother! She would NOT have them as her bridesmaids! She would NOT marry my bloody husband, whether I wanted him or not!

I re-ran my mental video, in reverse motion. Victoria and Lucy walked backwards down the aisle, pulling Lynnette behind them by the end of her train. Ha! That was better. Paul was looking round at her with a surprised look on his face, and then he, too, walked backwards away from the vicar, who was opening and shutting his mouth like a goldfish. I ran it right back. People were walking backwards out of the church. Wedding cars with white satin ribbons were driving backwards down the road. And who was that? I frowned in concentration inside my head, behind my closed eyes. Who was that sorry-looking figure in the sarong, walking backwards on her own out of the church gate? Was that ME? I really should lose a bit of weight before I appeared in any more wedding fantasies.

'I'm not standing for it,' I told Beverly over dinner, feeling better now I'd made up my mind. 'She's not marrying Paul. He's still married to me.'

'He might want a divorce.'

'He'd have said by now. He hasn't ever said he wanted one. He doesn't. He doesn't want to marry her. He wants to stay married to me. She's just a bit on the side.'

'Ally . . .'

'Don't look at me like that.'

'She probably loves him, Ally. She probably really loves him. Have you never thought of it like that?'

No, quite frankly. I hadn't, and I wasn't going to start now. Love, huh! I was beginning to wonder about the whole thing. I was beginning to see it as just another fairy

196

story. I think, actually, 'Snow White and the Seven Dwarfs', with its seven funny little men and its wicked witch and its poison apple, is a lot more believable than the idea of falling in love (and staying in love), which I think now is just a plot to get us to breed when we might prefer, otherwise, to have nothing to do with such a thing.

'No,' I said firmly. 'She doesn't love him. She just wanted to steal him from me and my children. Well, she can't. She won't EVER be his wife, and she won't EVER be their stepmother! I'd rather see her dead!'

I'd got myself a bit worked up by now.

'Ally!' remonstrated Beverly again. 'You shouldn't say things like that. You don't really mean it.'

'Don't I?' I retorted grimly. 'You watch and see if I don't.'

The wedding video began to play again in my head, only this time it was a funeral. Paul was in his other suit — the black one — without the carnation. I pressed 'pause' quickly. This was, perhaps, a bit sick. I hesitated for a while with my finger hovering mentally over the 'play' button, then pressed 'stop' quickly and turned off. I could always watch it again another time if I felt the need badly enough. It was something to look forward to.

'I don't know what you're grinning about,' said Bev, shaking her head, obviously shocked. 'I think it's a bit sick to say things like that.'

'Yes,' I grinned. 'I suppose it is.'

★ ★ ★

I was actually asleep when Victoria phoned.

'Mum? You're not in bed already?'

'Well . . . ' I'd been lying on top of the bed, fully dressed, contemplating a few things, like whether I should go on a diet and whether Lynnette should be allowed to live, when I'd just kind of dozed off. It was only half past nine. Funny how you could get exhausted doing nothing.

'Have you heard about Lynnette?' said Victoria, coming straight to the point without any preamble.

'What about her?'

I had to make a concerted effort not to start the video running in my head again. Surely not? Surely she wasn't talking about getting married?'

'She's ill.'

'Oh, dear. Nothing trivial, I hope?'

'Mum, that's awful!'

'Only joking,' I said hastily. I wasn't, of course, but I didn't want my own daughter thinking badly of me. 'So what is it? Flu? Measles? Work-related stress?' Perhaps it's catching, I don't know.

'No. Food-poisoning.'

'Food-poisoning! Christ!' Perhaps she should avoid eating her own cooking. 'Is Dad all right?'

'Yes, apart from being worried to death.'

'Oh, come on. Just a stomach upset . . . '

'No, it's been really bad. She's been in hospital.'

Oh. I sat up straight on the bed. This wasn't funny, after all. I'd spent the last couple of days thinking evil, nasty thoughts about the woman and there she goes, getting herself food-poisoning and being taken to hospital. It was scary. I felt as if I'd wished it on her. I'd better be careful what I thought about, in future. If I could cause as much harm as this by just thinking, what would I be like if I did something really spooky like sticking pins in a doll or cutting up her photo? Well, you hear of people doing it, don't you?

'Is she all right now?' I asked a bit shakily.

'Recovering. But very weak, very poorly, really.'

Bloody hell. I thought, with growing unease, about the funeral video. But I did press the 'stop' button, didn't I? Be fair, I did. I did think it would be a bit sick to continue

199

with it. Even if the idea was there.

'Well. I'm . . . er . . . sorry to hear . . . ' I said, trying to sound sorry.

'It's just that . . . ' Victoria hesitated.

'What?'

Paul's decided he wants to marry her? Because she's been ill, he feels he ought to suggest it. He feels sorry for her. Thinks it would cheer her up to get dressed up in white and . . . NO! I am NOT going to watch the video again . . .

'Dad thinks it's you,' she blurted out.

'Me? What's me?'

'He thinks you poisoned her. Lynnette,' she added unnecessarily.

I nearly laughed, but checked myself when I heard the tone of anxiety in Victoria's voice.

'He thinks you put slug pellets in her coffee,' she added, sounding close to tears.

'Oh, how ridiculous!' I exclaimed. 'For God's sake, Victoria, I hope you told him to grow up and get a life . . . '

'He's serious, Mum! I'm surprised he hasn't phoned you himself. He says you threatened to do it . . . '

'I was JOKING!'

'And then you made her a cup of coffee and told her you'd poisoned it!'

'JOKING, for Christ's sake! What's the matter with him? Can't he take a . . . '

Well, no, he obviously couldn't. I suppose he wouldn't, would he, with his girlfriend lying ill and feeble in a hospital bed. I began to feel a rising tide of alarm. He surely wasn't serious?

'That cup of coffee was AGES ago!' I said. 'And anyway, I don't even know what slug pellets look like! Or how to get hold of them.'

'So you did say it? You did tell her you'd poisoned her?'

'Victoria, you're not listening to this rubbish, are you? Has everyone gone mad?'

'No, Mum,' she said quietly. She sounded tearful.

Bugger Paul! I was furious with him. How dare he upset the girls with this nonsense! He was only trying to get back at me for teasing Lynnette. Hurting her precious little feelings.

'You and Lucy take no notice of this!' I ordered sternly. 'Understand? And tell your father . . . ' I ran out of steam. What were they supposed to tell him? That he was a total prat? That he should stop causing trouble and get back to looking after his sick girlfriend, try to stop her eating anything else that upset her? 'Tell him I'm on my way home,' I finished with sudden determination. 'Tomorrow. I'll see you tomorrow. OK?'

'All right,' sniffed Victoria. 'I'll tell him.'

Total prat.

It wasn't much of a homecoming. My own daughters looked at me as if I was an axe-murderer and even the cat wouldn't come near me, presumably because he'd heard I was handing out slug pellets like Smarties.

'Dad's coming round,' said Lucy.

'Oh, goodie.'

'Wants to talk it over with you.'

'I bet he does,' I said grimly.

'How are you?' she added, switching on the kettle.

How was I? I stared at her for a minute without comprehension. It was Lynnette that was supposed to be ill, wasn't it? Oh, hang on a minute — of course, the work-related stress! I'd forgotten all about it.

'Fine, fine,' I said vaguely. 'Be back at work on Monday.'

'If the doctor signs you off,' she warned.

'Well, it shouldn't be a problem if no one tells her I'm a mass-poisoner, should it.'

'It's not really funny, Mum.'

I'm not fucking laughing.

* * *

Paul sat down on the edge of the sofa, looking at me warily. How did I get to have such power? All the family tiptoeing around me, looking at me with a sort of respect mixed with fear. What I'd have given for that when the children were little and I needed them to do as they were told, and Paul to help me. Silly me. If only I'd realised all I had to do was start a rumour that I was a crazy woman with access to deadly poison!

'You've put some weight on,' he said.

'Thanks. You look good, too.'

A ghost of a smile. Perhaps he wasn't convinced, yet, that I was crazy.

'I mean, I'm surprised you don't look ... you know. Ill. Thin. Drawn. Wan. Wasted ... '

'All right, I get the picture. Instead, I look fit and fat. Could be because there's nothing wrong with me.'

He ignored this, like everyone did.

'Sorry to hear about Lynnette,' I said with a supreme effort.

'She's been very ill.'

'So I hear.'

We looked at each other. Your move. No, yours I think.

'Food-poisoning,' he said, nodding at me.

'Awful.'

'Something she ate, they say.'

'Usually is. That's why they call it ... '

'Ally!' he snapped. 'I'd appreciate you not

being flippant, just this once!'

'Sorry.'

'It affected her kidneys.'

'Poor her. Nasty. But she's getting better?'

'Yes. The point I'm making, Ally, or trying to make, is . . . '

I looked at him with interest. Polite, concerned interest. The point is . . . ?

'The cat. He had the same symptoms, didn't he. And it affected HIS kidneys.'

Actually, that was quite interesting, I had to admit. Quite a coincidence, that. What was the point he was making here? Lynnette was like a cat? Or she'd caught a disease from Apple Pie? I frowned at him, concentrating, really quite caught up in it all. Enlighten me, do.

'And the vet diagnosed poisoning with slug pellets.'

'The vet? Lynnette saw a VET?'

'Don't be obtuse, Ally. The vet you took Apple Pie to. He diagnosed . . . '

'Oh. Well, he said it COULD be slug pellets. He said cats often pick them up from gardens . . . '

I stared at him.

'You're saying I poisoned my own cat?!'

My hands flew to my mouth. This was horrific. I couldn't believe it. Christ, it was one thing to suggest I'd try to do away with

204

Lynnette, but my OWN CAT? What sort of a maniac did he think I was?

'Did you want to find out how much it would take, Ally? How many slug pellets would kill a cat, before you tried putting them in Lynnette's coffee?'

'I don't even know what a slug pellet IS!' I whispered.

'They kill slugs,' he said flatly.

'Paul, you're not serious about all this, are you? Come on, I know you want to get back at me for upsetting Lynnette, but this isn't really very funny . . . '

'No. It isn't.'

'I say these things. It's a sort of . . . outlet. For my feelings. For God's sake, you can't blame me for my feelings! I don't MEAN anything by them. Can you really imagine me trying to hurt anyone . . . '

'Not normally.'

'What's that supposed to mean?'

'Well, as everyone's been trying to point out to you, you're not exactly normal at the moment. Not exactly yourself, are you?'

I stared at my feet. They looked normal. My legs looked like mine. My hands and arms didn't look any different. My stomach was definitely a bit fatter, but still mine. I was ME. I hadn't changed! I hadn't turned into some sort of monster overnight, had I?

'You're not . . . going around saying these things to anyone else, are you?' I asked, quietly, hearing my voice wobble.

'Not yet,' said Paul.

Not yet. He made it sound like a threat. Not yet, but I might. I might tell the papers, the local radio station, the police.

I shuddered. There'd be a knock on the door in the middle of the night.

'Mrs Bridgeman? Wife of Mr Bridgeman, now living with Lynnette of the Private Hospital? We're arresting you on suspicion of the attempted murder, by poison, of one black and white cat and one skinny red-haired woman. You're not obliged to say anything but . . . '

'I didn't do it!' I'd scream. 'I love that cat! He's my only friend in the whole world! Ask him! Go on, ask him! He'll tell you how much I love him, how I talk to him when I dish up his Whiskas, how I cuddle him when he jumps on my lap, how I rushed him to the vet when he was sick . . . '

And couldn't pay for his treatment.

'The only witness for the defence,' the judge would be told at my trial, 'is a black and white cat who refuses to answer any questions.'

'Has the cat taken the oath?'

'Won't hold the Bible, M'Lud.'

'Arrest that animal for contempt of court!'

'Apple Pie!' I'd wail as he was led off in chains, miaowing pitifully.

'You won't get apple pie where YOU'RE going,' the prison officer would growl, and I'd be taken away in a Black Maria, with a huge ugly crowd pressing against the windows, hissing at me with contorted angry faces.

'*The Slug Pellet Poisoner!*' the tabloid headlines would scream.

'Woman tested poison meant for husband's mistress on her own cat!'

And all the animal rights activists in the country would send me hate mail in prison, where I'd be kept in solitary confinement to protect me from the other prisoners, who wouldn't tolerate cruelty to cats. No one would mind about Lynnette, apart from Paul, who'd spend the rest of his life campaigning for my sentence to be increased. I'd languish in jail, slowly losing my mind, saying nothing to anyone and only occasionally being heard to cry 'Apple Pie!' in a plaintive wail. One kind prison visitor might take compassion on me and bring me regular fruit desserts, and try not to mind when I threw them on the floor and stamped on them, still calling out for Apple Pie, my only friend, the only one who could save me, if only he could talk.

'What?' snapped Paul.

'If only he could talk,' I repeated, realising with a start that I'd said it aloud. 'Apple Pie. He'd tell you I didn't give him any poison.'

'Sorry, Ally. Cat's CAN'T talk,' he said brusquely, getting to his feet. 'Which is why you used him to test the stuff, wasn't it.'

I stared after him.

'Paul! You don't REALLY think . . . ?'

'I'll see myself out,' he said.

* * *

Snotty-Nosed Nicola seemed surprised to hear from me.

'Oh yes! Ally!' she said, almost as if she'd forgotten who I was. 'How's it going? You . . . er . . . hurt your back, or something, didn't you?'

'No. I had stress,' I said, stiffly, wanting badly to include the 'work-related' but not daring to.

'Oh yes. So how's it going?'

She couldn't have sounded less interested if she'd tried. Probably had Simon's tongue in her ear.

'I'm better, thank you,' I replied with dignity. 'I'll be back at work on Monday.'

'Oh. Really? Are you sure?'

I didn't like the sound of that. They ought to be expecting me back on Monday. The three weeks would be up.

'Of course I'm sure,' I said, trying to sound positive.

'And has the doctor signed you fit now?'

'He will do, tomorrow. I've got an appointment in the morning. So I'll be back on Monday.'

'Do me a favour then, Ally. Phone us again when you've been to the doctor, all right?' She was crooning at me as if I was a poorly child with a hearing problem. 'Then we can discuss it further.'

Discuss it further? Discuss WHAT further? And why the hell was I getting myself into the situation of discussing anything at all with this jumped-up bloody receptionist?

'I'd like to speak to Simon, please,' I said firmly. 'Now.'

If he can get himself out from under your skirt.

'I'm sorry, Ally,' she crooned sweetly. 'He's out of the office just at the moment.'

Yes, I bet he is.

'I'll ring him again later, then,' I said.

'Yes, that's the best thing. Ring him after you've seen the doctor. All right, Ally? Then we can discuss it properly.'

I spent the rest of the day worrying about what 'it' was and why we needed to discuss it properly. Eventually I couldn't stand it any more, and dialled the direct line number to my own office. Liz would be able to reassure me that nothing sinister was going on. She, at least, would be pleased to hear I was better. She'd be looking forward to me coming back to work, wouldn't she. I smiled to myself in anticipation of being welcomed back.

'Don't overdo things the first few days,' she'd say. 'Just settle yourself back in gently, let me take your phone calls and get your tea from the machine for you . . . '

'Good afternoon. Can I help you?' said a strange voice, jolting me out of my smiling anticipation.

'Er . . . sorry . . . who's this?' I stammered.

'Tracey McMarn, temporary secretary. Can I help . . . '

'No, you can't help me!' I snapped. 'Is Liz there?'

The call was transferred with a cold offended silence.

'Hello?' said Liz warily, having obviously been warned that there was a madwoman on the phone.

'Liz, it's me. Ally! Who's that snotty-nosed Tracey person and what's she doing on my phone?'

'Hello, Ally! How ARE you? Feeling any better?'

Funny, Liz was sounding almost as croony as Nicola.

'I'm fine, thank you. But who . . . '

'Did you have a lovely time in Cornwall? With your sister? Was the weather lovely?'

I felt like a baby lying in a pram, with adults hovering over me making goo goo noises. Any minute now I'd get a nursery rhyme sung to me.

'Yes, it was great, thanks. But listen, who's the . . . '

'And did it make you feel any better? The holiday? Are you nice and brown?'

Yes, and I'm also fifty years old and capable of listening to sentences of more than five words. And I want some answers.

'Liz,' I said loudly, 'Who's the temp? Tracey McWhat's-her-Face? How long has she been there, and how long does she think she's staying?'

'Yes, Tracey's settled in very nicely,' said Liz, in much the same tone I might have used about my daughters when they started playgroup. 'She's getting on very well with everyone — aren't you, Tracey?'

It's me paying for this phone call, actually, not fucking Tracey. You can talk to her later.

'Got her family photos on my desk?' I

asked bitterly. 'Cleared out any of my desk drawers yet?'

'Oh, she's handling things VERY well,' Liz said cheerily, ignoring me. 'She's already got to know most of the clients — haven't you, Tracey?'

I hated her. The bitch.

'Going out to the pub with you on Fridays, I suppose, is she?' I persisted, clenching my fist around the phone.

'Yes, yes, we've had a few little drinks — haven't we, Tracey?'

'And I suppose she's looking for a permanent job?'

'Well, you ARE rather hoping something might come up — aren't you, Tracey?'

Well, you're in for a big bloody disappointment then — aren't you, Tracey? Because I'm getting my arse back into that chair quicker than you can say 'Can I help you?', and I'll erase every little sign of you from that office, every file you've opened, every document you've produced, every coffee stain on the mouse-mat, before you're out of the door! Stick THAT up your temporary contract, you conniving little cow, you!

'I'll see you on Monday,' I said to Liz, and hung up abruptly before I had to listen to her expressions of surprise and warnings about not rushing back too soon as Tracey was quite capable of covering for another six years.

It's a fragile thing, is loyalty.

* * *

Just when you think things can't get any worse, they inevitably get worse. I was running late for my doctor's appointment in the morning so I decided to take the car.

'Where's my car, Victoria?' I called out, staring blankly at the space where it was normally parked.

'Oh!' she smiled at me. 'I forgot to tell you!'

You may think it slightly strange that I'd been home from Cornwall for two days without noticing my car wasn't there, but when you consider that since I'd been home I'd been accused of two counts of attempted murder and threatened with replacement by a temp, you might begin to understand that my mind had been just a tad preoccupied elsewhere.

'What,' I asked Victoria very nervously, 'What have you forgotten to tell me?'

Not that it had been stolen. Please, God, please, not that. I don't deserve any more bad luck, do I? Whatever I did in my previous life, or my childhood, or my adolescence, or last week even, that was so bad, surely I've paid for it by now? Surely there isn't MORE punishment to come? I closed my eyes, waiting for the blow to be dealt.

'We decided to give you a surprise,' she smiled again, looking very pleased with herself. 'Lucy and me. We wanted to treat you.'

'So you gave the car away?'

I might have threatened to do it myself on occasions, but I didn't mean it! You should know by now that I don't mean half the things I threaten! Murders, poisonings, car abandonment — they're all just idle threats . . .

'No! We put it in for its MOT, Mum!'

'Oh!' I gave her a hug. Nice to know they still loved me, despite having doubts about my sanity. 'That was very sweet of you!'

'Yes. We paid for it. Between us. As a sort-of birthday present.'

'Well, I'm very grateful. That was a lovely thing to do.' I waited. She smiled back at me happily.

'So where is it?' I asked. 'The car. Where is it now?'

'Oh.' She looked down, the smile fading a little. 'Still in the garage.'

'They're bringing it back? What time . . . ?'

'No. They're keeping it there. Till we decide what to do. Well, till you decide, really.'

'Sorry?'

'We could only afford the test fee, Mum. And it failed. It failed on six different things. It'll cost about three hundred and fifty pounds to get it through. I said you'd think about it.'

I walked to the doctor's.

9

I was pleased it was Dr Lewis I was going to see this time. I'd liked the little girl locum, particularly after she seemed to know such a lot about my pretend symptoms, but at the end of the day she'd done nothing but get me into more trouble. Giving me a certificate for work-related stress had been a stupid move, and as for giving me three weeks off work, well, she might just as well have written to Snotty Simon and suggested he gave the job to Tracey whenever he liked. Dr Lewis knew me. He'd see straight away that whatever minor, temporary little touch of stress I might have had, it was no big deal and certainly not enough to keep me off work. He'd probably tell me to go straight back this afternoon, car or no car. He'd probably get little Dr Holcombe on the phone straight away and tell her off for over-reacting.

'Hello, Alison,' he smiled warmly, stretching out his hand to me as soon as I walked into his surgery. 'Long time no see!'

You see? He knew I wasn't a sick person. Sick people are regular visitors to their doctors, aren't they. Me, I was so healthy I

216

had to ask the times of the surgery hours every time I phoned for an appointment because it had been so long since the last time.

'And how are you now?' he continued as I sat down. 'I see you've had a few problems recently?'

'Not really,' I smiled, trying to brush my few problems aside with a little toss of my head. 'Nothing that a little bit of rest couldn't take care of. You know how it is, Dr Lewis. Sometimes you just get a bit overtired, and things seem a bit worse than they really are . . .'

He was nodding at me with grave concern, which I was finding very off-putting whilst I was trying to maintain my smiling and my head-tossing.

'And have you been able to sort out any of your anxieties now?' he asked me quietly, looking straight into my eyes as if he was trying to hypnotise me.

'Anxieties?' I laughed, flicking my hair back gaily. 'Oh, they weren't really ANXIETIES, you know, just little niggles like we all have . . .'

'Worries about losing your job?' he asked, looking down at my notes and then back into my eyes. 'About your boss not liking you? Anxieties about your financial situation?'

Bloody hell, she'd told him the lot. What happened to patient confidentiality? I sat up a bit straighter in the chair.

'The anxieties are . . . sorting themselves out,' I said uneasily.

'And your age-related concerns?'

'Pardon?'

'Dr Holcombe thought you might have had a problem with approaching your fiftieth birthday?'

I smiled to myself briefly, remembering the morning of my fiftieth birthday. I'd probably never have another orgasm like that as long as I lived.

'You coped with the occasion?' Dr Lewis prompted me. Not half.

'Oh, yes, I coped, thank you, doctor,' I smiled.

He was approaching me with the blood pressure machine.

'And the rest from work has done you good?'

Until I heard about Tracey McMarvellous, the temp sent from heaven to change the world . . .

'Yes, thank you.'

We both waited in tense silence for the reading from my arteries, whilst he continued to look into my eyes as if he was examining them for specks of dirt. Just as I was beginning to feel uncomfortable with the scrutiny, he announced:

'It's higher than it should be. Your blood pressure. And I've got no doubt about the reason.'

I'm dying? I'm having a stroke? A heart attack? I'm on my last legs, not likely to last the night?

'Physically, you're in very good shape.'

So the blood pressure machine's on the blink?

'Psychologically, I think you're in trouble.'

The silence lasted for a good thirty seconds before I yelled at him, smiling and head-tossing having completely gone out of the window:

'Well, thank you very much! I thought at least YOU would stand by me! Everybody else thinks I'm raving mad, even my kids, even my husband, even my best friend at work doesn't want me back! Even the bloke I screwed on holiday thought I was having a breakdown . . . '

'You had casual sex on holiday?' he asked me calmly.

'Yes! And it was great!' I retorted.

'Did you use a condom?'

'Of course I did . . . what is this, sex education for the over-fifties?' I snapped.

He looked back at me, his calm, caring eyes

resting impassively on my face, waiting. He didn't have to wait long. I'd known this man since I was a new bride. He'd seen me, as I've said before, in every position known to man (or woman). He knew me inside out. Literally. Under his gaze, I suddenly felt overcome with something like shame. I don't know why. After all, I was a free woman, a deserted wife for Christ's sake. I could go and have sex with the whole of the county of Cornwall and nobody could blame me. I could have it off with every man I looked at and . . .

'All right,' I said. 'I suppose it was pretty stupid.'

'You're an adult,' he replied.

'I hardly knew him.'

'You make your own decisions.'

'It was a bad one.'

'It happens all the time. You're human. Don't be hard on yourself.'

'I'm not.'

Am I?

'Then what else is wrong?'

'Nothing.'

'Nothing? I don't think many people could say that, Alison, and certainly not many single parents with financial difficulties and job pressures, to say nothing of the worry of caring for elderly parents . . .'

'I told you, my anxieties are resolving themselves. My mother's gone, for a start.'

'Gone?' He shot me a look of acute concern.

'Oh, no. Not gone as in . . . departed this life. Just departed this country. She's gone to Majorca with a toy-boy to open a cockney bar.'

I felt myself frowning.

'How the hell she hopes to survive out there, I just can't imagine. What on earth does she think she's doing, taking such a risk at her time in life, and I don't even know this Ted — he could be after her money — not that she's got any . . . '

'But your anxiety about her has resolved?' he pointed out gently.

'Well. You know. Perhaps only partly,' I conceded.

'But the girls are well?'

'Fine. Victoria buys *Brides Magazine* every time she meets a new boy and Lucy's taking her first-year exams. No worries there,' I said, feeling my jaw tense as I said it.

'And Paul?' He did that thing again, where he looked straight through my eyes so that he could tell if I was lying. 'You're getting used to being on your own, now, Alison? How long has it been?'

'Two years,' I said tetchily. 'But that's no

reason why I should accept it!'

'No?' he prompted.

'No! And I wouldn't accept them wanting to get married, either, not ever! I'd rather see her dead!'

I nearly bit straight through my lip after I'd said it. Shit! Why did I keep on saying that? Me and my big mouth!

'But I didn't MEAN that!' I added hastily, watching him scribbling in my notes. 'Don't write that down!' He put down his pen and looked at me again. 'I'm not saying I'd want to actually . . . you know . . . murder her. Not with poison, not with anything else. I wouldn't even know where to get hold of slug pellets, for God's sake! And my cat! I love my bloody cat! It's not my fault he was ill!'

Jesus Christ, I was crying now. Blubbing out loud. I could actually hear myself, making these big sobbing noises while I was still trying to speak.

'I wouldn't hurt my cat! I love him! I wouldn't hurt anyone, not even Lynnette, the stupid cow, she probably just ate some of her own cooking . . . '

A box of tissues appeared in front of me. I groped for one and blew my nose violently.

'I want my job back!' I howled, changing the subject abruptly. 'I want that bitch Tracey out of my seat! I need the money more than she does! I want my friends to like me again! I want my daughters not to be scared of me! I don't want everyone thinking I'm a mad woman! I'm as sane as you are, Dr Lewis! Tell them!'

The strange sobbing noise carried on for a few more minutes, getting gradually quieter, while he wrote in the notes and I soaked a few more tissues. I looked at my watch. I'd been in here for fifteen minutes. How had he done that? How had he reduced me to a snivelling wreck in fifteen minutes? I'd been perfectly all right until I walked in here.

'I'm sorry,' I muttered, sniffing. 'I don't know what came over me. I was perfectly all right until I walked in here . . . '

'I don't think so,' he replied, very seriously.

He passed two pieces of paper across the desk to me. I picked them up, shakily. One was a prescription for Diazepam. The other was a certificate for a further three weeks off work.

★ ★ ★

I don't know why I didn't argue. I should have put up a fight, refused to accept the certificate, told him I wouldn't leave until he'd signed me back for work. Instead I listened meekly while he told me I was to rest completely, have no contact with work whatsoever, and if I wasn't feeling any different after these three weeks were up he'd refer me to 'one of his colleagues'.

'A psychiatrist,' I said dully.

'It probably won't be necessary. Maybe just a stress counsellor. In the meantime, Alison, there are some self-help steps you can try.'

Oh yes? Self-counselling? Sounds like talking to yourself to me, and everyone knows what that's the first sign of.

'You can think about your diet,' he went on, writing 'DIET' on a piece of paper.

I stared at it.

'You think I need to lose weight?'

'That's not the issue here. The objective is to achieve a healthy mind through a healthy body. Stay off the junk food, the alcohol, the caffeine, the chocolate — all stimulants . . . '

All the things that keep me bloody going.

'And exercise.'

He wrote 'EXERCISE' under 'DIET' on the paper.

Exercise? I might have no choice if I can't find the money to get the bastard car through its MOT.

'Something strenuous, Alison. Something that will get you really out of breath . . . '

Walking up the stairs? Making the beds? Reaching for the remote control?

'Jogging, or swimming, or aerobics. Join a gym!'

'A gym!' I exploded. 'I haven't even used the word since I left school! I hated all that stuff — vaulting over bloody great horses and somersaulting over bars. I couldn't even do the run-up, never mind the somersault. And I hated wearing those navy blue knickers, anyway.'

I was getting stressed just thinking about it. He was out of his mind!

Oh no. It was me that was supposed to be out of my mind, wasn't it.

'Health clubs aren't like your old school gym lessons at all, thank goodness!' he laughed. 'They're very popular, Alison. And you don't have to wear navy knickers, trust me.'

'So that's it, then? I cut out all the pleasurable things I normally eat and drink, and put myself through physical torture, and then you'll let me go back to work?'

'I'm only suggesting things that might help,' he replied gently. 'And the other thing, of course is breathing.'

Well, I hadn't been planning on stopping that.

'Learn some relaxation techniques. You can get tapes from the library. When you feel yourself getting tense and worked up, you can learn to cope by relaxation and deep breathing . . . '

He wrote 'RELAXATION' under 'DIET' and 'EXERCISE', and passed the piece of paper to me with a smile and a putting down of his pen that indicated my time was up. Well, to be fair I had been in there quite a while. The baby in the waiting room who'd been brought in for his vaccinations was probably a teenager now.

'Thanks,' I said, putting the paper in my pocket with the prescription and the certificate, and left the room feeling a hundred times worse than I had when I'd gone in.

How did this happen? How had I gone from making up a few little, tiny, harmless lies about some trivial symptoms, to get a few days off work, to having a full-flung breakdown that required drugs, rest, diet, exercise, relaxation and possible psychiatric counselling? When did I cross the line from pretend to real?

Was it real?

Or was I still pretending?

Why couldn't I tell the difference any more?

Was I really as mad as everyone seemed to think I was?

Or was I the only sane one left around here?

I was lying on the floor when Lucy came home, listening to *Floating*. *Floating* was one of two tapes of relaxation music I'd got from the library whilst waiting for my prescription to be processed at Boots. The other one was *Drifting* but I hadn't tried that yet. *Floating* had loads of floaty music interspersed with some bird with an irritating sleepy voice telling you how to relax each bit of you in turn. It reminded me of those awful childbirth classes where you had to tense and then relax muscles in your toes and face and buttocks and pretend they were the muscles of your cervix. As that was possibly the most stressful memory of my life, it wasn't doing a great deal to relax me, but I'm open to all suggestions so I had my eyes closed waiting for the next bit of advice.

'Are you asleep, Mum?' asked Lucy without much interest. She turned off *Floating* and replaced it with her new Boyzone CD.

'No,' I said, opening my eyes. 'I was relaxing.'

'What, listening to that shit?'

Boyzone began to sing out lustily that they loved the way I loved them. They should be so lucky. I closed my eyes again and tried relaxing to Ronan Keating's dulcet tones. Certainly no worse than *Floating*, and no insinuations about childbirth classes.

'The exam was crap,' said Lucy mildly, throwing herself down on the sofa and stuffing two chocolate digestives into her mouth at once.

I sat bolt upright, clasping my mouth in horror, all thoughts of relaxation shot to dust.

'Your exam! I for . . . didn't forget . . . I just . . . had a few other things . . .'

'Don't worry, Mum.' She wiped biscuit crumbs off her chin and swung her feet up on to the arm of the sofa. 'It was awful. I revised all the wrong things.'

'Oh, Lucy!'

'But never mind. Three more to go next week. As long as I do better in them . . .'

'How much better?'

'Brilliantly. I need to do brilliantly, now, to make up for the rubbish I've done today. If I don't, I'll be redoing the whole year.'

She spoke with a shrug, nonchalantly swinging her legs in time to Boyzone, but she didn't fool me. She was staring straight ahead of her at the framed picture of herself and Victoria on the fireplace. I followed her gaze. Two little blonde toddlers, the elder's arm protectively around the younger's shoulders, turning her face towards the camera. I could hear her now, as if it was yesterday:

'Look at Mummy, Lucy. Look at the camera, Lucy. Smile like me, Lucy, like this. Come on, Lucy, do like I do.'

Do like I do. It was hard to break out of the little sister thing, to NOT be in Victoria's shadow, to NOT do like Victoria did. Victoria had got a job straight after doing her A-levels. Lucy had gone to college. It wasn't that she had to be better than Victoria — she just had to be different. I could understand that. She had to succeed.

'You'll do it, Luce,' I told her gently, levering myself up off the floor to perch on the sofa arm next to her feet. 'You'll pass, I know you will . . .'

'You've got no idea!' she suddenly snapped, leaping to her feet, making the sofa tip up from my weight on its arm. 'You've got no IDEA how hard it is! I wish I'd never done this course! I'm no good at it! I can't do it! I'm going to fail all the exams! I might as well give up! I might as well leave now!'

★ ★ ★

She stamped up the stairs to her room in much the same way as she had when I'd refused to buy her another My Little Pony about fifteen years back.

229

'What's with HER?' demanded Victoria, coming in at the front door just as the house was shuddering from the slamming of the bedroom door.

'Exam nerves. Just leave her alone,' I snapped.

'I AM leaving her alone.'

She looked at me bleakly, her lower lip wobbling, her eyes filling up with tears.

'What's the matter?' I asked, taking a step towards her.

'Nothing,' she sniffed, tears pouring down her face.

'You don't want to tell me?' I prompted.

'Oh, what do you THINK it is?! It's just MEN. I hate them! All of them! I'm never going out with another one as long as I live! I'll be a nun! I'll be a lesbian! I'll be a virgin! They're all PIGS!'

And she followed her sister's route upstairs, her bedroom door closing more quietly but with a kind of sustained misery. Reece, I presumed, had joined Darren and all the others in the 'Ex' file.

I turned off Boyzone, who were by now singing some very inappropriate lyrics about love being for ever, no matter what, and went into the kitchen to peel some potatoes. *Floating* would have to wait. It seemed to me that everyone else around here was a hell of a lot more stressed out than I was.

I spent the weekend, in between coaching Lucy on her exam techniques and counselling Victoria about life without love, shopping around for gym memberships. And I got a few shocks, I can tell you.

'Do you mean to say,' I asked the bright young thing who'd taken my call at 'Fitness Is Fun', 'That not only do I have to pay £500 for a year's membership, but on top of that I still have to pay every time I want to come and use the equipment?'

To be honest I didn't understand what the equipment was, but I did understand what being taken for a ride meant, in a gym or out of it.

'That's right, madam,' trilled Sammy-Jo or Billy-Bo or whatever stupid thing she'd said her name was. 'But you get a Special Introductory Rate for the first month, entitling you to Free Advice and Health Check from our Fitness Instructor.'

'I'd expect him to take me out to dinner every night at that price!'

'Sorry, Madam, although food is available at our Fitness Food Bar, your membership doesn't include . . . '

'Oh, forget it,' I sighed, putting down the phone.

The next one was the Wesley Manor Golf and Country Club with Swimming and Leisure Facilities.

'What sort of leisure facilities?' I asked the young man warmly, picturing wide-screen TV and leather armchairs, open fires, perhaps a decent bar with basket meals.

'Olympic-size pool, sauna, jacuzzi . . . '

'And?'

'Eighteen-hole championship golf course . . . '

'And?'

'Squash courts, tennis courts . . . '

'And?'

'Fully equipped gymnasium and cardiovascular fitness training centre . . . '

'No bar?'

'Health food bar, yes, Madam.'

And how much for this purgatory, this hell on earth, this masochist's fantasy world?

'Seven hundred pounds annual membership, Madam, plus green fees for golf of course, and court fees for squash or tennis, and pool entrance fees for swimming, and . . . '

' . . . and is this a Country Club or a brothel?'

'I BEG your pardon, Madam . . . ?'

'Sorry. But it seems to me you're screwing all your customers.'

*   *   *

But not me. Even if I'd HAD seven hundred quid, even if I knew what it looked like, what it felt like to hold it in my hand or even see it in my bank account before it was direct-debited away from all sides as soon as it was paid in, there was no way in the world I'd ever spend it on the Health Club from Hell. I'd rather have a holiday. I'd rather get the bastard car through its MOT. I'd rather buy a complete new outfit of clothes that fitted me. Sarongs, whatever. By the time I'd worked my way through the health clubs and fitness centres section of the Yellow Pages I was feeling far more stressed than I'd ever imagined possible, and had to have a lie-down with *Floating* to calm me down. As this, by now, was inducing panic attacks about childbirth every time I heard it, it was beginning to be a fruitless exercise so I turned it off and was considering pouring myself a stiff gin instead when Beverly phoned.

'Are you back to work tomorrow, then?' she asked cheerfully.

'No. Can you believe the doctor's given me another three weeks off?' I admitted miserably. 'I don't know what's the matter with him. He seems to think I've got a problem.'

'What did you say that made him THINK that?' she asked suspiciously.

'Nothing! What do you mean? Why would I say anything to make him think I was off my trolley? All I want to do is to get back to work. Especially now they've got a temp in who thinks she knows my job better than I do. She's probably writing her application for my job even as we speak! She's probably sabotaged my files, erased all my data from the computer and made it look as if everything I ever did was wrong, to say nothing of undermining my relationships with the rest of the staff and taking my name off the coffee rota . . . '

'Not that you're paranoid or anything?'

'No! It happens, Bev, I'm telling you. You know how Snotty-Nosed Nicola and Slimy Simon hate me. And now I can't even drive to work because the bastard car's failed its MOT and I haven't got the money to get it patched up again.' I sighed deeply.

'Anything else wrong?' asked Bev.

'Yes. Victoria's broken up with the love of her life and wants to become a lesbian nun, and Lucy's going to fail all her exams and leave college. And Paul thinks I poisoned Apple Pie!'

At this, this most hurtful of allegations, this most wounding of all the insults that life had thrown at me, I began to sniff a bit with a bout of self-pity. Well, you couldn't blame me, could you? I wasn't exactly crying, though God knows any lesser person, any more STRESSED or depressed or neurotic person might have done and nobody would have minded in the least. I was just having a bit of a sniff.

'Cry!' exclaimed Beverly loudly, making me jump and stop sniffing in surprise. 'That's right! Let it all out! Have a bloody good cry, that's what you need, girl! Go on, cry as much as you want! Don't bottle it up inside you! That's what's making you ill, if you ask me — bottling it up!'

'Is it?' I asked timidly, having lost all desire to so much as grizzle, the moment she'd started shouting about it.

'That's your trouble!' she asserted, still shouting. Why did everyone seem to think that as soon as you had problems (real or imaginary) with your mental health, your hearing packed up too? 'You stifle your emotions! You bury your instincts! You don't give vent to your anger!'

I will in a minute, if you're not careful.

'You need to practise shouting and screaming!'

'I don't see how that's going to help to calm me down,' I said wearily. 'And to be honest with you, Bev, I'm sick of listening to advice. The doctor gave me three words on a piece of paper, which roughly translated spell out misery and deprivation. I've tried following them. I mean, I do want to get better and get back to work — that's if there was really anything wrong with me in the first place. Relaxation got me stressed out because the woman's voice on the *Floating* tape reminded me of ante-natal classes. Diet's making me stressed out because the girls want to pig out on comfort food whilst their lives are going through mega crises, and they snap at me every time I produce a tomato out of the fridge, and as for Exercise, just finding out how much it costs to join Wesley Manor Golf and Country Club is enough to give anyone a nervous breakdown!'

This was probably the most I'd said, calmly, for a long time to anyone. Beverly was obviously impressed. There was silence for a good ten seconds while she thought it over.

'Well,' she said eventually, a little more quietly. 'I can see what your problem is.'

'You've already said. I don't give vent to my primal feelings.'

'That too. But what you're doing here is, you're aiming too high.'

'I am?'

'Yes. Look at yourself. The doctor tells other people to relax, diet and exercise, and they go home, have a sit in front of the TV,

236

eat some fruit and go out for a walk. You? You have to go over the top. Relaxation tapes! *Floating* indeed!'

'But Dr Lewis recommended it!'

'And trying to give up junk food! Honestly! As if you could! As if anyone could! No wonder the girls are resentful. Go and buy them a bag of doughnuts, for God's sake, and stop fooling yourself . . . '

'But Dr Lewis said . . . '

'And as for joining a HEALTH club! In your dreams, Ally! In your dreams!' She was laughing uproariously now. Glad my little misfortunes served to bring light into someone's life, anyway. 'You'll be telling me next you're going to wear those awful navy blue knickers! Remember? Like we wore in school gym lessons?'

'Yes,' I said tersely. 'I do remember, thank you, and I don't intend to ever wear them again.' No, nor stand in a queue for a vault over a horse that looked like it was going to damage my gynaecological health for the rest of my life. 'Dr Lewis said health clubs are nice, friendly, helpful places and loads of normal people go to them nowadays . . . '

'I bet he bloody did. Probably owns shares in one.'

'But I can't afford it, anyway.'

'Of course you can't. Take no notice. Just

do the sitting down in front of the TV bit, Ally, and eat some lettuce if you like.'

'But I would quite LIKE to get fit, Bev, as it happens. Specially as I've got three weeks off work to do it in.'

'Three weeks? It'll take more like three years, girl. You've got decades of bad habits to make up for!'

'Well, thanks for the encouragement!'

I managed a laugh, just a little one. See? Even talking about exercise was making me feel better.

'Go for a walk,' said Bev more seriously. 'Go for a jog, go for a swim, go for a bike ride . . . '

'Haven't got a bike!'

' . . . but for Christ's sake stay out of those navy knickers! All right?'

It was all right for HER to talk. She used to be good at gym. She used to be good at netball, and hockey, and all those other torments that I used to hate. I used to lose my navy knickers, and my plimsolls, and my hockey boots and that horrible little pleated netball skirt, as often as I could manage so that I could be excused and keep my clothes on, but it didn't often work. If ANYthing in my life has damaged my psyche, I tell you what, it's school PE lessons. They have a lot to answer for.

I started keeping a 'Relaxation, Diet and Exercise' diary on the Monday, just to show I was serious about it all, and also to show Dr Lewis when I went back, in case he thought I hadn't been trying.

'Monday 23rd June', I wrote very neatly on the first page. Just like being at school. I always wrote very neatly on the first page. I used to sit and look at my very-neat writing with fondness and pride, turning the page this way and that, admiring the perfect symmetry of my letters, the straightness of my lines, the eveness of my spacing and paragraphing. Then on the second page I'd either make a blot or make a cock-up of some sort that involved erasing a word with an ink-eraser. Remember those? They never worked, did they? They just made a horrible bloody mess on the page, and then, inevitably, as I got crosser and more frustrated and rubbed harder and started to panic, I ended up with a hole. A hole that went right through the page and ruined my perfect neat writing on page one. So that was the end of that. By page three, I'd stopped caring and resorted to my usual scrawl with doodles in the margins, that used to get me into trouble.

'Monday 23rd June,' I underlined twice with neatly ruled lines.

'*Relaxation: managed five minutes of listening to Floating without thinking about childbirth. Lay in front of TV on cushions and practised breathing whilst watching* Neighbours.

Diet: breakfast: grapefruit and muesli (excellent). Lunch: lettuce and tomato sandwich (excellent). Mid-afternoon: two Penguins. One chocolate digestive. Five Jaffa cakes. Dinner: chicken with salad (excellent). Later: a few chips off Victoria's plate. Later: the rest of the Jaffa cakes. Bedtime: corned beef and pickle sandwich (very hungry).

'*Exercise: found on old pair of trainers and tried them on, with a view to starting a jogging regime.*'

All in all, not a bad start. Tomorrow would be even better. And as for the neatness of my first page!! — it was beyond reproach.

★ ★ ★

Things were definitely looking more cheerful in the Bridgeman household by the next day. Lucy had apparently managed to answer all

240

the questions on her exam paper that morning, and despite all her answers being total crap and it probably being the worst paper any student on that course had ever handed in, she was talking a little less about killing herself and hadn't mentioned leaving college more than four times during the evening meal. Victoria had been lent a book by a friend at work called *Nobody Needs A Man In Their Life*, and was eagerly quoting passages from it to anyone who'd listen, which basically meant me because Lucy plugged her CD Walkman into her ears as soon as she started.

'Listen to this, Mum! 'The period of history during which men were looked up to as head of the household, leader of the tribe, is coming to an end and will probably not last another decade.'! Wow! Do you think that's true?'

'Perhaps,' I conceded vaguely, trying to concentrate on the neat writing of page two of my diary.

''Men are lost and confused,'' she went on.

Join the club.

''They have no identity, no purpose, no place. They have become irrelevant to the majority of women in the civilised world. Their aggression is not only unnecessary but unwanted in our lives.''

You could almost feel sorry for the poor little sods.

''Millions of years of patriarchy are being turned upside down . . .''

'Victoria, do you think you could just read that to yourself?'

I'd come very close to writing a wonky 'D' on 'Diet' and I really, really, didn't want to spoil this page.

'But Mum! It's absolutely amazing! Don't you think?'

'I've heard it all before, to be honest,' I said wearily. 'We're supposed to be able to do without men and live happier, more fulfilled lives without them. Great! So why do we all sit glued to the TV when George Clooney's in *ER*, and gasp and sigh every time he smiles?'

'It's pathetic!' she agreed. 'Well, I for one refuse to be at the mercy of my hormones for the rest of my life!'

I looked at her in alarm. What was she considering? Hysterectomy? Sex-change surgery?

'I'm giving them up!' she declared stoutly with the religious conviction of a saint. 'For life!'

'So what's it to be? The convent or lesbianism?'

She shot me a scathing glance.

'Self-control.'

I dropped the pen, smudged the word 'Diet' and tore the page, all in one go.

'Sod it!' I exclaimed crossly. 'Now look what you've made me do!'

'Celibacy!' she went on cheerfully. 'It's the only way.'

'Is it?'

'It's gaining popularity. Take my word for it, Mum, in a few more generations, everyone will be doing it.'

Oh well. By the time she'd realised the difficulty there, at least she would have finished the damned book. And at least she was more cheerful again, even if it was going to be slightly wearing having a celibate in the house, coming off the Pill and refusing to watch *ER*. When the doorbell rang, my only concern was that if it was a man, Victoria might treat him to one of her quotations. I got to the door just ahead of her, in case.

It was Simon the Slime, from work. And he was carrying a basket of flowers. And smiling.

Perhaps celibacy had its points after all.

10

I said the first thing that came into my head, which tends not to be a good idea.

'What are you doing here? I'm not allowed to have any contact with work. My doctor said . . . '

'Sorry,' he said, and that was strange for a start — Simon saying sorry. He even looked it. He stood there on the doorstep, clutching the basket of flowers and looking sorry, whilst Victoria hovered behind me with almost tangible vibes of hostility radiating from her. I expected her at any moment to call him a superfluous remnant of defunct male superiority or a testosterone-charged genetic design fault.

'Go and . . . er . . . feed the cat, please, Victoria,' I said firmly.

I felt the sigh of her disapproval on the back of my neck, but she went, and I heard her banging tins of cat food about in the kitchen.

'You'd better come in,' I told the superfluous remnant of defunct male superiority. 'Or my neighbours will talk.'

He stepped into the hall, looking even

more uncomfortable.

'These are for you,' he said, not meeting my eyes, putting the flowers down on the hall table.

From the girls? A collection?

A Get Well present?

Or a leaving present?

What was he trying to tell me?

Why, after all, would he come round here, Simon of all people, Simon who hated me, who held the power of work and unemployment over me, Simon the Slime-man, in my home, bearing flowers, looking shifty. Very shifty.

'You're getting rid of me,' I said, my voice shuddering on the edge of control. 'Aren't you? That's what this is about, isn't it — getting rid of me and replacing me with Tracey McMarvellous.'

'No!'

I was surprised by his vehemence. He almost stamped his foot.

'What?' I continued with the merest suggestion of sarcasm. 'No as in 'Not Yet'? Or No as in 'Not Tracey'? Come on now, I've heard how good she is! And I've heard she's looking for a permanent job. I bet you can't wait . . .'

'No! Not Tracey, and not anyone.'

I stared at him. He really was very agitated.

It flashed through my befuddled brain for just one fraction of a millisecond that he was really, underneath all the previous antipathy, madly in love with me, hence the flowers, hence the agitation . . . but I quickly recovered my senses, which was reassuring.

'Can we . . . er . . . do you think we could sit down?' he continued miserably.

I led him into the kitchen, where Apple Pie was gulping Whiskas down with greedy self-absorption and Victoria was pretending to stack the dishwasher.

'Thank you, Victoria,' I said in my new firm voice.

She sidled out of the room without looking at Simon but giving me a reproachful glare as she passed.

'He's my boss,' I tried to mouth at her, but this obviously impressed her not at all. He was still the enemy, the endangered species, the outdated relic of paternalistic society.

'The thing is . . . ' said Simon nervously as he sat down on a kitchen stool.

Nervously! How the tables had turned! How the worm had squirmed! If only I'd been able to foresee, that day he'd made me beg and plead for my job, facing him across his huge and shiny desk, that he'd be sitting here tonight in my kitchen, SQUIRMING nervously!

'The thing is, Alison, I need to talk to you about this business of work-related stress.'

'You can't stop my pay!' I said at once, with more confidence than I felt. Actually, I realised with some surprise that I probably DID appear confident. For once in my life, I had the upper hand. I had a few definite advantages, such as:

1. *It was my house.*
2. *He was sitting down, I was standing up.*
3. *This was my kitchen. My KITCHEN, of all the rooms in the house. My domain, where I'd spent nearly all my bloody life, peeling potatoes and feeding the cat, feeding babies and cleaning the sink, emptying bins and buttering bread, frying eggs and unpacking shopping, drinking coffee and . . . well, you get the picture. And furthermore:*
4. *This was where I kept the knives.*

Now, don't get me wrong. I wasn't anticipating needing one. I hadn't flipped so seriously that I was contemplating sticking the bread knife in his back or cutting his throat with the grapefruit knife. But — well, it was reassuring to know that this was where I kept them. I always used to be reassured by that thought, when I was sitting lonely in the kitchen drinking coffee when Paul used to be out at night and the babies were asleep in bed. There were enough sharp knives in that kitchen to defend myself against the Russian army, should they be planning an invasion.

'You can't stop my pay,' I repeated, calmly, folding my arms and staring at Simon across my kitchen table. 'I've been certified sick by the doctor.'

'I know,' he said. 'We've got no intention of stopping your pay, believe me.'

I didn't like this new, nervous, squirming, oh-so-sincere and here's-a-basket-of-flowers Simon. I didn't like it at all. It made me very, very suspicious and very, very irritated. Just looking at him now, and remembering how he'd treated me that day in his office, so supercilious, so dismissive, so arrogant . . . I wanted to punch his lights out. Or take the grapefruit knife to him?

I could just see the headlines in tomorrow's tabloids:

'Insurance Magnate's Son Found Dead in Employee's Kitchen!' 'Mad Cat Poisoner Stabs Boss With Grapefruit Knife!'
('He brought her flowers,' says daughter, 21 and celibate.)

I took a knife out of the dishwasher, tested

its blade against my finger, held it up to the light, put it back again. Not sharp enough.

'Are you . . . all right?' asked Simon.

'Fine, fine. Just testing the knives.'

'Listen,' he tried again, evidently anxious to move the conversation on, 'The point is, nobody at the office realised you were . . . '

Crazy?

Such a superb worker, an asset to the company?

So beautiful?

Human?

' . . . under stress.'

'I wasn't. I mean . . . not until recently,' I corrected myself quickly. I looked at him with increasing dislike and added: 'Only since the interview in your office when you issued me with my Serious Warning. You know, the one that was going to go on my Personal File.'

He blanched. He really did! He turned white, looked like he was going to throw up, then went abruptly pink, then had a coughing fit from which I began to have doubts that he would ever recover. Save me a job with the knife.

'Want a glass of water?' I asked eventually out of mere politeness and to pass the time before he stopped breathing.

He nodded, eyes popping, tongue lolling in a most unattractive fashion. I'd seen healthier sights in geriatric wards.

'Consider it . . . ' he choked over his glass of water.

'Consider it . . . '

'Done?' I prompted, bored.

What the fuck was this all about? I'd been hoping to watch a new series of *Two Point Four Children* at nine o'clock.

'Consider it struck off!' he managed eventually, loosening his collar and spitting up the last mouthful of water. 'The Serious Warning. Struck off your Personal File. As from today.' I stared at him, suddenly not bored any more. This was, suddenly, interesting. It might even be worth missing the programme for.

'Why?' I asked, simply.

Could it be? Could he be in love with me after all? Not realised it till he heard I was ill? Oh, I do hope so. It would give me such enormous pleasure to turn him down, the nasty, two-faced, ignorant, obnoxious, unpleasant little git. I wouldn't sleep with him if he was the last man in the universe. I'd even sign up for celibacy with Victoria.

'Because we want you back at work, fit and unstressed,' he said, unconvincingly. So much for rejecting his sexual advances. Pity. It was almost as good as the knife fantasy.

'Why?' I persisted.

'Because you're . . . a good worker . . . of course!' He was wriggling uncomfortably on his stool. He was hating this, hating every minute of it. Why had he come, if he hated it so much? What had forced him to come . . . ? Or . . . WHO?

'Who made you come round here?' I demanded, already knowing the answer. 'And don't try to pretend you made the decision yourself, out of decency, humanity, or compassion, because I'd have no choice but to stab you.'

His eyes bulged again and I thought he was about to start another coughing fit.

'Well?'

'My father,' he admitted, looking at his shoes. 'My father was very concerned to hear about your work-related stress . . . '

'Yeh,' I smiled. 'Yes, I bet he bloody was! I bet he's shitting himself, isn't he? I bet he's hurrying back even as we speak from his golf course in Portugal, or his whore-house in France, or wherever it is he hangs out when he's pretending to be abroad on business, jetting back with sixteen changes of under-wear he's so shit-scared about the possibility of me taking the company to court for causing my illness!'

Simon continued to study his shoes.

'Isn't he!'

'Probably,' he admitted finally in a whisper.

'Well, you can tell your old man something from me,' I said, folding my arms again and giving him the most evil look I could manage.

Oh, this was lovely, this was! I could get used to this, this having the upper hand. It was almost orgasmic. No wonder people get hooked on power. I watched him squirm and wondered how it would feel to throw him on the floor and stand with my foot hovering over his bollocks.

'Tell him I MIGHT decide to sue the company, and I might NOT. It depends.'

'Depends on what?' he asked fearfully. He obviously had to get the message right, to report back to Dad.

'How I get treated when I come back to work, of course,' I replied scathingly.

'So what are your demands?' he said.

'Demands? Demands?' I retorted. 'What do you think I am? A blackmailer?'

Honestly. My reputation was shot to buggery these days, what with accusations of poisoning and all.

'Of course not,' he said at once.

He'd agree with anything I said, right now. I could ask him to kiss my feet, and he'd be kneeling on the floor slobbering over my socks before I could blink.

'All I'm saying is,' I continued, and I had to

think about this to make sure I got it right, said exactly what I meant, because I'd never get another opportunity, 'I don't want it to be the same old thing when I come back. Being picked on for every five minutes I come in late, even if I work hours later than I should in the evenings. I want a bit of understanding if I need time off for my car, or my cat, or my mother, or any of those things we all can't help. If I make up the time by working late, or working my lunch-breaks, why can't you be reasonable about it? Why is it one law for Nicola, and another law for me? I expect to be treated the same as her. Except, of course, for the sex, because that would make me puke.'

A bit daring, that. In normal circumstances I'd never have gone that far, but we weren't in the workplace now, were we — we were in my kitchen. With the knives.

'I understand,' he said quietly.

I didn't really need to say any more, so I didn't bother. Quit while you're ahead. Simon left, hurriedly, still looking at his feet, promising things would change, things would be different, everyone at work would live happily ever after and all the angels in heaven would sing. I shut the door after him, wondering if I'd just had an out-of-body experience in a time warp on another plane.

The whole thing seemed so completely unreal. Nothing for it but to sit down with a glass of wine and a box of Jaffa cakes, and watch the end of *Two Point Four Children*.

★　★　★

I went jogging the next day. Well, to be absolutely honest, I put on the trainers, went out, jogged to the end of the road, stopped for breath, walked round the corner and then it started raining so I jogged halfway home. And walked the other half. When I got home I had to have a cup of tea and two slices of toast and jam to get over it. But it was a start, wasn't it?

The next day I jogged to the bus-stop before getting the bus to Tesco, but that was a bad idea because I then felt too knackered to push the trolley round the shop. However, by the end of the week I was jogging for England. I could keep going all the way to the end of the road, round the corner and almost back again without dying. My diary (apart from the smudge and tear on page two) was looking impressive. I'd cut down on chocolate to the point where I only ate one Jaffa cake at a time, and had started doing the relaxation exercises to Boyzone, as their CD was always playing anyway and they didn't remind me of childbirth.

I came back from my morning jog on the Saturday morning to find a motorbike parked outside our house. I slowed down (well, I was slowing down by now anyway on account of the sweat dripping down my neck and the pains in my sides), and stared at it. I didn't KNOW anyone who drove a motorbike. I didn't even know anyone who knew anyone who drove one. Then I remembered, just at the same moment as the front door opened and he came out with all his limbs wrapped around my younger daughter. Neil.

'Morning, Ally!' he called out cheerfully from somewhere around Lucy's neck.

'Mrs Bridgeman', I felt, would have been more acceptable for the first few encounters, but at least he wasn't ignoring me.

'Morning,' I puffed and wheezed. 'What are you doing here?'

It took me a few seconds to realise how ungracious that sounded, and I followed it up quickly with:

'I mean, all the way from Cornwall?'

'I drove down this morning. To see Lucy,' he explained with a wide grin as she gazed into his eyes with the adoration of a new convert at a shrine.

'He's staying the weekend,' she smiled, stroking his hand.

'Where?'

'Here,' smiled Lucy again.

The smile was so soppy it made my stomach heave. Lucy had had boyfriends before, but so far she'd managed to avoid getting that look on her face. She'd always enjoyed making fun of Victoria whenever she'd fallen madly in love, and now . . .

Victoria!

The man-hater!

The chastity fighter!

The born-again virgin!

'Where's your sister?' I asked sharply.

'Sulking in her room,' said Lucy without taking her eyes away from Neil's. 'We're going out on the bike,' she added, putting both arms tightly around his waist as if they were already on it.

I looked at the bike suspiciously.

'Be careful . . . ' I warned with the automatic and irrepressible fear of a mother about to put her offspring into the hands of an unknown stranger and a dangerous machine.

'Don't worry, Ally,' said Neil with perfect seriousness, putting a helmet on Lucy's head and smiling at her as if it was the latest fashion and suited her more than any Paris model. 'I'll look after her better than anyone's ever looked after her in her life.'

She simpered and giggled and obviously thought it was the most romantic thing anyone had ever said to anyone in the whole history of the universe, whilst I fumed with annoyance at the implied insult that anyone could EVER look after either of my babies better than I'd been doing for the past couple of decades. AND I'd be the one to mop up the tears and soothe the heartache when he disappeared back to Cornwall on his bloody bike. But did she even give me so much as a backwards glance as she sailed off into the distance clutching him tightly from behind, with her face pressed against his leather-jacketed back?

Motherhood's a bastard at times.

★　★　★

'I can't believe it!' exploded Victoria, pounding down the stairs as soon as I set foot in the door. 'What's come over her?'

'The same thing that came over you, with Reece,' I sighed wearily, 'And Darren. And . . . '

'Yes, but I was allowing myself to be dictated to by my hormones. I allowed myself to believe it was love, but really it was just

257

irrational biological instincts . . . '

'I know.'

She stared at me.

'What do you mean, you KNOW?'

'I know, because everyone does it.'

'You KNEW? And you never TOLD me? You allowed me to make an absolute IDIOT of myself . . . ?'

'Victoria, can you imagine how you'd have responded, when you were dancing around the house singing love songs, reading *Brides Magazine* from cover to cover and grabbing the phone on its first ring, if I'd told you: 'You're not in love, it's just your hormones'?'

'Well, thanks very much! I thought I could have relied on YOU . . . '

'And I suppose YOU're going to tell Lucy, now, are you?'

'I already have done.'

Oh, great. World War Three must be about to kick off in my own house.

'And how did she react?'

'Told me I was jealous!' exclaimed Victoria furiously. 'Can you imagine?! ME, jealous of her with that scruffy, long-haired prat . . . '

'So she didn't listen to your reasoning?' I pointed out gently.

'No! She totally ignored me!'

'She obviously hasn't read your book yet,' I smiled.

'Oh, OK! Take the piss out of me, go on!'

She turned her back on me and started to raid the fridge for comfort food.

Like I say, motherhood! It's a bastard at times.

★ ★ ★

Lucy and Neil roared back up to the house at somewhere round about feeding time. Love didn't seem to have dulled their appetites.

'Can we have chips?' shouted Lucy, taking off her crash helmet and cuddling it like a baby. Neil's spare helmet. Did it smell of him? Of his after-shave or his hair gel?

'Chips sound great!' grinned Neil, and they sat down together on the sofa and proceeded to stroke and tickle each other's necks.

'Oh, yuk!' exclaimed Victoria. 'Do you MIND?'

'Lucy, if you want chips, go and start cooking them,' I told her in the no-nonsense tones of an in-control mother. A non-stressed, non-psychotic, non-sick mother.

'Yeh, go on, go and cook them,' repeated Victoria nastily, sneering at Neil as she said it.

'Mind your own business,' snapped Lucy.

'Thought you were stressed out over your exams?'

'Thought YOU were stressed out about being dumped!'

'Dumped? Huh! No fucking man's gonna dump ME! I'm never giving another one a chance! I'M not going to prostitute myself for . . . '

'You calling me a prostitute?' glared Lucy.

'You acting like one?'

'Hey, that's ENOUGH!' I decided to intervene, just as Lucy aimed the first swipe at Victoria.

Victoria squealed and lashed out blindly, knocking her cup of tea over the cat, who'd been dozing on her lap. Apple Pie ran yowling out of the room, closely followed by Neil, who was obviously embarrassed by the girls' fighting and pretended to need the toilet.

'Wimp!' muttered Victoria.

'Shut up!' returned Lucy.

The doorbell sounded. Probably the neighbours complaining about the noise or the RSPCA having heard reports of a scalded cat. I opened the door cautiously.

'Hello!' sung out my mother, who was leading by the hand a dapper little man in a blue suit. 'This is Ted! Can we come in?'

★   ★   ★

260

They made Lucy and Neil look like a rather reserved old married couple. Mum sat in an armchair and patted the seat next to her, shifting over so that Ted could squeeze in beside her. They held hands and smiled cheesily. Victoria was elected to go out and get a take-away, which she did with obvious relief, muttering 'Yuk' viciously to herself.

'We got a taxi from the airport,' explained Mum, patting Ted's hand with every syllable. 'Didn't want to bother you.'

Just as well. With my poxy car in the garage without its MOT, and Victoria's current mood of hostility towards any suggestion of heterosexual behaviour, their only hope would have been a ride on Neil's bike.

'So you're back to sort things out?' I asked.

'That's right, dear.'

Dear? My mother calling me 'dear'? Had she flipped? Too much Spanish sun?

'We've got a lot to do. Packing everything up, sorting out . . . '

'You're not selling your flat?'

'I'm not stupid!' she retorted with a flash of her old bad humour, softening again quickly as soon as Ted squeezed her hand. 'We're both keeping our properties here, just in case,' she smiled.

'Not that we expect any problems out there,' added Ted. It was the first time he'd spoken apart from 'Pleased to meet you'. 'British bars are big business in Majorca.'

He said it like an advertising slogan:

'British Bars Are Big Business In Majorca! Buy one now — special half price offer till the end of June!'

'Good,' I said weakly, still having great difficulty imagining my mother behind the bar, pulling pints.

Had I ever really known her? I stared at this stranger sitting in my lounge with her boyfriend and her deep Majorca tan. She looked younger, slimmer and fitter than I remembered her. What had happened to the arthritis? The headaches, the bad chest, the skin conditions and the unmentionable problems with her bladder? How was Ted coping with her insomnia? Her food fads? Her allergies which changed according to the season and her moods which swung more violently than the weather? He didn't LOOK worn-down and defeated. He looked at her with the kind of devoted affection I'd only really ever seen before in the eyes of that old spaniel I used to have.

Only one possible explanation for it. Love. Love had tamed her. Love had changed her from a fearsome old biddy into a new and gentler person. Eat your heart out, Victoria! — and the author of *Nobody Needs A Man*

In Their Life! Here was living, breathing evidence of your fallacy!

My mother ate her way through chicken tikka masala with onion bhaji and pilau rice without once complaining about her digestion, or complaining about anything else for that matter, and we talked about Majorca, and the British Bar Business, and the legalities and practicalities of starting up in it, and Ted came to life and opened up and told us about his years of running The White Hart pub in Tottenham, and the characters he met there, and the things he learned, the wealth of experience he built up. He told us without a trace of coyness or embarrassment how he had met my mother and fallen in love with her and how he'd throw himself into the pit of Hell before he'd see any harm come to a single hair on her head. Lucy and Neil looked at each other with dewy eyes and even Victoria swallowed back any sarcastic reply that might have been brewing and gazed at her wineglass in silence. The wine had no doubt helped towards the silence but it was welcome in any case.

When their taxi arrived to take them back to stay at Mum's flat for a couple of nights ('We'll sort out my stuff first and then go on to Ted's'), I hugged her and said a few affectionate things that I'd probably never said before, and which owed less to the wine than to Ted's speech and, to be fair, the change in her own demeanour.

'It's a strange thing,' I admitted to Victoria as we scraped the curry plates and loaded the dishwasher, 'to suddenly start liking your mother at the age of fifty, and just as she's about to leave the country for good.'

And Victoria gave ME a hug and said how lucky she was that she'd always liked HER mother and didn't have to wait till she was fifty to find out. And I laughed and said she must be as pissed as a fart, but I shed a tear or two when I went to bed, and whispered one of those rare little prayers that you say on these occasions, thanking God a thousand-fold for letting me have two lovely daughters — one of whom was sleeping off her excess alcohol in front of the TV and the other of whom was sleeping with her new boyfriend (and hopefully adequate contraception) in the room next to mine. I put the pillow over my head and fell asleep thinking about James.

*　*　*

'No,' I told Bev on the phone the following day, 'I never think about James at all. Why would I?'

I'd phoned to tell her about our mother,

264

reassure her about Ted and their chances of future happiness, but she seemed determined to discuss me instead.

'Any other men on the scene?' she asked casually.

'No. Not unless you count Simon the Slime-man, the most repugnant lump of flesh outside of an abbatoir, who spent most of Tuesday evening shitting himself in my kitchen over the possibility of me suing the company for giving me work-related stress.'

'Wow! What an idea! Are you going to?'

'For Christ's sake! I've got enough to worry about, haven't I? But I did send him off with his tail between his legs, jabbering frantic promises about treating me more fairly when I go back to work.'

'Good for you.'

'Yeh. I feel so much better. What with that, and Mum, and the jogging.'

'You've started jogging?'

'Getting good at it! Next time you see me I'll be slim, and fit, and athletic, and energetic . . . '

'Don't overdo it, girl. I'd settle for seeing you happy and rational, and together with some horny man.'

'I thought you said rational?' I laughed.

'Are you off men? James finished you for life?'

What a way to finish!

'No . . . although Victoria and her book do make a few good points. My problem's not giving them up, it's finding any. Always supposing I wanted to,' I added quickly.

'So Paul's out of your system?'

Crash. Just when you manage to spend about twenty-four hours not thinking about somebody, you hear their name and the walls come caving in again.

'Paul's got Lynnette,' I said dully. 'And he thinks I'm a mass-poisoner.'

'But you're not giving up hope altogether, eh?'

Oh, very funny. I seem to remember she said the same thing when I got turned down for the school swimming squad, and with the same degree of sarcasm.

And the same accuracy of assessment.

★　★　★

I knew I had to make a decision about the car, but how? Where was the money going to come from to get it through its exam, and if I couldn't find the money, how was I going to manage without it when I went back to work? Two buses and a tube to get across London for the pleasure of working for Slimy Simon. Or two tubes, one bus and a ten-minute walk if I went the other way. I couldn't afford the extra time. I'd be late every morning, and then I'd be REALLY handing him a reason for sacking me. On a plate, work-related stress or no.

I jogged past the garage where the bastard car was languishing, and pulled faces at it behind its back. The bastard! I'd loved it, cherished it, cleaned it at least once every couple of months or so, bought it unleaded petrol and even put one of those little hanging things in the windscreen that smell of pine. And this was how it paid me back! It sat there, bloody sulking, and didn't even CARE that it had failed its test, miserably failed, failed to the tune of three hundred and fifty quid. It didn't even have the decency to throw an exam-stress wobbly like Lucy did!

'You'll be sorry,' I told the car as I jogged past it for the second time, having now built my stamina up to the point where I could do two whole circuits without completely collapsing. 'You'll end up being sold to some maniac boy-racer who drives you through built-up areas screaming at sixty miles an hour on two wheels. Or a used-car dealer!' (I thought I noticed the car shudder at this, but it may have been a trick of the light, or the effect of the sweat dripping into my eyes.) 'A used-car dealer who dissects you whilst you're still alive, and sells your internal organs for spare-part surgery! And serve you bloody right!'

Actually, after saying it I felt sorry, and wished I hadn't been so cruel. The car would never forgive me for that, and if I did manage to get it back, it would stall on hills and roll backwards into buses, and break down on dark winter mornings with no anti-freeze in it, and . . .

I did a third circuit, which came close to killing me, and made parts of my legs ache which hadn't been used since I (once only, and never again) tried horse-riding; and on passing the garage this third and final time, I smiled sweetly at the car and wished it well, and reassured it that I'd either be back one day soon to liberate it from its forecourt purgatory, or I'd sell it to a good, kind, caring retired vicar who'd polish it every week and never drive it above the speed limit or swear at it when it dropped a bumper.

Picture me thus, if you will, jogging in a very slow and exhausted manner on my knees, sweat sticking my T-shirt nastily to my chest and running down my neck, conversing in frantic gasps with a car on a garage forecourt, when a shiny silver BMW passed me at a gentle cruise and the driver, leaning casually on the half-open window, caught my eye from above his dark glasses and smiled.

And for some reason I smiled back, although it hurt all my muscles to do so and made breathing even more difficult. And as he accelerated away at the green light, I stopped to recover from cramp in my side and found myself staring after him. And feeling like I knew him from somewhere, or that he reminded me of someone, which considering the dark glasses was a pretty unrealistic thought.

But for some reason or no particular reason at all, I memorised the number plate of the shiny silver BMW. It wasn't difficult to memorise. It was IOU 1.

11

'*Monday 30th June.*

Diet: excellent. Run out of Jaffa cakes. Too knackered from jogging to cook dinner. Lucy pining over Neil, Victoria moody about Lucy pining, so nobody eating much. Found an old tin of chicken soup in the cupboard, past its sell-by date but tasted OK.

Exercise: excellent +++. Will probably enter next London Marathon. Did THREE circuits of usual route past the garage today and was admired by a BMW driver. Will borrow Lucy's sweat-band tomorrow. Might get hair cut. Need to buy tracksuit.

Relaxation: given up. Two out of three's not bad. How can you relax when your car's glaring at you from a garage forecourt and your husband STILL hasn't phoned you since calling you a poisoner?'

The other thing I'd done, was to forget to take the Diazepam. Well, I couldn't really have needed it, could I, if I only took it for two days and then forgot it? I felt guilty about even having been given it on the NHS when there were probably people out there, REALLY stressed-out people, who needed it. I resolved to take the rest of the pills back to Boots next time I went shopping. Dr Lewis would never know.

'You're looking better, Mum,' said Lucy a few days later, having started to recover from Neil's visit to the extent where she could look around her again and notice other things in the world.

'Better than what?'

'Just better. You look . . . different.'

I looked at myself in the mirror. It was true! You really ARE the fairest of them all, Snow White! I'd lost a bit of weight already. Some of my clothes were feeling more comfortable, and others, the ones that had already felt comfortable on account of their elastic waistbands or huge baggy nature, were starting to look like maternity smocks. I'd had my hair cut shorter so it didn't fall all over my face when I was jogging, and my skin somehow looked better. Lack of Jaffa cakes? I'd avoided the aisle in Tesco where they lived, when I'd done that week's shopping, and thereby also avoided Kit-Kats, Penguins and everything else associated with chocolate comfort.

'You ought to go out and buy yourself some new clothes, Mum,' said Lucy generously.

'What with?' I smiled ruefully.

'Well, you're not spending anything on petrol at the minute, are you?' she pointed out.

* * *

I sat down and worked out that three weeks' petrol to and from work (I didn't count the first three weeks I had off, because I had petrol to Cornwall then to pay for), plus a couple of weeks' worth of Jaffa cakes and Penguins, chocolate digestives, doughnuts, crisps, nuts & raisins, Mr Kipling mini apple pies, treacle tarts and chocolate mini-rolls, would amount to at least fifty pounds. I was so surprised, I added it all up four times, and to be honest fifty pounds was on the conservative side. I then spent a further ten minutes (no longer) debating the issue of whether I ought really to put that fifty pounds somewhere safe in the hope that it would somehow, magically, grow into three hundred and fifty pounds so that I could save the life of the car. Towards the end of the ten minutes, Victoria came in from work and said:

'Mum, is there some reason why you keep on wearing baggy clothes?'

She looked pretty startled when I leaped up

272

and kissed her. The car could wait. If I gave up chocolate and cakes for life, I could perhaps save up for its operation in about five years.

And so it was that I was in Dorothy Perkins that Friday lunchtime, trying on skirts in a size I used to be before I started the normal expansion programme of middle-age (to say nothing of the extra pounds the comfort eating of my more recent Worrying Things had made me gain), when I met Liz. I turned round from the mirror to see her staring at me across the changing room.

'Ally! My God, I didn't think it was you at first!'

'Hello, Liz,' I said a touch frostily. Well, be fair. The last time I'd spoken to her, she'd hardly been able to spare me a word, she'd been so busy gushing about bloody Tracey.

'I can't believe it!' she continued in great apparent excitement. 'You look so WELL! Have you been to one of those . . . health farmyards?'

'No. One of the pigs came to see me, though.'

'Sorry?'

'Simon. Last week. Bearing flowers . . . '

'Oh. Yes. I heard about that.'

'You did?'

We stared at each other for a moment, me

273

in my old baggy T-shirt with a smart blue Dorothy Perkins skirt (size twelve), Liz holding an armful of blouses she'd apparently already tried on, and then before I'd even realised I was going to do it, I was letting her have it. All my bitterness and frustration, right there in the changing rooms in front of a line of mirrors and an assortment of semi-naked females of varying ages and shapes.

'You could have bloody well phoned me! I know you've got Amazing Trace now, and I realise I can't compete, but I AM coming back Monday week, whether you like it or not, and after all the years we've worked together, I thought we were friends, Liz! Whatever happened to sticking by your friends, that's what I'd like to know! You and Mary, both of you! Once, one measly time, you came round to see me before I went to Cornwall, and then when I got back it was like I had some contagious disease, not a single sod has come anywhere near me! Well, thanks very much, all of you, for your concern, and you can go back and tell them, all of them, that I think they're a selfish, uncaring load of shits and I just hope nothing ever happens to THEM, because . . . '

I ran out of breath. It was very quiet in the changing room, embarrassingly quiet. People were doing up buttons and zips quickly, hanging things on hangers and getting out of there. I unzipped the blue skirt and stepped out of it.

'But you and Mary, most of all,' I added, quietly, not looking at her. 'I'm gutted, to tell you the truth. I thought you'd have stuck by me, at least.'

I picked up my bags, and turned to go, still not looking at her.

'Don't just walk out,' Liz called after me.

'Why not?'

There was a silence. I turned my head back to look at her. I was glad I'd managed to say all that without losing my temper or crying. I could make a dignified exit now.

'Why not?' I repeated calmly.

'Because you're only wearing your knickers,' she replied.

★ ★ ★

We went to Burger King. It was supposed to be her lunch break, but she phoned Simon and told him she'd been stricken with a migraine and couldn't make it back to the office.

'He's so different,' she said, 'Since his encounter with you. Even if I'd told him I just fancied the afternoon off he probably would have said 'Fine, fine, whatever you say, take as long as you need'. What exactly did you do to him?'

'Not as much as I'd like to have done,' I said, thinking again about the knives in my kitchen drawer. 'So what have you heard?'

'What haven't we heard!' she said with relish, taking a bite of her burger. 'The place is a hot-bed of rumours and gossip!'

Things must be looking up, then. The only stuff we normally get to gossip about is the state of the toilets and whose turn it is to make coffee.

'But I want to clear something up first,' she added more seriously, putting the burger down on her tray. 'We didn't phone you, or come and see you, because Simon told us not to.'

'He WHAT?'

'The day after he came to see you, I asked him how you were, and whether you were well enough for me and Mary to visit you. As soon as I mentioned your name, he went pale and started trembling. 'No way!' he shouted. 'She's got to have complete rest, and no contact with anybody from work whatsoever! Her doctor has ordered her to have no contact! No one's to go round there or bother her on the phone!' It was really bad, like you'd scared the shit out of him.'

'I think I did! It's true my doctor did say all that about no contact with work, but I still would have liked the odd spark of concern from someone. But no,' I scowled, remembering. 'No, you only had time for bloody Tracey, didn't you. You couldn't even be bothered to talk to me when I phoned. It was Tracey this, Tracey that, Tracey's wonderful and she's my best friend now . . . '

'She was awful,' interrupted Liz bitterly.

WAS?

'Was?' I repeated. 'Was, as in, she's not awful any more?'

'No. Was, as in She's Gone.'

'Gone for good?'

'Too bloody right.'

'But I thought you really liked her?'

'No. I didn't, but I had to pretend to. Oh, come on, Ally, don't look at me like that. Don't make out you wouldn't do the same. You know what office politics are like. We all have to pretend to be nice to people, like Nicola and . . . '

'But I don't understand it. Tracey was a bloody TEMP. You'll be telling me next that SHE was having it off with Simon!'

Liz stirred her milk-shake and stared into its creamy foam in silence.

'Bloody hell,' I said. 'I HAVE been missing some scandal, haven't I!'

★ ★ ★

You can't believe it, can you? Life goes on in the same dull, monotonous way for year after boring year, nothing more interesting ever happening than the occasional visit by a photocopier engineer or the appearance of an unusual stamp on a letter. And then, overnight, as soon as I take time off, all hell lets loose. Amazing Tracey McMarvellous, the best-looking and most efficient temp ever to set foot in the office, catches Simon's eye and decides to make a play for him. 'She toyed with him like a cat with a mouse', was Liz's graphic description of the flirtation process. Except it ended up with the mouse getting the cat's knickers off across his desk, which may or may not have been a shock to Tracey, but was definitely a shock to Snotty-Nosed Nicola when she walked into the office and caught them in the act.

'Jesus!' I exclaimed, gobbling up chips with tomato ketchup. Nothing like a good bit of juicy gossip for improving the appetite. 'What did Nicola SAY?!'

'Apparently she threw things around the office, stamped her feet, tore things up, and ended up telling Simon that if he didn't get rid of 'that slag', she'd tell his father what he'd been doing during office hours . . . '

'On his nice polished desk!'

' . . . and with the phone switched over to answerphone!'

'Causing irritation to any possible clients trying to get through . . . definitely not very good for business.'

'Exactly. Well, before she'd hardly had time to get her clothes back on, Tracey was hustled out of the door with Nicola snapping around her heels like a rabid terrier.'

'So all's well that ends well?'

'Oh, that wasn't the end of it. The next day, Ian Unwin himself turns up at the office!'

'WHO?'

'Come on, Ally, how long have you been away?! Mr UNWIN? The owner of the company? Simon's father . . . ?'

'Oh, Christ! I've never even met him!'

'Nor's anyone else, as far as I know — apart from Simon, of course, and that's not too often, from what I hear.'

'He spends all his time abroad!'

'Yeh — Portugal. He only comes back at Christmas, or when there's a problem with the business.'

'And there was a problem? He heard about Tracey being screwed on the desk?' I asked, my eyes popping with excitement.

'No, you idiot. The problem was YOU.'

I dropped a handful of chips in my surprise. Me? A problem? A big enough problem to bring the great, the rarely glimpsed Mr Unwin rushing home from Portugal?

'In what respect?' I almost whispered.

'You KNOW in what respect! In respect of your work-related stress! Simon had told him about it on the phone, as soon as you sent in the certificate for your second lot of time off. He was worried enough about the first certificate, but the second one had him running to the toilet all day, I can tell you.'

'Good!' I smiled smugly.

'So Dad turns up in the office,' she continued, 'Straight off the plane from Faro. He marched through reception, with Nicola running after him asking who he was and where he thought he was going! . . . Can you imagine it?!'

I could, and it was giving me great, great pleasure.

' . . . Straight into Simon's office, where Simon was apparently sitting with his feet on his desk listening to a Tom Jones CD.'

Sad git.

'And he slammed the door behind him so hard, the CD jumped and kept playing the same line over and over: 'My, my, my Delilah!', while the whole company and probably the whole bloody street could hear him shouting and swearing at Simon, calling him a Fucking Useless Lazy Bastard and a Pathetic Little Shit.'

Not a bad judge.

'And Simon started shouting back, saying his father had buggered off to Portugal leaving him to take all the responsibility and cope with all the worry, with staff who let him down and wouldn't do as they were told . . . '

'Fucking cheek!'

'Yeh, but do you know what Mr Unwin said?'

No, but I'm sure you're going to tell me . . .

'He said that if he treated staff with more consideration they'd repay him with more efficiency and loyalty, and wouldn't end up being signed off with work-related stress and be possibly on the verge of suing the company, and that if the company DID get sued, it would be Simon standing up in court answering for it, and furthermore, if he insisted on shagging the receptionist he should be more discreet about it because it was perfectly obvious that everyone knew about it and he, personally, couldn't see what he saw in the cheap little tart anyway!'

'NO!' I breathed, loving it.

'And then he flung open the door and

Nicola fell in on to the floor at his feet!'

'She'd been listening to all that from outside?!'

'Ally, I'm telling you, it was so loud we could hear it all from our office!' she insisted gleefully.

I finished off my chips and took a long, blissful drink of Coke. Lovely. I felt almost sensual with pleasure.

'So what happened then? After Mr Unwin went?' I demanded, eager for more.

'Simon came out of his office with his eyes downcast, got in his car and drove off. We all wondered if he'd gone to throw himself off a bridge. Tom Jones was still going 'My, my, my, Delilah', and eventually someone went in there to turn it off because it was doing all our heads in, and discovered Nicola still lying on the floor, crying her eyes out.'

'Why? Because of Tom Jones?'

Understandable but somehow unlikely.

'No. Because Simon had dumped her.'

'OH!'

I clapped my hand to my mouth with excitement. This was getting better and better. I hadn't had a Friday afternoon like this since I was a teenager and we used to swap diaries and read all of each other's secrets.

'He dumped her because his FATHER disapproved?'

'I think he just wanted to take his anger out on someone because HE'd been given a bollocking, and she literally fell at his feet at just the wrong moment. He told her he couldn't look at her in the same light after she'd treated Tracey so badly, and that he couldn't carry on with her any more knowing that everyone knew about them, even his father knew about them!'

'He must have known everybody knew about them! She practically hung her underwear on his door handle! She bought chocolate condoms from the machine in the toilets and filed them under 'C' in his filing cabinet . . . '

'Yes, well, he obviously believed that was their little secret. ANYway,' went on Liz, obviously enjoying herself as much as I was, 'next thing we know, Simon comes back carrying a huge basket of flowers . . . '

'For me!'

'As it turned out, yes. But Nicola obviously thought different. She jumped up from blubbing on the carpet, wiped her eyes with paper from the fax machine, and went running out to meet him, arms outstretched like something out of *Wuthering Heights* . . . '

'Heathcliff, Heathcliff!'

'Well, more of a 'Simon, Simon'! But you get the picture. She thought she was forgiven. She had one hand on the basket of flowers and the other hand round the back of his neck before he'd had time to blink.'

'What did he do?' I gasped, my drink halfway to my mouth, suspended in horrified fascination.

'He put down the flowers, peeled her off him, sat her down on the nearest chair and said 'Fuck off, Nicola. I've told you already — it's over.''

'What? In front of everyone?!'

'Everyone,' declared Liz solemnly. 'Well, Chloe and Laura from Accounts, anyway, but they told Jason, and Jason told . . . '

'Poor Nicola,' I said, and I ALMOST, almost, meant it. 'She won't be able to look anyone in the eye for a while.'

'She won't have to. She's left.'

Wow.

It was going to be fun going back!

★ ★ ★

We carried on shopping after we'd finished our lunch, and I spent the fifty pounds that didn't get spent on petrol or comfort food, on a dress and jacket. Well, to be honest it came to just a little bit more than the fifty pounds but I borrowed the extra out of the following week's money that wouldn't be spent on petrol or comfort foods. Or had I already allowed for that in the fifty pounds? I was frowning to myself over the mental arithmetic involved in this, on the way home on the bus, when I saw the silver BMW again. Same driver, same dark glasses, same strange feeling of déjà vu about him. It bothered me just enough to make me forget about the business with the money, which was a relief, as I could then go home and show off my new clothes to the girls without feeling guilty.

'Where are you going to wear it, Mum?' asked Victoria.

'What do you mean — where?' I snapped. Anybody would think I never went anywhere where I could wear a nice dress and jacket.

'Well. I mean, it's very nice. Very, very nice!' she said tactfully. 'But, well, you never really go anywhere where you could wear it — do you?'

'Yes, I do! I go to places! I go out to places . . . all the time.'

I felt stupid. Annoyed and stupid. It was horrible to think that I was the type of person who never went anywhere to wear anything nice.

'I'm going out tomorrow night!' I lied.

Anything to stop thinking of myself as that sort of sad person.

'Are you?' Victoria looked interested. 'Where? Who with?'

'With the girls from work. Up the West End.'

'Good for you!' she said approvingly, giving me a kiss. 'It'll do you good. Do you far more good than all those bloody pills!'

The bloody pills. That reminded me. I still hadn't taken them back to Boots.

★   ★   ★

'Liz,' I whispered into the phone so that Victoria couldn't hear me. 'Do you fancy going out tomorrow night? Up West? You, me and Mary?'

'Yeh, why not!' she agreed, to my relief. 'What's the occasion?'

'Nothing. I just need to wear my new dress.'

★   ★   ★

We went to a wine bar just off Piccadilly. We bought a bottle of Italian red and managed to get the last free table, away from the crush at the bar.

'It looks very nice,' said Liz generously,

indicating my dress.

'Thanks. Victoria said I'd never go anywhere to wear it.'

'Huh. What do they know? We ought to do this more often.'

'Well, not too often,' said Mary cautiously. 'Derek might get upset.'

Sod Derek, I found myself thinking ungraciously. I bet he went out whenever it suited HIM.

'We could go and see a show,' went on Liz, 'or go out for a meal. It's stupid living in London and never going anywhere.'

'Derek and I go out quite a lot,' said Mary. 'We've seen *Les Miserables* four times.'

'Why? Didn't you understand it the first time?'

'Ally, you can be quite cutting at times,' Mary reproved me.

We sipped our wine in silence for a while, watching the people around us as the wine bar started to fill up. Snatches of conversation drifted through the cigarette smoke.

' . . . AWFULLY difficult for her, now the au pair's gone . . . '

' . . . SO frightful, the Daimler needed servicing so we had to use the Rover . . . '

' . . . and where they live now in Hampstead, they've only got two bathrooms, and the master bedroom isn't even en suite . . .'

We raised our eyebrows at each other across the table.

'Awfully difficult for me,' I muttered. 'The Metro's failed its MOT so I have to use the tube.'

'Ally,' said Liz, looking past me towards the door. 'Isn't that Paul that's just walked in?'

He had his arm around Lynnette, shepherding her in through the crowd. She looked little and fragile, and people made way for her.

'Thanks, old chap,' I heard Paul say to some guy who'd got off a bar stool and let Lynnette sit down. He clumped the old chap on the shoulder and the old chap clumped him back on the shoulder and said Not At All, Old Chap.

'Is she anorexic?' whispered Mary.

'No,' I whispered back. I wasn't whispering on purpose, it was just that my voice wouldn't come out properly. It felt shaky and sort of strangled. 'She's been ill.'

'Christ. Something serious? She looks . . .' Mary shrugged and shook her head.

She looked dreadful. She must have lost about two stone, and she hadn't been big to start with. She looked pale and tired, her cheeks were hollow and her eyes, those grey-green eyes that used to sparkle and twinkle, looked huge in her tiny pinched face. Paul still had his arm protectively around her. He hadn't seen me yet, but as I stared at her, Lynnette looked up and caught my eye.

'Ally!' she mouthed, and whispered something to Paul. I looked away quickly as he turned in my direction, but it was too late.

'Oh, God,' I said into my drink as they made their way towards our table.

'Ally! This isn't one of your usual haunts, is it?' said Paul.

'I don't have any usual haunts,' I returned, not looking at him. 'Not being a ghost.'

'Still the same old sense of humour,' he said without laughing.

'How are you, Ally?' asked Lynnette in a sad little voice.

'I'm OK, thank you.' I made a huge effort. 'It's me who should be asking you, I think.'

'Oh, I'm much better,' she said bravely, leaning on Paul's arm for support. 'I've started going out for little walks and I think I've put a little bit of weight back on. The doctor says I'm over the worst now.'

'That's good,' I said politely.

This was hell. It was like a scene from a nightmare. Were they going to stand there all night, staring at me, thinking thoughts of poison and waiting for me to break down and confess? Yes, she looked awful. Yes, I was shocked, I was horrified to see how ill she must have been — yes, I felt sorry for her. I really did feel sorry for her. I even felt sorry for him because he must have been scared, her being so ill like that. But it was nothing to do with me. Nothing! To! Do! With! Me! I felt myself shiver with fear. They SURELY couldn't really believe I'd do anything like that? It was horrible.

'I think we'd better go, actually,' I said suddenly, in the middle of something Lynnette was saying about her employers at the private hospital being so understanding and paying her full sick pay.

Mary and Liz both looked at me uncertainly.

'We're going on to see a film,' I said, scrabbling on the floor for my handbag, desperate now to get out, get as far away from there as I could, quickly, now, immediately.

'Yes, that's right,' said Liz, catching on at once. She stood up and put on her jacket. 'Come on, then, or we'll miss the start . . . '

'Which film are you . . . ?' began Lynnette, but we were already walking away.

'Nice to see you,' I called back without turning round.

It wasn't until much later that I realised I'd acted exactly like someone with a guilty conscience. And I didn't even have one.

'Paul must be worried sick about her,' said Mary as we strolled up towards Leicester Square.

'Yes.'

'She's a lovely-looking girl, isn't she. I mean, she obviously WAS, before she was ill.'

'Yes.'

'What exactly did you say was wrong with her? Food-poisoning?'

'Yes.'

'Must have been bad.'

'Yes.'

'You can see he's obviously devoted to her . . .'

'Mary!' said Liz. 'I don't think Ally wants to discuss . . .'

'It's all right,' I said, sighing deeply. I looked at the pavement as we walked along, weaving our way through crowds of theatre-goers and tourists. It was late, but here in the heart of the West End it was still as bright as midday on this summer night, with the glare of neon everywhere. I wanted it to be dark, the sort of dark you only see out in the countryside where there are only stars in an inky black sky, dark to match my mood. 'I don't mind talking about her. Or him. I need, really, to talk about him.'

I needed to hear myself saying out loud the

things I knew in my heart to be true.

'I don't mind any more. About him and Lynnette.'

'That's good,' nodded Mary wisely.

'I don't want him back.'

When did that happen? When did I stop wanting him back? Or did I never really want him back, but just wouldn't admit it?

'I'm not even sure if I really loved him at all.'

'Love's a funny thing,' said Liz, slipping her arm through mine. 'Who really knows what it means? Who can really say when it starts, when it ends, whether it's real or not?'

I thought of Victoria, with her succession of 'The Real Thing's, who'd all now been contemptuously dismissed as hormonal blips, and smiled to myself.

'I assumed I still loved Paul, and I assumed I'd do anything to get him back,' I admitted. 'But I think it was just a habit, really. If I'd still been in love with him I wouldn't have jumped into bed with James the way I did . . . '

'James!?' squealed Liz and Mary together. 'Who's James? And when did you jump into bed . . . ?'

'Let's find somewhere to have another drink,' I laughed. 'And you wait till I tell you about James! He was the best-looking thing I've ever seen in my life . . . '

* * *

'You were late home last night,' commented Lucy as she buttered her toast the next morning.

'Yes,' I said, smiling.

'Have a good time?'

'Excellent, thanks.'

One drink had led to another, and another, and then to a curry. One shared secret had led to many more and by the end of the evening the three of us had been laughing and giggling like schoolgirls. Even Mary had agreed that we were going to make a habit of our nights out together, and Derek would have to get used to the idea.

'I think I'm going to enjoy being single,' I confided to Lucy. 'Now I've finally got used to the idea.'

She looked at me with a frown of disapproval.

'You're not even divorced yet.'

'No, but I think your dad and I ought to start discussing it.'

Lucy's eyes opened wide in surprise.

'He and Lynnette are a couple now, Luce,' I said gently. 'He's not going to leave her and come back to us. I've had to learn to accept it.'

'Accept it? It sounds as if you're GLAD about it!' she retorted.

I sighed.

'Would you prefer me to be miserable and pine for him for the rest of my life? I've got to pick myself up and start again, Lucy. It's all right for you and Victoria. You've got your own lives to live. You'll eventually be moving out and . . . '

'Actually, Mum . . . '

She suddenly put down her toast and wiped the crumbs from her mouth.

'Yes?'

Something about her manner startled me. Something about the look on her face. Serious, nervous, but excited. I didn't like it. It looked Worrying.

'What?'

'Well, I wasn't going to tell you yet. But I don't think I can wait. It's going to happen sooner than you think.'

'What is? What's going to happen?'

'Me moving out. We're planning it now. As soon as we've found somewhere . . . '

'We? We who?'

'Me and Neil, of course! Mum, you must have guessed! You must have realised how right we are for each other! As soon as Neil's found somewhere for us to live I'll go down and look for a job and . . . '

'Down where?' I asked with a heavy heart. A heavy, sinking, aching heart that was going to break at any moment. My child. My little girl. I couldn't bear it. I wasn't ready for it. It was too soon. Not yet, please! Next year, perhaps, or the year after. I'd be ready then. I wouldn't mind, honestly, I wouldn't try to hold her back, but not yet . . .

'Cornwall, of course!' she laughed with excitement. 'I'm going to live in Cornwall with Neil. We'll probably get married. And we want loads of babies. Are you looking forward to it, Mum? Being a grandma?'

12

'What's up?'

Paul sounded slightly irritated, like he'd been disturbed whilst watching *Match of the Day*.

'Can you come round? Now? Please? It's Lucy.'

'What's wrong with her?'

Sharp with concern now, no doubt imagining appendicitis, or a car crash.

'Nothing, no, she's not ill, nothing like that. Sorry. I just . . . need you to talk to her. Come and talk to her, please, Paul.'

'Why . . . ?'

'Paul. I don't often ask for your help, do I.'

I was surprised by the tone of my voice. So, I think, was he, because he immediately agreed:

'No. OK. I'll be there in half an hour.'

'Just you.'

'OK.'

★   ★   ★

His forehead was creased with anxiety.

'What's the problem?' he asked as he

stepped into the hall. 'Her exams?'

'No. She doesn't get the results till next month, but I think they went all right in the end. It's this new boyfriend — Neil. She met him in Cornwall and . . . '

'Hey, Dad!' shouted Lucy, coming down the stairs. 'Didn't know you were coming!'

'Hi, Dad!' echoed Victoria, leaning over the bannisters. 'You staying for dinner?'

'No. I . . . just came to . . . see you. Talk to you,' he said, frowning at me.

'She's not PREGNANT?' he added under his breath, walking ahead of me into the kitchen.

'Pregnant?' said Lucy, whose hearing was better than her father obviously remembered. 'Who is?' She stood stock-still and stared at Paul. 'Lynnette?'

'No. Nobody,' he said. He sat down at the kitchen table and I put the kettle on. 'So tell me,' he said to me at length, looking from me to Lucy, to Victoria, and back to Lucy again.

'Tell your dad,' I said to Lucy. 'About Neil.'

Victoria bit into a biscuit, looking puzzled. 'What about him?'

'Oh, thanks, Mum!' exclaimed Lucy. 'I wanted to tell Dad myself, in my own time, when I was ready . . . '

'Tell him what?' asked Victoria.

'Why did you need to tell him?' went on

Lucy. 'You have to make a drama out of it, don't you, and get everyone all worried . . . '

'Worried about what?' demanded Victoria, her mouth full of biscuit.

'Well, of course I'm worried!' I shot back. 'You're only nineteen, and what about your college course? You're just going to give all that up? After all the hard work . . . '

'I can go back to it later. After I've had my babies!'

There was a silence. Victoria started choking on biscuit crumbs. Paul put his hand to his forehead and swayed slightly.

'My God,' he said softly. 'You are, aren't you. You're pregnant.'

'No!' she said crossly. 'Not yet!'

'What do you mean, not yet?!' cried Victoria. 'Are you TRYING to get pregnant? For fuck's sake, Lucy!!'

'Watch your language, Victoria,' said Paul unnecessarily. 'Lucy, what's all this about? Why are you leaving college? I thought it was all going well?'

'I'm in love,' she declared with an expression of self-righteousness.

'For fuck's sake!' repeated Victoria under her breath.

'I'm going to live with him. In Cornwall.'

'I don't think so,' said Paul.

'Well, I DO think so!' she returned. 'And

I'm over eighteen, so I can make my own decisions!'

'Please,' I said, banging cups of coffee down in front of everyone. 'Let's not start getting angry. Let's try and discuss this calmly and sensibly, like adults.'

'There's nothing to discuss,' said Lucy flatly. 'I'm going to Cornwall to live with Neil.'

'You've only just met him,' I said, my voice wobbling.

'You're out of your mind,' said Victoria.

'Shut up, Victoria! You're just jealous, because Reece dumped you!'

'Jealous! Do me a favour! I think you're pathetic! You need to learn how to live without a man in your life. They're an anachronism, a relic of paternalistic society . . .'

'Thank you, Victoria,' I said quietly.

'I love him!' asserted Lucy, pushing away her coffee.

'It's only your hormones!' said Victoria. 'Isn't it, Mum! Tell her! You said you knew it was only my hormones every time I thought I was in love with someone. You should have told me, and you should be telling Lucy now! Go on, tell her!'

'Victoria, do you really expect Lucy to listen to a word I say?' I hissed at her. 'Any more than YOU would have done?'

'I wasn't so stupid to want to go and live in Cornwall and have babies . . . '

'You weren't really in love!' threw back Lucy.

'And neither are you!' I retorted. 'You just think you are! It just feels like it!'

'And what would you know about it?' asked Lucy scathingly.

Paul looked at me with raised eyebrows.

'I just do,' I said, reddening slightly. 'Believe me.'

'You should listen to Mum,' Victoria told Lucy aggressively. 'She knows more about life than you do. She's old.'

Not that bloody old.

'Nobody knows how I feel!' returned Lucy dramatically. 'Neil's the only one who's ever understood me.'

Oh, spare me the violin music, please.

'Thank you very much,' I said in peevish martyred tones. 'I suppose I didn't under-stand you when you cried for your feeds in the middle of the night, or when you screamed because you were scared of the window-cleaner when you were two, or when you didn't want to go to playgroup because Jason Johnson was laughing at your red shoes, or . . . '

'You know what I mean,' she sighed. 'You KNOW.'

Yes, of course I did know. And so, of course, did Victoria, despite her new and superior knowledge of the subject, and so, perhaps more than any of us, did Paul, who when all was said and done had walked out on a wife who'd been understanding him since he was little more than a child, to live with someone who'd infected him with just exactly the same sort of madness as his younger daughter was displaying here today. Whether it was the result of following this same train of thought, or whether he'd just decided to try a different tactic, Paul suddenly took a deep breath, took a gulp of his coffee and began again:

'OK, Lucy. Fair enough. It's not that we don't understand your feelings . . . '

But before he got any further, the phone started ringing and Lucy was upon it with the speed and agility of a rugby tackle.

'Neil! Hello, darling!' we heard her gush, and then the door was shut hard behind her.

'I can't stand any more of this,' said Victoria. 'I'm going out. 'Bye, Dad.'

'Who does she go out with,' asked Paul, watching her from the window as she got into her car and drove off, 'Now that she's given up men?'

'Her friend Hayley. They go out drinking and clubbing,' I smiled. 'I'm sure it's only a phase. The next good-looking lad that chats her up, I bet all this anti-men stuff goes straight out the window. But I think it's doing her good being single for a while.'

I paused, and looked at him pointedly.

'It can be fun, being a single girl,' I said. 'And it helps you sort yourself out. Who you are, without being part of a couple.'

'Is that right?' he said, looking back at me equally pointedly.

'Yes.'

'You look different,' he said after a while. 'Better.'

'Everyone keeps saying that. Did I look so terrible before?'

'That's not what I meant. I just said you look better.'

'I've been exercising. And eating better. It's what the doctor said. I couldn't cope with the relaxation. The tapes reminded me of childbirth classes.'

He laughed.

'What am I going to do about Lucy, Paul?' I said, a lump coming to my throat. The childbirth classes had been a nightmare, the childbirth itself had been worse than a nightmare, but look what it had produced. The best two things in my life. I couldn't lose her now, could I? But I couldn't stop her, either! 'She's nineteen! She's an adult. If she insists on going . . . '

'Listen.' Paul sat down next to me and took hold of my hand. I stared at it. It seemed odd, now, after all this time, to see his hand holding mine like that, as if he still cared about me. As if he'd never said all those things to me, terrible things about poisoning Lynnette and the cat. 'I don't think we should fight her too hard,' he said gently. 'She'll run to this guy all the faster if we do. And cling to him all the more.'

'So what do we do? Just let her go? She hardly knows him . . . '

'Let her go and stay with your sister. Bev wouldn't mind, would she? Then she can see as much of this Neil as she wants, without rushing to move in with him . . . '

'What about college?'

'By the start of term, I wouldn't mind betting the love affair will have run its course. If not, then perhaps it will deserve us taking it more seriously.'

I held onto his hand for a minute or two more, thinking this over, nodding slowly to myself as the sense of it sunk into my brain and calmed the panic that had been threatening a take-over bid.

'Why didn't I think of that?' I said eventually.

'Because you're here all the time, getting all

the worry and all the crap, aren't you. I just get called in at times like this, on a . . . consultation basis. I can look at things more clearly, perhaps.'

'Will you always? Always come if I call you for a consultation? Even if . . . if we get divorced?'

There. I'd said it. I'd been the first one to suggest it. My heart was racing. It sounded such a desperate thing to say. He looked at me with surprise.

'If we do. Yes, of course. You know I'll always be there for the kids. And for you, Ally. I've always wanted us to stay friends.'

'But I didn't give anyone poison,' I said quickly. 'Not Lynnette, and not the cat. Especially not the cat!'

He shrugged.

'I don't suppose you did, really. But I didn't know what to think . . . '

'Think about what?' interrupted Lucy, coming back from her phone call with the pink excited flush of someone who's just been giggling and soppy for half an hour.

'We think this is what should happen,' I said firmly. 'I'm going to phone Auntie Bev tonight . . . '

★ ★ ★

It went surprisingly well, Lucy having stopped protesting the minute she realised she could be on her way to Cornwall and in her lover's arms within twenty-four hours if she played her cards right. Bev was unlikely to be a very serious chaperone.

'I'll start packing!' she announced, a little prematurely, bouncing up the stairs singing something yukky about love.

'Thanks,' I told Paul, going to see him out.

'Glad you're looking better,' he said again. 'What tablets did you say the doctor gave you?'

I didn't.

'I'm not taking them. Didn't need them. I wasn't really stressed, just needed a bit of rest and exercise . . . Dia-zie something. Hang on, they're here in the kitchen. I'll tell you . . . I'm sure it was Dia-zie something . . . Where are they, now?' I moved a pile of bills and yesterday's paper to one side. 'Sure I left them here, 'cos I kept saying I ought to take them back to Boots. Where the hell have they got to? Lucy? Lucy, have you moved those tablets that were on the side here in the kitchen? Lucy?'

She was bounding back downstairs, looking worried.

'Mum! Have you seen Apple Pie? He's been on my bed, and he's been sick all over the duvet, and it's absolutely horrible . . . What did you say about tablets?'

★　★　★

The first time you prowl around your garden for hours shouting out 'Apple Pie, where are you?', your neighbours might well assume you just have a temporary problem. The second time, they could be forgiven for calling the nearest mental health authority. And God knows I had enough people concerned about my mental health already.

'He might be lying dead somewhere!' I cried, peering under shrubs and staring into the murky depths of the fish-pond once again. 'I can't believe it! I just can't believe he managed to get the top off the pill-bottle. It was a childproof top!'

'Don't jump to conclusions,' said Paul. We hadn't found the pill-bottle, and there hadn't been any definite evidence of pills in the vomit, although to be fair we hadn't done an in-depth study of it yet.

'Well, what else am I supposed to think? The pills are gone, and the poor cat's been poisoned again. Paul, he's already got dodgy kidneys! He hasn't even had tonight's dose of his drug! I'll never forgive myself, never! How could I have been so stupid, leaving tablets lying around the house like that! Any little child could have got them!'

'We don't KNOW any little children,' pointed out Lucy.

'Well, any little CAT, then,' I said. 'Apple Pie! Apples, darling, come on, where are you? Come to Mummy! Please don't be dead!'

I'll never leave pills around the house again.

I'll never even HAVE pills in the house again.

I won't even let the doctor give me any, I won't buy any from Boots, I won't even get Vitamin C supplements from Tesco. Nothing.

Apart from the cat's kidney pills, of course.

If he turns up safe and well.

Please, God, please don't do this to me all over again. Please don't make us have to drain the fish-pond, I really couldn't stand it, but on the other hand if we do have to do it, thank you for making Paul be here.

'You'll have to drain your fish-pond,' I told him snappily.

'No, I won't,' he retorted.

'If we don't find him, you will. What do you care most about, Apple Pie or your silly fish?'

'They're not silly. They have feelings too. They're living, breathing creatures. They fall in love, and have babies, and get sick, and die, just like . . . '

'Oh, please! Fishes don't fall in love!'

'Of course they do! Look at that bright orange one there. I bet he fancies the little silvery-pink one rotten.'

'Paul, you don't even know if it's male or female, so . . . '

'I can't believe you two!' protested Lucy. 'Poor Apple Pie is probably throwing up and dying somewhere, and you're arguing about fishes fancying each other! Christ! It's almost like having you LIVING together again!'

Despite everything, we looked at each other across the pond and we both smiled. It wasn't ANYthing like living together again. But it was still nice, and comforting, to be arguing in that careless, joky, married sort of way again. I had a strange flash of passing thought that, now I'd decided I didn't love him, I could really get to like Paul again. But then I went back to panicking about the cat and forgot about it. Just as well. Not a good idea to indulge too much in those sort of thoughts while you've still got a possible poisoning charge pending.

★ ★ ★

It was beginning to get dark when we finally heard it. A faint, very faint, very feeble miaowing.

'Mum!' shouted Lucy. 'I heard him!'

'Where?'

'Ssh! Listen!'

We all crept quietly towards the house.

'Miaow! Miaow!'

It was plaintive and pitiful, and it seemed to be coming from . . .

'The shed!' called Paul, running to the kitchen drawer, where he knew we still kept the key to the old potting shed.

'It's not locked!' I called after him.

He stopped in his tracks and stared at me.

'Why not?'

'Does it matter? Let's just get the door open . . .'

It was stiff, so stiff it hadn't seemed worth bothering to lock it any more. Paul used to preside over its security with the rigour of a prison warder. You'd have thought he had the Crown Jewels in there, but in fact it was just the sort of stuff men like to play with out of doors: bags of compost, lawn fertiliser and peat; pots of Creosote and varnish; flowerpots, seed trays, spades and shovels; jars of screws and nails (why DO they keep them?); inexplicable bit of things that had broken and other things that had bits missing . . . you know what I mean, don't you. Things they play with for hours while you're doing the housework, thinking they're fooling you that they're busy when really we all know it's just an extension of infant school play therapy: sorting and stacking, cutting and sticking, painting and modelling. Maybe that's why they're so secretive about it. Anyway, suffice it to say I hadn't seen any reason to keep the bolt, the chain or the padlock on the shed door since he'd moved out, since there hadn't been any reports of flower-pot thieves in the neighbourhood for quite a few years. I tended to leave the little window open, too, in the summer, because it got disgustingly hot and smelly in there and I hated it when I went in occasionally to look for something and found a bee or butterfly killing itself against the window in its desperate bid for freedom.

'The window's open!' Paul said accusingly.

'Only a fraction . . . '

A big enough fraction, apparently, for a medium-sized elderly cat to squeeze through.

★ ★ ★

Apple Pie was lying on the floor of the shed, panting lightly and looking apologetic about the pool of vomit beside him.

'My poor baby!' squealed Lucy, rushing to pick him up.

'Careful, Lucy,' I warned her, remembering his delicacy of digestion on the previous occasion, but he allowed himself to be lifted gently into her arms without further mishap.

'I'll get straight on the phone to the vet,' I said.

'It's Sunday night.'

'The emergency service, then. They'll have to see him, won't they. It looks like poisoning again.'

Paul was staring at the floor.

'What?' I asked sharply, following his gaze.

'Fishing bait,' he said, pointing.

'Sorry?'

'All over the floor, look. The cat must have knocked the jar over.'

'So what!'

This was hardly the time for an argument about who might, or might not, have been responsible for disturbing the neatness and order of his sanctuary.

'I didn't realise I'd left it there. It's been there for years. It must be absolutely rank by now.'

'I wondered why it smelled so awful in here.'

'Ally,' he said, very quietly, very slowly, still

311

looking at the mess on the floor of the shed as if he was hypnotised by it, 'Ally, I think this is what Apple Pie's been eating. I don't think it was slug pellets at all. I think we ought to take some of this to the vet and tell him it's probably what poisoned the cat.'

I'd already started dialling the emergency vet's number.

★ ★ ★

If you have to be in the position of tearing through the London suburbs in the dead of night with a retching cat on your lap, it's better to be doing it with your ex-husband driving you in his Vauxhall Primera than sitting alone on the District Line of the Underground. I wasn't unaware of the fact that it could have been a lot worse. Indirectly, Lucy had done us a favour by announcing her elopement plans and getting her father over that day, whether she saw it that way now or not. The reason I mention this was that she was now on the back seat of the Primera holding a sample jar of foul-smelling fishing bait on one side of her and a sample jar of cat vomit on the other.

'This is DISGUSTING!' she cried for the fifteenth time as Paul turned right, then left at the traffic lights, then left again at the second roundabout after the pub, as per directions given to us on the phone. 'Hurry up! I can't STAND it! It's . . . eurggh!'

'Miaow!' cried Apple Pie, coughing weakly.

'Paul, hurry up, I think he's getting worse!' I said anxiously. 'Is it much further?'

'I don't think so. Stop nagging, both of you, and look out for Greenway Road on the right, will you?'

We got to the emergency vet at half past ten. By eleven o'clock he'd anaesthetised Apple Pie and washed out his stomach, examined the contents of both our sample jars and agreed that the decaying fishing bait was indeed responsible for his food-poisoning but that we'd found him soon enough this time, before any of it had been completely digested and had time to cause any serious damage.

'Thank God!' I breathed, tears not far away now as I looked at the lifeless little form in his recovery cage.

'Will he be all right, then?' asked Lucy, reaching out to hold his paw through the wire.

'Hopefully. We'll keep him here overnight for observation . . . '

'We don't have Pet Save . . . ' I began, shutting my eyes tight against any random images of supercilious know-it-all families

313

with irritatingly healthy labradors and beaming, goody-goody children.

'It's all right,' interrupted Paul at once. 'How much is the bill?'

He handed over the cash with a strange expression in his eyes. I didn't recognise it at first, but on the way home I suddenly knew what it reminded me of. Victoria, when she stole my box of Quality Street once when she was about seven years old. She gave me back what was left of the chocolates and said she was sorry, but then she burst into tears and said:

'I should be giving you ALL of them back, but I can't! I ate them!'

It was guilt. Guilt and regret. Well, it served him bloody well right.

* * *

You can see what I'm getting at here, can't you? Even if I'd knocked the jar of fishing bait off the shelf myself, even if I'd taken Apple Pie out to the shed and put him on the floor and said 'There you go, boy, lovely fishing bait! Come on, eat it all up!' — even if I'd mashed it in with his dinner and spoon-fed it to him . . . Well, it was hardly likely I'd been able to do the same to Lynnette, now was it? I'm pretty sure that even in his most irrational moments — and I have to add here to be strictly fair to him that he's normally a fairly rational man — even in his most delusional of moods, Paul could never have seriously imagined Lynnette consuming anything containing that revolting, putrid, vile, mess of slimy, mouldy, stinking rotten maggots. How the cat could stand to eat it was beyond me, but a human being? Never. Never in your wildest nightmares, not even if it was baked in a champagne gravy and served with chocolate sauce. No way. So I was perfectly aware that the silence in the car on the way home owed more to guilt and regret than it did to concentration on the homeward directions, tiredness, or even anxiety about Apple Pie's condition.

'I'll pick him up tomorrow night and bring him home to you,' he said quietly as he turned back into our road. 'And don't worry about the rest of the fees. I'll take care of it.'

'If you're sure.'

'Of course.'

'Thanks, then. Do you . . . want to come in for a coffee or anything?'

'No. I'd better get back to Lynnette.'

'Yes.' I opened the car door and started to get out, then added: 'I'm glad you were here, Paul.'

'So am I. Glad we've sorted out . . . what the problem was.'

He couldn't meet my eyes. I'm not a vindictive person, but I have to say this: he DESERVED that guilt. Hope it was screwing him up.

*   *   *

There were two messages on the answerphone when Lucy and I let ourselves back into the house. I pressed 'play' half-heartedly whilst I waited for the kettle to boil. They were bound to be for Victoria or Lucy but you never know, it could always be the Lottery organisers telling me I was the missing winner of a million pounds, or it could be George Clooney's agent saying George had spotted me when he was in town and wanted to take me out for dinner.

'Hello, Ally, love. It's Mum. Just phoning to say goodbye.'

I stared at the phone as the long beep sounded at the end of the message. Goodbye? Was that IT? She was going off to live in Majorca for the rest of her life and she couldn't even be bothered to say Take Care, Keep in Touch, Have a Nice Life? No mention of missing me? No regrets at leaving me behind, after all I'd done for her, with her

316

corns and her hip and everything? After we'd finally managed to become friends — or so I thought? Didn't I even deserve a visit? Well, great! Wasn't that just great! Well, if she thought I was going to go running after her to Majorca . . .

'Message Two', said the annoying smarmy voice of the Answerphone Man, and then my mother's voice began again:

'Oh. Ally, you're still not home. Oh dear.'

BEEEEEEP! went the answerphone.

Oh dear? Oh fucking dear?! Is that all you can say?

I threw coffee into mugs and slopped boiling water on to it in a reckless and dangerous fashion, steaming with anger. What sort of mother leaves messages like that on her daughter's answerphone? It would have been better not to phone me at all. She could have just buggered off back to Majorca and let me find out in my own good time that she couldn't be bothered to say goodbye to me, instead of advertising the fact and rubbing my nose in it.

'Have you heard from Mum?' I demanded, phoning Beverly a few minutes later.

'Oh, God,' said Beverly, yawning.

'What do you mean, OH GOD? Oh God, what?'

317

'I mean Oh God, not another phone call. I was in bed, Ally, for Christ's sake. Do you know what the time is?'

'You never go to bed early. And what do you mean, another phone . . . Oh. I see. In bed with who? Whom?'

'No one you know.'

I heard the smile in her voice, the smile that said that the No one I knew was nibbling her ear or nuzzling her neck or . . . whatever . . . right at that moment as she was speaking to me. And I felt cross, and frustrated, and jealous and left out. Inexplicably, suddenly, I wanted to be in bed, too, with someone who was doing things to me that made me smile like that on the phone.

'Can't you just stop that for a minute,' I said, sulkily. 'I want to talk to you.'

'So does half the world, apparently.'

'What do you mean? Who?'

'Lucy, and Mum . . . '

'LUCY? She's phoned you ALREADY? When the HELL did she get the chance . . . What did she say?'

'What is this? *Ask The Family*? She said: 'Hello, Auntie Bev, it's Lucy' . . . '

'Very funny. What did she . . . '

'She said: 'I'm phoning you straight away because I'm so excited I can't wait for Mum to phone you tonight and ask you, but Guess

318

What!!' And then she said: 'Oh, shit! The cat's been sick on my duvet! Oh, fucking hell! I'll phone you back!''

'Sneaky little cow. She should have waited. I was going to phone you and ask you . . . '

'Ask me what, Ally? I'm a bit bored of these guessing games, and I really have got a lot on my mind right now . . . '

I could hear that smile in her voice again. I scowled to myself. Lucky bloody cow.

'I wanted to ask you if Lucy could come and stay for a while . . . '

'I guessed it must be something like that. Can't tear herself away from the new boyfriend?'

'Talking about having babies, for God's sake. Don't let her, will you?' I added with sudden alarm.

'What do you take me for? I keep condoms in every room of the house. Even the garage.'

'Yes, well. We'd better discuss Lucy a bit more when you haven't got . . . other things on your mind. Just tell me what Mum said.'

'Mum?'

'Yes, come on Beverly, concentrate. You said Mum phoned you.'

'Three times.'

'Three times!' I screeched. 'Oh, that's great, isn't it! She phones you three times, and can't even manage to leave a decent message on my answerphone! Well, as a goodbye I think that's absolute crap . . . '

'She phoned once, said 'Hello, Beverly,' dropped the phone and cut us off. She phoned a second time and Lorenzo answered.'

'WHO?'

'Lorenzo.'

She even said his name with that smiley voice. She even said it with an Italian accent. It made me want to puke.

'And Lorenzo said: 'Yes, plis? Who EEZ THEEZ, plis?'' I could quite happily do without the phonetic imitation of Lorenzo's undoubtedly very charming and sexy telephone manner.

'And she said . . . ?' I tried to hurry her along.

'She must have thought it was the wrong number and hung up.'

So the point to this story was what? That Lorenzo frightened off our mother with his sexual charisma? That our mother couldn't understand Italian accents?

'And then she phoned again?' I encouraged her wearily.

'Yes. Ten minutes ago.'

'Whilst you were in bed.'

'Well, yes. But I mean to say! It IS late . . . '

'And she said?'

'Oh, she said goodbye.'

'And that was it? Goodbye? Just like that? Nothing else? Just a measly goodbye, before she jets off to spend the rest of her days on foreign soil, cut off for ever from her family who've given up their lives for her? Just goodbye!?'

'Well, no, not exactly.'

I sighed.

'What do you mean, not exactly? Can't you put that . . . that Italian Job down for a minute and JUST TELL ME?'

'Sorry. Yes. She said she'd been trying to phone you. She said . . . ' I could almost hear her trying to concentrate. Must have been difficult. Lucky cow. 'Yes, she said she'd planned on going to see you tonight, to say goodbye and do all the stuff, you know, have a drink and kiss you goodbye and all that. But you weren't in. And the taxi was on its way to take them to the airport.'

'Oh,' I said, only slightly mollified. 'Well, she could have tried . . . '

'And she said she couldn't talk any longer 'cos the taxi was just pulling up outside.'

'And that was it? That was all? That was her goodbye?'

'Oh, yes! And then she said she'd get the taxi to stop off en route to the airport, and . . . '

The doorbell rang just at the point where Lorenzo had obviously got fed up waiting and the phone was thrown on the floor amidst a wail of giggling.

*   *   *

Apparently they'd been on standby and had got flights back to Majorca at very short notice, so I suppose it was understandable that, after all, I only got time to wish Mum and Ted all the best, kiss her goodbye and exchange a few tears, whilst the taxi waited outside for them. Almost everything they possessed had been packed up and shipped off, and the whole thing felt final and permanent to the point of unreality. The trips to the hospital with a moaning, ungrateful old woman who seemed to enjoy her ailments and enjoy upsetting everyone, seemed now to have no connection whatsoever with this excited and spritely lady, but it was a shock when the last thing she said to me was:

'You're much better now, Ally, dear. Much more bright and cheerful, and you look younger too. You should keep up this diet and jogging or whatever it is you're doing!'

Much better? How come everyone was saying that to me, when there hadn't been anything wrong with me in the first place? It was HER that looked better ... She was probably just seeing me in a different light, now she felt happier herself.

Victoria came home just as they were getting back into their taxi, so both the girls were able to say their goodbyes to their grandma, and we then sat up together drinking tea and talking about Serious Issues.

'Lucy's going to stay with Beverly for a while,' I told Victoria.

She nodded.

'Good idea.'

I stared at her.

'You don't mind? It doesn't bother you?'

'Why should it bother me? I can phone her. She'll be home again by September.'

'I won't!' asserted Lucy. 'I'll stay down there and marry Neil! You see if I don't!'

'If you say so,' shrugged Victoria, sounding bored.

'I do say so!' said Lucy, obviously spoiling for a fight.

'Well, Auntie Bev will soon sort you out. She's an arch feminist, isn't she, Mum!'

'In some ways,' I said evasively, thinking of Lorenzo and wondering if he was going to be wandering around the house much while Lucy was staying there.

'I bet SHE doesn't need a man in her life!' said Victoria.

No. She needs several. At the same time. The only way she was likely to 'sort Lucy out' might be to persuade her against settling down too soon with just one. And that, in my view at least, would be a good thing anyway.

'It's a temporary measure,' I warned Lucy. 'We'll see how the situation goes.'

'We'll be looking round for our own place while I'm down there,' insisted Lucy. 'I won't have to stay with Auntie Bev for too long.'

'We'll see,' I repeated.

I was buying time, and I knew it.

★　★　★

'I can't understand WHAT I did with those tablets,' I commented as I put the cups in the dishwasher before we went to bed.

'What tablets?' asked Victoria.

'Those Diazie-thing. The ones the doctor gave me, that I didn't need. I thought the cat must have got them, but . . . '

'No! I've got them.'

'You?'

I stared at her in horror.

'Yeh. They're in my bag. Look . . . '

I knew it. I always knew it would happen. I couldn't have been lucky enough to get both girls through to adulthood without one of them turning to drugs. Stealing pills from your own mother, admitting to it openly . . . Christ! It all pointed to her being beyond help. I looked at her closely, trying to remember the things you were told to watch for on the leaflets they used to bring home from school. 'Drug Awareness — A Parent's Guide', and 'How Do I Know If My Child Is On Drugs?' Were her pupils perhaps a bit dilated? Or did her breath smell funny? Or was I just imagining it? Perhaps it was garlic?

'What are you staring at?' she asked me curiously.

'What other drugs have you been taking?' I asked, sighing.

Let's get it all out in the open.

'Taking? Drugs? What are you talking about?'

'The Diazie-stuff. What else? How long have you been doing it?'

'Mum. I can't believe you're saying this. You know perfectly well I don't do drugs. For God's sake! I just put them in my handbag to take them back to Boots for you tomorrow, 'cos you said you kept forgetting.'

'Oh.' I looked at her helplessly. 'Well, thanks. Sorry.'

She raised her eyebrows and shook her head.

'Over-reaction, or what!?' exclaimed Lucy. 'Is it all right if I take a Paracetamol for my headache, or do you want to phone the Drugline?'

'All right, I said I was sorry,' I said, feeling absolutely ridiculous. 'I'm going to bed.'

'She's still behaving a bit weird, don't you think?' I heard Lucy saying in a low voice as I climbed the stairs.

'Yeh,' answered Victoria. 'I mean to say, as if I could get a high from Diazepam anyway. It'd just send me to sleep.'

'Yeh. Anyone knows that,' laughed Lucy.

Anyone.

I never did read those leaflets properly, did I.

13

'Monday 7th July.
Diet: breakfast — stayed in bed and couldn't be bothered, so —

Lunch — bacon sandwich with tomato sauce.

Dinner — very, very good — cottage cheese salad with a jacket potato.

Later — used up the rest of the bacon and it looked kind of lonely on the plate so fried two eggs, two tomatoes and some mushrooms with it.

BUT no chocolate and no biscuits, all day!

Exercise: excellent. Jogged for miles and miles, past the park, down to the canal, back up past the garage (to pull faces at bastard car), round by the pub and back again. So impressed with myself, went out for another jog in the evening (to work off the egg and bacon).'

Of course, I didn't mention in the diary about the BMW.

It was getting to be uncanny. I'd seen it several times now, and the driver always looked at me as if he knew me. Or fancied me? It seemed unlikely. The weather had turned very hot and I was jogging in an old pair of blue and white striped shorts, a pink vest-top of Victoria's with a Union Jack on the front and skull and crossbones on the back, and a baseball cap. Add to this the fact that I was very red and sweaty and you can see why it was strange that anyone would look at me at all, but because of the unusual registration I noticed the BMW every time. And then, that Monday, when I came back from the morning jog, it was parked outside my house.

I slowed down as I came round the bend and saw it there. This was strange. This was very bloody strange. The driver was sitting in the car with the window right down, leaning out of it and smoking a cigar. 'I Want to Break Free' by Queen was playing very loud, and he was tapping his hand in time to the music. Funny, the little things you notice. As I got closer I noticed that his shirt was cream, short-sleeved and expensive-looking, and his arm, the arm outside the car window, was lean and tanned and that there was a big chunky gold ring on his right hand, the hand holding the cigar.

'God knows, God knows I want to break free . . . '

I walked, very slowly now, past the car, trying to resist the urge to stare in the window, and turned into my front path.

'I've fallen in love . . . I've fallen in love for the first time; this time I know it's for real . . . God knows . . .'

I fumbled in the pocket of my shorts for my door key. Wrong pocket. I was all fingers and thumbs, wanting desperately, out of curiosity, to turn round and look back at the car, see if he was looking at me.

'I can't get over how you love me like you do . . . I've got to be sure, when I walk out that door . . .'

Got it. Got the key now. Put it in the lock, come on, just open the door and go in. No need to look round. Just being bloody nosy, that's all. Nothing to do with you if he chooses to park his BMW outside your house, just coincidence.

'Oh how I want to be free! God knows I've got to . . .'

Clunk. The music went off. The silence was appalling in its abruptness. Key in my front door lock, door half open, I swung round in surprise as I heard the door of the BMW slam shut. I stared in surprise as the BMW driver stood up, smoothed his smooth brown trousers and his smooth grey hair, took off his dark glasses and looked straight at me.

'Mrs Bridgeman? Alison Bridgeman?'

Quite a few possibilities went through my head in those next seconds. He could be the psychiatrist, sent by Dr Lewis to check up on me, see if I was behaving strangely or doing anything dangerous. Or an RSPCA inspector who'd heard about my cat-poisoning reputation. Or worse, a detective called in by Paul whilst he suspected me of poisoning Lynnette. Then again, it could always be someone from the National Lottery about that missing million-pound ticket . . . or George Clooney's agent . . .

'Who wants to know?' I asked cagily.

'Sorry,' he said, smiling and holding out his hand to me. 'I should have introduced myself. I'm Ian Unwin. I believe you work with my son Simon in my company?'

That's who he reminded me of. Slimy bloody Simon. I should have known.

★ ★ ★

We went through to the kitchen, me in my shorts and sweaty pink Union Jack vest, him in his crisp, smooth slacks and cream shirt, and it reminded me so much of the episode with his son and the basket of flowers that I couldn't concentrate properly on what he was saying. As soon as I'd made some drinks I

330

suggested: 'Would you like to sit out in the garden?' in the tone of a duchess inviting someone for Pimms on the terrace, remembering too late that I hadn't cut the grass for four weeks and that there was still the ghastly remains of a sparrow that Apple Pie had killed and then got bored with, lying on the patio.

'Lovely,' he said, nevertheless.

We carried tea and biscuits outside and I arranged our chairs either side of the sparrow corpse, which we both pretended not to notice.

'I've called round a few times,' he said. 'But you've always been out.'

'Jogging. I've been doing a lot of . . . '

'I've seen you. I didn't realise it was you, of course, but I noticed you. Jogging.'

'I noticed you, too.' My face flared with embarrassment. 'I mean, the car. The registration — IOU. It's . . . noticeable.'

'My initials,' he laughed. 'Ian Oswald. Awful names, but the initials are catchy.'

There was an awkward silence. What DID he want? Perhaps he was going to reprimand me for threatening his son with a grapefruit knife?

'Sorry I've been out,' I said.

'I could have phoned. But I really wanted to speak with you in person.'

Must be serious. Must be the grapefruit knife.

'Your son . . . ' I began.

'Is a prat,' he said with a shrug.

Oh.

'My fault, of course. I probably shouldn't have left him in charge of the place. Too much responsibility for someone of his limited capabilities.'

Oh.

'But I had a hell of a lot to do, setting up the branch in Faro.'

Oh! There really WAS a branch in Faro?

'Despite all the rumours about it being a golf course!' he added with a broad smile.

What a nice smile that was. How the hell did a man like this manage to have a son like Simon? How unfair the laws of genetics could be.

'So how's it going?' I asked, out of politeness. 'The branch in Faro?'

'Getting off the ground now. I've left everything in the charge of a manager out there who seems to be a lot more capable than my own son,' he said ruefully.

I felt quite sorry for him. It wasn't his fault Simon was a prick, was it. We all do our best for our children, but at the end of the day if they're going to behave like turds can we blame ourselves?

'I've shaken things up a bit, at head office,' he added.

'I've heard,' I admitted.

He looked at me questioningly.

'Oh, come on, Mr Unwin!' I exclaimed. 'You must realise how people talk! I've got friends . . . '

'And they're saying?'

'Well.' I stirred my tea with my digestive biscuit, feeling uncomfortable. 'Well, just that you and Simon had a few words . . . ' I smiled. 'No wonder he came round to see me bringing flowers and all . . . '

'Did he?' He looked surprised. 'He didn't tell me that!'

Not even about the knife?

'Well,' he added, 'I hope he expressed our concern. About your stress.'

'Oh, yes. Yes, he did,' I said into my tea-cup.

This was so embarrassing. He could surely see from looking at me that I wasn't remotely stressed. Stressed people don't jog around the streets, looking fit and tanned, in old shorts and pink vests. They don't go on jaunts to Cornwall and have passionate affairs with gorgeous men. They don't go on shopping sprees and buy new clothes that they have to go out to wine bars to wear. I suddenly knew with absolute certainty that the whole thing had been a complete and utter fraud. I'd never been stressed in my life. It had all started off as a lie, but Dr Holcombe and Dr Lewis, between them, had done such a good job of diagnosing my symptoms that they'd begun to have even me convinced. It had been good to see Simon squirming in my kitchen, scared shitless that I was going to take him to court. It had served him right and it had made the whole thing worthwhile, but somehow it wasn't half so much fun doing the same thing to his father, who seemed like a nice guy, a genuine and fair man who liked Queen and smiled as if he meant it. It was no good. I had to come clean.

'I haven't had stress at all,' I told him, putting down my cup and looking him in the eye.

'You haven't?'

He looked puzzled. He went to put his cup down too, but the dead sparrow was there.

'No. The doctors . . . I saw two different doctors. They both thought I was suffering from stress, and I believed them. But now, now I'm feeling better . . . '

I stopped, suddenly confused. If I was feeling better, then I must have had something wrong with me, mustn't I? So the whole thing couldn't have been a complete lie after all. I frowned, trying to understand.

'Perhaps it was something else?' he prompted me. 'Something . . . less serious? A virus?'

'Perhaps,' I agreed uncertainly.

'You hear a lot of stories,' he went on, quite earnestly, 'about people who have a virus, sometimes just an insignificant virus, not much worse than a cold or a minor flu, who then end up with a sort of fatigue . . . '

'Post-viral fatigue syndrome,' I nodded eagerly. 'I've read about it in the paper.'

'And it can last for months, even years in some cases.'

'Well, I certainly hope that's not what I've got . . . '

'No, no, I'm sure it isn't, but . . . '

'But perhaps something similar?' I wondered.

'You could have been tired. Run down. Overworked. Anxious.'

Oh yes. All of those, and more besides. Worried, frazzled, fed up and worn out were just a few that sprung to mind.

'But I really don't think it was stress,' I added more confidently. 'Not work-related, or any other related.'

'Well,' he said, and I could hear the relief in his voice. I could almost feel it coming out of his pores. 'Well, I'm so glad to hear that, Alison.'

'Thank you.'

'I came along, as you can probably guess, to apologise. Apologise on behalf of my stupid son, and his even more stupid girlfriend . . . '

'Ex-girlfriend, from what I hear!'

'Yes,' he smiled. 'Stupid bitch! I'm glad she's gone. Well, on their behalf, I want to apologise anyway, even if you're NOT suffering from work-related stress, for the awkwardness and unpleasantness they may have caused you . . . '

'It doesn't matter,' I told him. It really didn't, any more. 'It's all in the past, isn't it. He won't dare mess with me any more, Mr Unwin.'

'Call me Ian, please,' he said. 'Why won't he?'

'I think he's scared of me,' I smiled, remembering his face as I sorted out my knife drawer.

'I'm looking forward to you coming back to work, in that case,' he said. 'It would do Simon good to be scared of someone. Make him get off his ar . . . his backside and do some work.'

'I hardly think I'll ever have that sort of influence over him.'

'Perhaps not. But at least that silly bitch Nicola won't be around any more to waste his time.'

He got to his feet, narrowly missing stepping on the sparrow.

'Would you like me to bury that for you?' he asked calmly.

'That's probably the nicest thing anyone's offered to do for me for a long time,' I laughed, and was amazed at myself afterwards. Amazed at myself, and amazed at him. He got a shovel from the shed, he dug a hole in my garden, he buried my sparrow corpse, and for God's sake! — he was (a) almost a complete stranger and (b) my boss. And I stood by and watched him do it, laughing with him, having a chat about cats in general (he had one himself, apparently, called Captain), and Apple Pie in particular, and how ill he'd been and how we drained the fish-pond for him and then found him in the car. And he told me about an old cat he used to have, who had a habit of climbing into the bath and falling asleep in there, and how he'd once terrified a geriatric house-guest by rising up out of the bath as the old guy leaned over to turn on the taps. And by the time the burial of the bird was complete we were pretty relaxed and I wasn't embarrassed about calling him Ian or walking back into the kitchen with him past my clothes-line full of underwear.

'Well,' he said at the front door, 'I'm

pleased to have finally met you, Alison.'

'You, too,' I said, meaning it.

'Now you take care, and get yourself completely better before you come back to work, OK? Whatever it was you've had. Virus, flu, stress, strain or fatigue, whatever — we want you back fit.'

'OK.'

I held open the door. He hesitated, looking at his car from the doorway. Nice car, but no need to stand there looking at it. I waited. Couldn't very well shut the door whilst he stood there, and couldn't very well walk away with the door wide open, so I just had to stand there, holding the door, waiting for him.

'Just one other thing,' he said at last after I'd begun to get pins and needles in the arm holding the door open.

'Yes?'

'Do you like Thai food?'

I looked at him with the sort of level of comprehension I'd have felt if he'd asked me to solve an algebraic equation in Japanese.

'Pardon?'

'Thai food. It's very nice. A bit spicy, but not quite like Indian. More like Chinese, but . . . '

What? Was he flogging cookery books in his spare time?

'I know what it is. I just don't understand the question.'

'There's a nice little Thai restaurant out on the New Park Road. Next to the Gold Digger wine bar, opposite the . . .'

'I know. I know where it is. I still don't understand . . .'

'I wondered,' he said, still looking out at his car. Then he turned to look at me and added all in a rush, 'I wondered if you'd like to go there. One night.'

'Sorry?' I asked.

Spell it out, go on. You'll have to. I won't believe what I'm hearing until you do.

'With me. Would you like to come out for a meal with me? Please?'

'I don't think so,' I said.

* * *

Oh no, I don't think so, do you?

This is the trick, you see.

Go round and see her. Be friendly, drink her tea, eat her biscuits, give her a load of sympathy about her so-called stress. Get her on your side by moaning about your son and his girlfriend. Bury her sparrow cadaver and share a few jokes about cats jumping out of baths. Butter her up. Smile at her, tell her to call you Ian. Then go in for the kill. Let her

339

really think she's special. The boss offering to take her out for a meal! Wow! She'll think she's really made it. She won't believe her luck. She'll be the envy of all the other girls at work. She'll be eating out of your hand.

She'll be no threat.

You'll never hear another word about work-related stress out of HER.

Well, sorry, IAN, but I'm not buying it. I may be dumb, but I ain't that dumb. You can stick your Thai food up your arse, and your flash car with it.

It put me in such a bad mood I ALMOST dug up the sparrow again.

★   ★   ★

Apple Pie looked so much better, when Paul brought him home from the vet, it was hard to believe he'd been rushed into hospital with the blue light flashing. Well, almost. He yawned and stretched when we let him out of the cat basket, flicked his tail at us disdainfully and strolled straight over to the catflap.

'Is he allowed out?' I asked Paul.

'The vet said he could go back to normal but keep him on a light diet for a few days.'

Apple Pie pushed open the cat-flap and climbed out. We watched from the kitchen window, like fond parents watching a baby's first steps, as he strolled nonchalantly across the patio, stopped, sniffed the ground, turned around three times, sniffed again, and stared at us through the window.

'He looks a bit disorientated,' said Paul.

'No,' I smiled. 'He's wondering where his dead sparrow went.'

★ ★ ★

We all went to the station on the Tuesday morning, to see Lucy off to Cornwall.

'Why have you taken the day off work?' she asked Victoria suspiciously.

'To say goodbye to you,' retorted her loving sister. 'In case you never come back.'

'Well, I might NOT,' declared Lucy. 'But that doesn't mean to say you can put any of your clothes in my wardrobe.'

'Girls!' exclaimed Paul, pulling Lucy's suitcase on wheels down the steps to the platform. 'Come on, try to be civil. You'll miss each other . . . '

'Yeh,' shrugged Lucy. 'Like you miss a spot after you've squeezed it.'

'You should know,' shot back Victoria.

It bothered me more that Paul had taken time off work than Victoria. Victoria would take a day off sick with the least provocation, but Paul was a different matter. It made it feel serious, like Lucy was really leaving home. Like he really thought he might not see her again. I felt tears prickling the backs of my eyes as I looked at her, bright-smiled and excited, clutching her train ticket and a magazine for the journey. Going off to be with the man she loved. Leaving us behind without a second's thought. It was the natural order of things, the normal course of events. In prehistoric times she'd have been clubbed over the head and carried off by Neanderthal Man to his cave in Cornwall. In more recent history, she'd have been married off by now and consigned to a life of domesticity and babies. Today, in our more enlightened society, she was acting with her own free will. Making a choice. Wasn't she? Or was Victoria's new philosophy correct, that she was merely a victim of her own hormones? I looked at her sadly, remembering the little pink bundle I'd brought home from the hospital nineteen years before; the toddler in red velvet dungarees following her big sister adoringly around the house; the pretty girl with her long hair in pigtails and ribbons going to birthday parties in her best dress . . .

'What are you crying for?' Victoria suddenly asked me accusingly.

'Nothing. Just something in my eye.'

'Why do you think she's crying?' Paul snapped at her, to my complete surprise. 'Your mum's going to miss Lucy, and so will you, Victoria, even though you might not like to admit it.' He put his arm around my shoulders, making me jump in even greater surprise. 'She's not going to be very far away,' he said to me gently. 'You can easily go and see her. It's not Australia.'

And I couldn't even reply, I was too surprised. And too choked up.

We didn't say much on the drive back from the station.

'Just drop us on the corner,' I told him as we approached our road, 'if you want to get straight back to work.'

'Don't be silly.'

He pulled up outside the house and Victoria jumped out.

'Cup of tea, then?' I asked him.

'No . . . no thanks.'

He was just sitting there, frowning, holding on to the handbrake.

'Well. Thanks for taking us to the station, and . . . '

'Wait. I need to tell you something.'

My mind reeled with possibilities.

I've decided to come back to you.

I've realised I never really loved Lynnette.

I want a divorce.

I want to bring Lynnette to live here with you so we can all be one big happy family.

I haven't paid the vet's bill.

The vet told me something else was wrong with Apple Pie, something serious.

I've lost my job.

I've got a new job in Australia, I'm leaving tomorrow.

Each possibility was more worrying than the next.

'You're scaring me,' I told him, not liking his expression.

'No. It's nothing bad. It's just . . .'

I waited, trying to stop Worrying Possibilities flooding my brain and spilling out all over my body.

'It's just that we've found out how Lynnette got ill.'

Go on. Not fishing bait poisoning, then? I looked at him with sudden real interest.

'Yeh? What was it? A dodgy pint?'

He laughed. I think it was what's called a rueful laugh.

'You're closer than you think. Not a dodgy drink — a dodgy meal. In a dodgy restaurant.'

'How did you find out?'

'The restaurant's been closed down. They had public health inspectors in. There's been a spate of food-poisoning cases and all of them had eaten there during the few days before they got ill. It was traced to their kitchens.'

'Christ. Not good for business.'

'No. Like I say, they've been closed down. You'll probably see it in the local paper.'

'Which restaurant?'

'The Thai one down the New Park Road. Next to the . . . '

'Gold Digger wine bar.'

'You know it?'

'No.'

And not likely to, now.

'Lynnette loved Thai food,' said Paul. 'But I don't think she'll ever eat it again now.'

Me neither.

'Well, at least the mystery's solved,' I said.

'Yes.'

He looked wretched. Served him right. Suspecting his own wife of poisoning mistresses and cats.

'I owe you an apology. For the suspicions. It was out of order. Totally.'

'Apology accepted,' I said flatly.

'If you hadn't been acting so strangely . . . '

'I wasn't.'

'If you hadn't kept making threats to Lynnette . . . '

'I was joking.'

'Yes. Well, I'm sorry. We both are.'

'Good.'

I let myself into the house. Victoria was playing her music loudly upstairs. I shut myself in the kitchen and sat down at the table, staring out at the garden. So my reputation was saved. I was no longer a suspected poisoner. Well, great. He was sorry, Lynnette was sorry, we were all bloody sorry, but it didn't change the fact that he'd suspected it, even for a minute, even for a second. If he could suspect me of doing something so hideous just because he thought I was acting a bit strange, just because I'd made a few jokes at Lynnette's expense, well then, it just showed what he thought of me, didn't it. It was a good job we were separated, because I'd have to leave him if we were still together. He could beg, he could plead, but I'd never have him back now. Lynnette was welcome to him.

A bouquet of flowers was delivered during the afternoon. Yellow roses and blue irises. Lovely. Must be for Victoria from some poor young man trying to break down her resolve.

'They're for you!' she said indignantly, almost throwing them at me. She stared at the writing on the card. 'What does IOU mean?'

★　★　★

346

He phoned a few hours later.

'Did you get the flowers?'

'Yes. Thank you. Very nice.'

'You don't sound impressed,' he said.

Oh, don't I? Perhaps it's just that I have this funny side to me. This tendency not to want to be bought by bribery.

'I've got something in the oven,' I lied.

'All right. I'll talk to you again another time, then . . .'

Don't bother.

* * *

Chocolates arrived the next day, champagne the day after that. I threw them in the bin, I tipped it down the sink. I let the answerphone take the calls, and didn't return them. You think I was over-reacting? No, look! HE was over-reacting. Who sends flowers, chocolates and champagne to someone they hardly know? Only someone who's after something, and I don't mean something nice. Only someone who wants to be sure that they won't get taken to court. He was no better than his son, with his basket of flowers and his pathological fear of knives. No, no, let me get this straight. He was ten times WORSE than his son, because I disliked Simon anyway, whereas Ian . . . I could have liked him. That was what made me so angry. I felt a fool. I'd started to like him, in that very short time, sitting on my patio with the sparrow's rotting corpse between us and the tea and digestives. I'd thought to myself that he was a decent guy, a father who didn't deserve his son. And now I just felt stupid and naive, and I didn't want to speak to him any more. I didn't care what he sent me, it would get thrown in the bin. I didn't care how often he phoned, it would get picked up by the answerphone and ignored.

★ ★ ★

'Why don't you answer the phone any more?' demanded Lucy crossly from Cornwall towards the end of the week.

'I've had some funny phone calls,' I said with some justification. 'How are you settling down?'

'OK.'

'Only OK?'

Alarm bells sounded in my head. She was homesick. She missed me. Or perhaps she missed Victoria. Or her bedroom. Her stereo system.

'No, fine. Everything's fine.'

She paused.

'Auntie Bev's got some strange friends,

though, hasn't she?'

'You could say that, yes,' I smiled. 'But it takes all types . . . '

'And . . . '

'What?'

'Well, I don't think it's going to be so good here, with Neil, as it was when he stayed in London with us. He spends too much time surfing.'

Cracks in the beautiful relationship!?! After only these few days! My heart leaped with hope. It could be all over soon. She could be home to lick her wounds in time for the new term.

'But I think it'll be better once we've got our own place,' she went on cheerfully. 'And get married.'

Yeh. And have roses round the door for ever and ever. Dream on, my poor baby. Dream on.

★   ★   ★

I could ignore Ian as long as he kept phoning, but it wasn't so easy when he turned up on the doorstep. It was Friday morning and I was getting ready for my appointment with Dr Lewis. I'd made an effort with my appearance. I know you don't normally set out to impress your GP, but I was desperate for him to sign me back to work, so I wanted him to see me at my best. I wanted him to see me as a normal, relaxed, calm, pleasant person. Someone without an ounce of stress in their entire life. Someone whose daughter wasn't considering marriage to a beach-bum in Cornwall, whose mother hadn't eloped to Spain with a toy-boy, whose car wasn't sitting outside a garage glaring at her and whose cat hadn't twice survived traumatic poisoning and emergency hospitalisation. I practised smiling at myself in the mirror, the calm, relaxed smiles I was going to smile at Dr Lewis. When the doorbell rang, I was in the middle of practising my prepared speech about how much better I felt now that I exercised regularly and ate no chocolate, and I'd opened the door before I had time to think. Or time to check through the window.

'Oh,' I said, politeness (only just) preventing me from shutting the door again in his face.

'Sorry,' he said, fidgeting with his car-keys like a nervous schoolboy. 'But I've kept trying to get you on the phone, and . . . '

'I've been out a lot,' I lied. 'And in fact I'm just going out now.'

'I see. Yes.' He managed to meet my eyes

and added, 'You look very nice, too.'

Of course, this was all part of his buttering-up and bribery business so I took no notice whatsoever. It was, however, reassuring to know that the efforts I'd made for Dr Lewis seemed to have been worthwhile. I almost asked him if I looked like a calm, sensible, unstressed person but then I remembered I didn't really want to talk to him.

'I've got to go now,' I said, pointedly, keeping him on the doorstep whilst I picked up my handbag.

'Of course. I'm sorry. I've called at a bad time.'

Any time's a bad time, mate. Get the message.

'But please let me just tell you . . . '

Funny. People seem to keep doing this to me. 'Let me just say one thing': and then they seem to get struck dumb and it takes them half an hour to spell out the One Thing.

'It's about the Thai restaurant.'

And the One Thing always seems to be about the Thai restaurant!

'The one that's been shut down for food-poisoning?'

'So you did know about it!' He struck his forehead in such a theatrical way that I almost laughed despite myself. 'No wonder you refused to come out with me! No wonder you haven't answered my calls! You must have been so insulted! What an idiot I am! How could I have been the only person in London not to know about it!?'

'But . . . '

'Please believe me,' he went on earnestly. Well, it LOOKED like earnestly, but I knew better, didn't I. 'I knew nothing about it. I wasn't trying to be funny, or nasty, or cruel, when I asked you to come there with me — I happened to like the place! I didn't get ill when I ate there . . . '

'My husband's girlfriend did,' I commented.

'You see!' he said, slapping his forehead again as if to beat his brain into action. 'No wonder you were offended! Your own family affected by the food-poisoning! Trust me to put my foot in it . . . '

'But I've only just found out about it.'

He was too busy berating himself to take this in. Instead, he continued at a rate of knots, as if he had to get this speech finished before he changed his mind, or more likely before I walked off down the path (which I was waiting to do):

'Now, I won't insult you again by suggesting another restaurant, and running the risk of finding out later it's infested with cockroaches or already been demolished!' — he laughed uncomfortably here at his own joke. Good job one of us did — 'So what I'm going to do is, ask you to do it.'

'Do what?' I asked, looking at my watch.

'Choose the restaurant.'

'What restaurant?'

'Any one. Anywhere you like. For whatever evening you like.'

'Mr Unwin,' I said, beginning to get really impatient. 'Ian. There isn't going to be a restaurant. There isn't going to be an evening. Now, if you'll please excuse me, I really am going to be late for an appointment . . .'

'Well, can I at least give you a lift somewhere?' he asked, a note of desperation in his voice. 'As I've made you late? And will you then at least THINK about the restaurant?'

I hesitated. Not about the restaurant, but about the lift. I WAS going to be late for Dr Lewis, by the time I'd walked round there, and this was very annoying as it would ruin all my good work at appearing non-stressed. I also quite fancied a quick ride in the BMW. Not that I'm a car snob or anything, but when your bastard Metro keeps glaring at you about its MOT failure, anything like this does appeal. I might even ask him to drive past the garage just so I can lean out of the window and put up two fingers at the Metro. Just as I was about to give in and agree to the lift, just as I had the word 'Well . . . ' forming on my lips, my mouth pursed into a thoughtful and considered 'W', I looked up to see another familiar can turn the corner and pull up behind the BMW.

'There's no need for the lift, thank you!' I told Ian, almost elbowing him out of the way. 'My boyfriend's here! Hello, darling!'

I watched his face drop as I tripped down the path towards the other car. But it was nothing compared to the expression on Paul's face as I kissed him extravagantly and noisily and jumped uninvited into his passenger seat, cooing: 'Where are you taking me, darling?'

Lucky for me that Lynnette wasn't with him!

14

'Are we going anywhere in particular,' asked Paul, fairly calmly I think in the circumstances, 'Or are we just running away from Mr Flashy BMW?'

I looked at him sideways as he accelerated on to the main road. Did I detect a slight, ever so slight, hint of jealousy in his tone there? Something to do with the flashy BMW? Or (surely not) something to do with the fact that another man had been chatting to me on my doorstep?

'The doctor's, please,' I said. 'And sorry for all that. Calling you my boyfriend and kissing you and everything.'

'Was he harassing you or something? The guy in the flashy shirt?'

Oh, so it was a flashy shirt now, was it? Not only a flashy car but flashy clothes, too. I smiled to myself.

'No. Nothing I can't handle . . . '

'Look, Ally, we may not be together any more, but I don't want to think of you . . . well, you know . . . '

Having a life of my own? Having any fun? Seeing any other men?

'Getting yourself into any situations . . . '

'Paul, what are you trying to say?'

He pulled up outside the Health Centre and turned in the seat to face me properly.

'You're an attractive woman, Ally, and a lot of men . . . well, they see a woman on their own, and they think . . . '

An attractive woman? I pulled down the mirror and stared at the little bit of my reflection that it afforded. Was I attractive? How long had this been going on, then, and why hadn't anyone told me before?

'If I was such an attractive woman,' I said dully, 'If I was so attractive that men were going to start beating down my door to get to me, then you wouldn't have gone, would you. You wouldn't have gone to Lynnette.'

'Come on, Ally. Let's not start all that, all over again. These things just happen. I'm sorry, but they do. It's nothing to do with how attractive you are, or how nice, and good, and . . . '

'I know. I know that, really.'

'You do?'

He looked at me in surprise.

'Yeh. I do. I understand. It's taken me a while, but . . . '

'Well, of course it has.' His voice was trembly with relief. 'It's only natural that it should have taken a long while. It was so hard on you. I didn't know how to make it any easier . . .'

'Don't worry, Paul. And don't worry about me, either. I don't have hordes of men fighting over me. That one . . . with the BMW . . . he's my boss. Slimy Simon's father.'

'Oh! I see!'

That made it all right, then, apparently.

'And he wanted to drive me somewhere out in the country and rip off all my clothes, tie me up, gag me, rape me, murder me and bundle my body into the boot of the car . . .'

'Ally! Sometimes, you know, I really do wonder about your sense of humour.'

So do I. I wonder where the hell I'd be without it.

★   ★   ★

'Alison!' Dr Lewis looked up with a beam. 'Well! You certainly look a lot better than last time I saw you!'

Thank God for those hours I spent in front of the mirror.

'Yes. I've followed all your advice about exercise and diet,' I gabbled. 'And I've lost some weight, and I've relaxed, and I go jogging every day. And . . .'

I'd forgotten it. I'd forgotten my carefully prepared speech. With all the hassle of Ian

Unwin turning up, and then the in-depth stuff with Paul in the car, my mind had gone a blank.

'And how are you FEELING?' prompted Doctor Lewis.

'Oh, fine. Yes. Much better,' I nodded brightly.

'Sleeping better?'

'Like a baby.'

'Still needing the Diazepam?'

'Oh . . . ' I blushed and bit my lip. Forgotten about those. 'No, I . . . didn't need them for very long . . . '

'And how are you coping now with your anxieties? About your job?'

'I can't wait to get back,' I told him earnestly. 'I think it's going to be fine. The Written Warning's been taken off my file and the temp's been kicked out . . . '

He smiled.

'There will always be other problems, though, Alison. Every day you'll have new problems to face. We all do. What I need to know is, are you ready to go back to facing them?'

'Well, I won't know till I get back in there, will I?' I retorted. 'No one ever solved any problems by lying at home on the couch listening to soppy relaxation tapes and eating celery, did they, doctor?'

He leaned back in his chair and laughed.

'Yes, I think you're better,' he said, starting to write out the form that would certify me sane and safe to return to work. 'And I'm very pleased to see it!' He handed the certificate across the desk to me. 'But come back if you have any more problems. Remember, you should be looking after yourself now. You've spent years looking after other people. Be kind to yourself now, Alison. You're a nice woman. You deserve a bit of happiness — go for it!'

'Oh. Thank you!' I stammered, completely confused. 'I will. I'll . . . er . . . go for it, then.'

What with Paul telling me I was attractive, and the doctor calling me a nice woman, this could all go to my head if I wasn't careful. I smiled to myself as I walked home. The sun was warm, I felt fit and relaxed and ready to take on the world. Go for it? I'd go out and GRAB it if I got the chance! If only I knew where it was and what it looked like.

★　★　★

'Do you want to go out for a drink again, tomorrow night?' Liz asked when I phoned her with the good news about being signed back for work.

'Yeh. Yes, why not! That'd be great!'

'Anywhere in particular you want to go?'

'No. As long as it's not the Thai restaurant in the New Park Road!'

'Have you heard about that? It's been closed down . . .'

'I know. Paul's girlfriend ate there and nearly died.'

'Bloody hell. Did you send them a bouquet?'

And Paul thinks I've got a problem with MY sense of humour!

* * *

It gave us the idea, though, of going to the Gold Digger wine bar, which was next door to the closed-down Thai restaurant. None of us had been in there before, but it looked all right from the outside and would save going all the way to the West End.

'You look nice, Mum,' Victoria commented, a bit grudgingly I thought, as I was getting ready to go out.

Again, I looked in the mirror in surprise. So what had happened recently, apart from losing a bit of weight, to make me suddenly look nice and be called a nice woman? Had passing the milestone of the fiftieth birthday somehow worked some magic spell? Perhaps I'd been granted three wishes by a fairy who came to my party. You know, the party I didn't have. Perhaps the good fairy had bestowed Youth, Beauty and Niceness on me as her three gifts for my fiftieth birthday. Now all I had to wait for was the bad poxy fairy to come along and take the gifts back and return me to my usual state of old age, ugliness and bad temper. There always has to be a bad fairy, doesn't there. That's one of the first lessons we all learn in life, sitting on our mother's lap listening to those scary stories everyone always seems to think are good for children in some obscure way, the ones about wolves eating poor little girls up, and giants killing people for the fun of it. No wonder kids have nightmares — we read this stuff to them and then kiss them goodnight, turn the light off, shut the door and leave them on their own in the dark. 'Sweet dreams!' we call out to them as they lie there shivering in fear under the bedclothes, imagining all sorts of monsters coming to get them. Then we tell them off when they won't go to sleep. Yes, the bad fairy was bound to come sooner or later, that was the one thing I could be sure of.

'Are you going out on the pull?' asked Victoria disapprovingly.

'I'm going out to have a few drinks and a chat with my friends,' I replied defensively, feeling again like the child instead of the

361

mother. 'But if there's anything out there worth pulling, that wants to be pulled, well . . . who knows?'

'Mother, honestly,' spoke the reproving tones of my own child, the born-again virgin, the voice of celibacy. 'I really think . . . '

'Don't worry, Victoria,' I said, kissing her hastily as I heard a taxi pull up outside. 'I promise I won't do any drugs, I won't drink and drive, and I won't get pregnant. I might be late, though. Don't lock the door!'

Perhaps she might let me stay out all night when I get a bit older.

★   ★   ★

'I'm so glad you're coming back to work on Monday!' said Liz for probably the twentieth time. I was pleased the first couple of times. Now I was beginning to think she was trying to convince herself. It was getting a bit wearing. Mind you, she was pretty pissed. We'd shared a bottle of red wine already and were well into the second one. 'It's been no fun while you've been away.'

I don't remember it being much fun while I was there, but perhaps I missed it. Perhaps I blinked while the fun was going on, or it happened while I was in the toilet.

'I'm glad I'm coming back, too,' I said

362

cheerfully. 'It's all very well being at home for a few days, but eventually you start feeling useless.'

'It's done you good, though, hasn't it,' said Mary. 'You look so much better.'

See? There it was again — this thing about looking better. What was wrong with me before? I must have looked terrible, and no one ever told me. Don't you think they should have told me? They were supposed to be my friends, after all.

'Talking about work,' said Liz suddenly, leaning across the table towards us with a sudden drunken lurch, 'Look who's over there, Mary!'

Mary turned to stare over her shoulder. 'Who?'

'You won't know him, Ally,' went on Liz in what she obviously believed to be a confidential whisper but which actually came out only a few decibels short of a bellow.

'It's Ian Unwin — Simon's father. You know I told you he was over from Portugal? Nothing like his son, is he?'

I froze in my seat. Literally froze. I had goosebumps all over me. I took a gulp of my drink. There was no way I was going to turn round. I didn't want him to see me. I could just sit here and pretend to be invisible and perhaps he'd go away.

'Actually I think he's quite good-looking,' went on Liz relentlessly. She seemed, if anything, to be getting louder. 'Don't you think so, Mary? What do you think, Ally? Look, he's over there ... what do you reckon? Not bad, is he? Must be about our age, but he's in good shape ...'

'Yeh, I'd give him one,' giggled Mary into her wine. 'What's the matter, Ally?'

'You all right, Ally?' echoed Liz. 'You look really red. Have you started getting hot flushes? You poor thing. Are you going to go on HRT?'

'Shut UP, Liz!' I implored.

'Oh, look! He's coming over!' Mary whispered, barely containing her excitement. 'He's seen us!'

Heard us, more likely. So have most of the people in the wine bar, and probably half of those in the pub over the road.

'You can start HRT even while you're still having your periods, you know,' Liz was continuing, well into her stride. 'And it keeps you coming on regularly every month. But I think you're still supposed to use contraception. You'd better check that with your doctor, Ally. But I suppose there's not a lot of need for that, at our age, eh! Chance would be a fine thing, wouldn't it! Ha!' She chortled merrily and then looked up and nearly fell off her chair in surprise. 'Oh, hello Mr Unwin! How nice to see you! Ally, this is Mr Unwin . . . Ally?'

Wishing only to die, preferably instantly and regardless of how painfully or messily, I was halfway under the table pretending to do something intricate and desperately important to my shoe.

'Ally, this is Mr Unwin,' she said again a little louder in case the people drinking in pubs in Manchester hadn't quite caught it the first time. For good measure she nudged me with her knee so that I hit my head on the edge of the table.

'I heard you,' I replied, straightening up and glaring at her.

'We've already met,' he said. 'Hello again, Ally.'

Liz and Mary looked at me open-mouthed, their eyes full of accusation.

You crafty cow, said their eyes. What's been going on here? What exactly have you been keeping from us, and why? If you don't tell us, we'll draw our own conclusions, and you know quite well what conclusions we're going to draw . . .

Later, I told their eyes. Later, I'll tell you, I promise. Just keep your conclusions to yourselves for a minute and don't say anything else to embarrass me, please, please, if you love me, if you've ever cared for me at all, however drunk you are . . .

'What's all this, then?' said Liz, ignoring everything my eyes had been trying to tell her eyes. 'You've already met?'

'Yes, we have,' I admitted in a miserable whisper. 'Hello, Ian.'

IAN! said Liz's eyes, wide open with shock. So it's Ian, is it? Bloody hell, it must be serious!

He pulled up a chair. Why don't you join us, I thought, even more miserably. Liz and Mary were both stunned into silence, which, although a profound relief from the point of view of saving me from any further discussion of my periods, meant that I felt obliged to talk to him.

'How's your boyfriend?' he asked me politely without meeting my eyes.

Mary choked on a mouthful of wine and Liz had to go to the Ladies. By the time they'd both recovered, I'd managed to change the subject but neither of them could stop staring at me, as if I'd suddenly grown horns or developed an interesting rash.

'Did you get to your appointment on time the other day?' asked Ian.

'Yes, thank you. Sorry I had to rush off, but . . . '

'No, no, I quite understand. Inconsiderate

of me, really, to turn up unannounced like that.'

I didn't dare look at Liz or Mary but I could tell from the continued unnatural silence that their eyes would be out on stalks by now.

'So I just wanted to apologise,' he went on. 'And buy you a drink. To show there's no hard feelings?'

'That's nice of you, but not necessary,' I said stiffly.

'Come on, let me treat all of you to a drink. Another bottle of red wine?' he insisted.

'That's be lovely, thanks,' Liz got in quickly, recovering her power of speech.

'Yes, lovely, thanks!' agreed Mary.

'So how long have you been seeing your boyfriend?' he asked me very quietly as he stood up to go to the bar.

'Oh . . . quite some time,' I replied, looking at my problem shoe again.

'Well, if the situation should change . . . ' he added meaningfully, hesitating, trying to make me look up at him. But my shoe was far more interesting and demanding of my attention. He wandered off to get the drinks.

'WHAT BOYFRIEND?' yelled Liz as soon as he was half a yard away.

'WHAT SITUATION?' spluttered Mary, dribbling in anticipation of a really juicy bit of gossip. 'And why did he turn up unannounced? And where? And when? What for?'

'You lucky cow!' said Liz, looking at his departing rear with open admiration bordering on lasciviousness.

'You crafty mare!' added Mary. 'How many are you carrying on with?'

'None!' I said. 'Ssh! Keep your voices down, for God's sake! He'll be back in a minute!'

'How did you meet him?' persisted Liz.

'He only came to talk to me about my work-related stress. He only wanted to apologise about Simon, about the written warning. He only wants to make sure I don't sue the company. That's all . . . '

'It doesn't look like it to me,' retorted Mary.

'Doesn't look like what?' I asked nervously, stealing a look behind me and seeing him heading back with the bottle of wine and another glass. He saw me looking and smiled at me. I felt the heat rise in my face again.

'Doesn't look like that's all he wants,' she replied, watching him too. She turned back to look at me and added, 'And it doesn't look like that's all you want, either.'

'No. It doesn't,' agreed Liz, slurring slightly. 'It looks like you're both just about gagging for it . . . '

'Here's the wine, then,' said Ian softly at my shoulder.

'Cheers,' I said.

If all else fails, getting pissed often seems like the best solution.

★ ★ ★

He drove me home. Well, he drove all of us home, but he dropped me off last. I wasn't really in any fit state to argue by then, and I DID fancy a ride in the BMW, anyway.

'Can you drive past the garage in Essex Road?' I asked him. 'I want my car to see me.'

'It's dark,' he pointed out, but nevertheless did so, and slowed down so that I could lean out of the window and blow raspberries at the Metro.

'I think that told it,' I said, sighing happily. 'Bloody thing.'

'What's it done?'

'Failed its bloody MOT. Wants me to take out a second mortgage to rescue it. Not that it even deserves it.'

I'd completely forgotten I wasn't supposed to be talking to Ian Unwin. I felt mellow and safe in the leather seat of the BMW, cocooned from the world and all its evils. I couldn't even remember what its evils were. We cruised gently home and he turned off the engine.

'I meant what I said,' he told me softly.

'What bit?' I asked, frowning, trying to remember. About it being dark?

'About your boyfriend. If the situation changes . . . '

'What situation?' I asked, still frowning, trying to remember.

'Is there really a boyfriend?' he asked, looking at me intently. 'Or was that guy just a friend . . . ?'

I tried hard to concentrate. I'd been off there in a dream for a few seconds, trying to imagine how it would feel if he kissed me. That's the only thing with being totally pissed. Your mind starts to play strange tricks and you forget what you're supposed to be talking about.

'Pardon?' I asked. 'You were saying . . . ?'

'Would you mind if I kissed you good night?'

Couldn't think of a damn reason why I should mind. Why should I mind? I leaned towards him and took hold of him round the neck. Yeh. Felt good. I kissed him long and hard and started to wish we were somewhere more comfortable than the front of his car, so we could really get down to it.

'Wow,' he said very gently when we

eventually paused for breath.

'Nice,' I smiled.

Then my head began to swim and I suddenly felt very, very sick.

'Thanks for the lift!' I muttered, struggling with the door handle. 'See you . . . '

Just made it to the bathroom in time.

★ ★ ★

'I don't know how you got yourself into such a state,' said the disapproving voice close to my ear. 'Coming home at all hours of night, rolling drunk . . . '

Mum! Don't tell me off, Mum! Please, I don't feel very well. Just let me lie here . . .

' . . . falling asleep on the bathroom floor . . . '

Bathroom floor? What are you talking about? Where's my pillow? Where's my duvet? Give me back my blankets, Mum! I feel so ill!

' . . . being sick all over the place . . . '

Sorry, Mum. Don't shout at me. I don't FEEL very well.

' . . . and as for that bloke that brought you home . . . '

Bloke? Bloke? What bloke? I don't remember any bloke.

' . . . parked outside there in the flashy BMW at all hours of the night. Well, I just hope he wasn't taking advantage of you, the state you were in!'

Sorry, Mum. Can't remember a thing. Please just go away and let me go back to sleep, Mum!

'MUM!!'

Mum? I thought YOU were the mum! I opened my eyes very cautiously, wincing as the bathroom ceiling came zooming down towards me and the bath tilted dangerously on its axis.

'Oh! Victoria!' I whispered, recognising her.

'Come on. Get up. Go to bed. You're cold. It's only three o'clock. Get into bed and sleep it off.'

'Oh . . . oh . . . oh,' I groaned, closing my eyes again as she pulled me to my feet. 'I don't feel well!'

'You'll feel better in the morning. Perhaps,' she said stonily.

'Sorry. I won't ever do it again. I promise. Just let me sleep for ever . . . '

★ ★ ★

I woke up again at half past ten and felt, miraculously, undeservedly, much better.

'Want a cup of tea?' asked Victoria, looking in at me as I sat up and rubbed my eyes.

I nodded and tried out my voice.

'Thanks. And — sorry, Victoria. About last night. You should have left me there. My own fault.'

'You were making too much noise, groaning. You woke me up.'

'Sorry,' I said again, sheepishly.

She shrugged.

'Suppose you've looked after me often enough.' This was true. This was very true. Probably cleaned up more vomit than she'd ever seen in her life, her comfortable, pampered, cleaned-up-after little life. Certainly didn't hurt her just once, just this one time ever, to look after her poor old sick mother, did it?

'But don't make a habit of it, eh, Mum? I mean to say, at your age! It's so demeaning!'

Just get the tea, there's a good girl. I'll decide what's demeaning around here!

★　★　★

'So?' demanded Liz as soon as I walked into the office on the Monday morning.

'So?' I repeated. 'What do you mean, so? What sort of a greeting is that for someone who's been off sick for the past six weeks? Welcome Back might have been nicer!'

'So,' she repeated, ignoring me completely, 'What happened? After we got out of the car?

Come on, come on, give, give! Did you have it off with him? Was it good?'

'Liz! No! Who? What do you mean?'

I sat down at my desk, not looking at her, readjusting the chair after its adjustment by Tracey McMarn who was apparently a short-arse. Switched on the computer, asked it to let me choose a new password. Rearranged the telephone, the mouse and the mouse-mat to suit my longer arms.

'Who?' laughed Liz. 'Who? Don't give me all that crap! You and Ian Unwin. Come on, what's the score? You know you'll tell me eventually . . . '

'There's nothing to tell,' I said stiffly. 'I had a bit too much to drink, AS you know, AS we all did, and he very kindly drove us home . . . '

'And?'

And. And that kiss.

Wow.

Nice.

I moved the mouse, crossly, jerkily, familiarising myself again with the icons, finding my way around the screen again. Don't think about it. The feel of the hair at the back of his neck, surprisingly soft and springy. The touch of his lips against mine, shockingly gentle but firm, disturbingly passionate but lingering and slow . . .

Click. Don't think about it. Click. Read e-mail. Click. New messages. Click. What's this?

'*To: Alison Bridgeman.*
From: IOU.
Subject: Proposed meeting.'

Proposed meeting? What proposed meeting? My fingers hovered over the mouse button. Delete? Save? Print? Reply? Read.

'*A meeting is proposed this morning at 09.30 in my office to discuss your reintegration into the company.*'

Reintegration?
Reinter-fucking-gration?
'What?' asked Liz, seeing the expression on my face. She got up from her desk to come and look at my screen. I clicked the mouse button quickly and told her:
'I've got to go to a meeting.'
'Meeting?' she echoed blankly. 'I don't know about any . . . '
It took me five minutes in the loo to do my hair and another five minutes to find out which office he'd taken over. It was still only nine-fifteen.
'What's all this?' I demanded, waving the

print-off of his e-mail at him as I walked into his office. 'Meeting? Reintegration meeting?'

'Welcome back, Alison,' he said, getting out of his chair to close the door behind me. He was smiling at me. 'Good to see you. Sit down. Please.'

I sat. I watched him walk back to his side of the desk and I suddenly felt nervous. Why? Well, there were a lot of things I'd have liked to say to him. Things like:

Cut the crap and let's get this straight. I was pissed when I kissed you and I want to forget it happened. I don't like you and I don't know what came over me. I don't have a boyfriend, I made that up to get rid of you, but I don't want to go out with you and I resent you thinking I can be bought off that easily.

Or that I need to be.

But at the end of the day, he was my employer, and this was my first day back at work. Dr Lewis had warned me that there would always be problems to face at work, but I bet even he didn't anticipate me having to consider telling my employer to fuck off within the first half-hour of my first day back.

'About the other night,' he said suddenly, watching my reaction.

'Yes,' I said, not reacting.

'I'm sorry.'

'So am I. I was drunk.'

'Yes. Exactly.' He looked down at his desk, doodled on a pad, and frowned to himself. 'I'm of the generation that was brought up to believe that only an absolute cad, a filthy bounder, takes advantage of a lady when she's drunk.'

I smiled, despite myself, which annoyed me. I smothered the smile, but admitted:

'I'm of the same generation, and I was brought up to believe that a lady doesn't get drunk in the first place. So let's just forget it, please.'

Forget the feel of that hair at the back of his neck. Look at it now, just where it meets the collar. Soft and springy.

'But I won't give up trying to make you change your mind,' he added.

'Well, you should do. I'm not interested.'

Not interested in those firm, passionate lips. Look at them now, remember how they felt. How difficult it was to stop . . .

'But I think you could be. Perhaps if it wasn't for the boyfriend?'

'Please, Mr Unwin. Ian. We have to work together, so I can't afford to be rude to you, but please don't waste your time . . .'

'You don't like mixing business with pleasure?'

I don't like being taken for a mug.

377

'Perhaps.'

'Well, I'll probably be going back to Portugal soon.'

So what was I supposed to do? Book his plane ticket? Wave him goodbye?

'OK,' I said.

'Perhaps just one night out together, then? Before I go?'

To safeguard the company? Bribe me into submission?

'No. I don't think so,' I said, again, getting up to go. 'Thank you for the meeting. I'll get back to my work now.'

'Yes. All right,' he said, opening the door for me.

I walked away, aware that he was watching me, and probably didn't breathe until I sat back down at my own desk.

'Tea?' asked Liz. 'Biscuits?'

Oh, yes. It was good to be back.

★   ★   ★

The roses were delivered at midday, red ones, a dozen of them.

This was not really on, was it. I mean, this was not really playing the game. Flowers arriving at home was one thing. Flowers arriving at work was a whole different matter. It got everyone talking, and it got Liz and

Mary into an absolute frenzy. They couldn't even eat their lunch they were so excited.

'They're from HIM, aren't they!'

'So are you going out with him? You ARE, aren't you?'

'I knew it! The meeting this morning . . .'

'It's no good you keep shaking your head at us, Ally. We're not stupid! We can see what's going on right under our noses . . .'

I sent an e-mail after lunch.

'To: IOU
From: Alison B.
Subject: Roses.
Please do not send any more flowers. People are talking. If I wanted flowers I would work in a cemetery.'

The next day, two dozen roses were delivered, accompanied by a card which stated in very large writing: 'LET THEM TALK. PS: The cemetery has no staff vacancies.'

I was getting dangerously close to having to tell him to fuck off after all. It was all very well for him, sitting in his private office, phoning Interflora, laughing to himself about my embarrassment. He didn't have to work with Liz, who spent every available minute between nine and five interrogating me and then phoned me at home in the evening to ask if there'd been any further developments. He didn't have to eat lunch with Mary, who was growing thin and anorexic with her obsession with my business to the exclusion of her own nourishment. He didn't have to run the gauntlet of nudges and winks from Jason, Carl and Daniel every time I moved from my office, or the knowing looks from Melissa and Roxanne when they met me at the photocopier.

'NO MORE FLOWERS PLEASE. I have an incurable allergy', I e-mailed him on the third day.

A basket of fruit was delivered that afternoon. I sent it, together with the four bottles of vintage port and the silk scarf, straight back to his office. This was getting ridiculous and would have to stop. If he carried on like this I'd be signed off with stress again by the end of the week. Nothing arrived on the Thursday, and I breathed a sigh of relief.

'I think he's finally got the message,' I said to Liz as we were clearing up to go home. 'Thank God for that. I was beginning to wonder what was going to turn up next.'

When I got home from work, there was a new white V-W Golf parked outside the house. Tied up with a blue ribbon, with helium balloons sprouting from its door handles, it grinned at me in a challenging way as I stood staring at it from the corner of the road. It was raining, and I'd walked from the tube station because the buses were on strike. I looked at the Golf, and it looked straight back at me.

'Now what are you going to do?' it said. 'You and your principles?!'

'Fucking hell,' I said.

15

The keys for the challenging white Golf had been put through my letter-box in an envelope, together with (by the feel of it) the paperwork. Nothing written on the envelope, of course. People who delivered new cars with balloons and banners on them to other people's houses presumed, I suppose, that the recipient would know who they were. And of course, I knew who he was, all right. My legs were shaking as I sat down, next to the window where I could look at the car, with the envelope in my hands, and thought about it. My legs shook so much, even whilst I was sitting there, that I had to go and pour myself out a brandy from the bottle I kept for emergencies. You know the sort of thing — resuscitation of collapsed invalids, treatment of colds, flu, toothache and stomach ache, anointing of Christmas pudding and mince pies. This was treatment of severe shock. I sat there, sipping the brandy, feeling the keys in the envelope, and staring at the car, for about half an hour. Every few minutes I closed my eyes, counted to ten, and opened them again, expecting the car to have disappeared and a TV crew from *Beadle's About* to have jumped out from behind the bushes shouting:

'So, Mrs Bridgeman. What have you got to say to the friends who played that little trick on you? Is it true that you've never had a nice new car like that in your entire life? Well, there you go! You've still never had one! Ha! Ha! Isn't she a good sport, everyone?'

Victoria's car pulled up behind the Golf and she got out, slowly, eyes riveted to it. She stared at the house as if looking for clues, looked all around (probably wondering about Jeremy Beadle too), then approached the car cautiously and touched its bonnet very gently. Was it a mirage? Was it going to melt away before her eyes?

She turned and ran up the path, let herself in at the front door and screamed:

'Mum! Whose car? Where's it come from? Is it a present? Who's it from? Why . . . ? What . . . ? Is it ours? Can we go out in it? When . . . ?'

'No,' I said, dully, still staring at it from the window.

'But why . . . ? Why not? Who . . . ? What . . . ?'

'Because I'm sending it straight back,' I interrupted before we could get any further

383

into the interrogation. 'It's not mine, and I don't want it.'

'But . . . ' She gulped, lost for words. 'But . . . '

I stood up, put down the brandy glass with a decisive thump and went out to the kitchen to make tea.

'Forget it, Victoria,' I told her brusquely. 'Forget you've seen it. Pretend it's not there. It'll be gone by tomorrow.'

I peeled potatoes viciously and stabbed sausages with a red-hot anger. Now I'd got over the shock and the disbelief, I was so angry, if I could have seen him right now he'd be in there with the sausages, stabbed and fried. How dare he? How dare he think he can buy me like this? What did he take me for? What sort of person would send back wine, chocolates and flowers but be won over by a car? I would NOT be that sort of person, however much I wanted the car, however much it hurt to send it back, however much it smiled and winked at me out there while the old bastard Metro sulked and languished at the garage. My moral indignation grew and swelled as the sausages spat and shrivelled. Did he really imagine I was going to sign some sort of declaration now, to say I accepted his gift of a car and would undertake never to sue his company for my work-related stress? Then, I suppose, he could fly off back to Portugal with an easy mind, leaving his slimy son in charge again, and the minute his back was turned, Simon would sack me. He would. He'd make up some trumped-up excuse to get rid of me, to pay me back for scaring him with the knives and everything, and he'd get Amazing Trace installed back in my seat faster than she could say 'Screw me slowly over the stationery cupboard, Big Boy'. And nobody could do a thing about it because I'd be driving around in the Golf, paid off and signed off, and out of a job. Well, if he thought I was falling for it, he had another think coming. I wouldn't drive that car, I wouldn't get into it, I wouldn't open its door or touch its door handle. I wouldn't even look at it. It was going straight back.

I didn't have his phone number. I had to wait until I got to work the next day (by tube, NOT thinking about white Golf GTi's at any stage of the journey, even when the tube stopped between stations for ten minutes due to signal failure), whereupon I went straight to his office and flung the envelope with the keys and documents in it, on to his desk. The gesture was spoilt somewhat by the fact that he wasn't there, but it would make its impact as soon as he came in and sat down. For good measure I sent a very curt e-mail:

'To: *Mr I Unwin*
From: Mrs A Bridgeman.
This is not acceptable. I do not accept it. Please remove it from in front of my house at once. I will treat any further offerings as harassment and may have to consult my solicitor.'

After I'd sent it, I felt a quiver of anxiety about the fact that he was, after all, still my employer. Also I didn't actually have a solicitor. However, I was still too angry and offended to really worry about it and when all was said and done, he wouldn't have a leg to stand on if this whole business came out, would he.

I worked like fury all morning, taking out my temper on the keyboard and refusing to answer Liz when she tried to find out what was wrong. It was nearly one o'clock, and I was just contemplating going to lunch, when Lucy phoned.

'Mum? Listen, I haven't got long . . . '

'What? Lucy, is that you?' It was a terrible line, sounded like someone was practising Morse Code in an aviary.

'Yes. Can you hear me? I'm calling from a pay-phone, and I haven't got any more money, so . . . '

'Why? What do you mean, you haven't got any more money? Where are you? Why are you on a pay phone . . . '

'Mum, just listen, or the money will run out! I'm coming home.'

'You're what?! Coming home? Why? What's happened?'

'Neil and I are finished . . . '

I knew it. The bastard. I'll kill him. He's taken her all the way down to Cornwall, she's given up everything for him, she's left her home and family, and . . .

'And I . . . er . . . need to get away quickly. So . . . '

'What do you mean, quickly? What's happened? Lucy, are you all right? Tell me . . . '

'Yes, I'm all right, but I'm coming straight home . . . '

'Where's Beverly? Let me talk to her.'

'She's not here. Look, the money's running out . . . '

'What's HAPPENED, Lucy?'

I was on my feet now, shouting into the phone. Liz was staring at me across the office, hand to her mouth, eyes wide.

'Has there been . . . any violence?' I

demanded, beginning to shake ever so slightly.

Silence. And then, in a very quiet voice:

'Well . . . sort of . . . '

'My God!' I practically screamed. 'I'm coming to get you! Stay there! Don't move! Don't let anyone in! I'll be straight there! Lucy . . . ?'

The line had gone dead.

*   *   *

I thought I'd been through some Worrying Things in my time, but believe me, at that moment I realised none of them had even been worth a moment's concern. They had been nothing but minor irritations, mere itches on the skin of my life. This was the Fear, the Dread so great and so awful in every mother's heart that it can't even be spoken about. The one that starts to bug you when you first get the result of the pregnancy test, and grows huge and desperate when you hold that newborn baby in your arms and understand for the first time the vulnerability of life and your role as protector. The real terror you feel as you watch your child cross the street, ride off on their bike, drive a car for the first time. It never goes away, it just lies there dormant, and then a phone call out of the blue brings all the monsters suddenly and horribly to life. My baby, hurt, crying, needing me, out of my reach. I had to get to her, now, instantly, and nothing else mattered. I couldn't think, I couldn't reason, I couldn't listen to Liz trying to calm me down, I just had to go. Now.

'Tell them . . . ' I said, my voice trembling, waving an arm in the direction of the management offices. 'I had to go . . . '

Liz was trying, gently, to hold my arm, stop me from rushing headlong out of the office.

'You can't drive in that state. You'll have an accident. Let me . . . '

'No. I'll be OK. I'll . . . oh. Oh, shit.' I sat down, my legs feeling hollow and wobbly. I couldn't drive. Of course I couldn't drive. I didn't have a car.

★ ★ ★

'I'm sorry. Mr Bridgeman's out of the office at the moment, Mrs Bridgeman', said his secretary sweetly. 'Can I give him a message?'

'Shit! Sorry. No. No message. Don't worry.'

I hung up and dialled Victoria's work number.

'No, sorry,' said a strange voice answering her phone. 'She's off sick today. Who's calling?'

Nobody. Nobody calling, and certainly not her mother, a mother who didn't even know her daughter was skiving off work. I phoned home. No reply. The crafty little minx had taken a day off to go out somewhere without even telling me. Great! Just great! Never mind about me, needing her, needing her car to go and save her sister's life. I felt tears threatening and blew my nose angrily. This was no time for self-pity. I had to think of something.

'Please. Let me drive you,' said Liz. 'I came by tube but I can pick up the car and come back for you, and . . . '

'No. It's all right. I'll get the train down there. It'll be quicker. Or I'll go and steal the Metro back from the garage . . . ' I stopped, suddenly remembering. 'No I won't,' I said, more calmly. 'I know what I'll do.'

Ian Unwin looked up from his desk in surprise as I flung open the door without knocking.

'I want the keys back,' I said abruptly, holding out my hand. 'I haven't changed my mind. It's an emergency. I need to use the car.'

'What keys?' he asked.

The tears overflowed and started running down my face. He jumped to his feet, looking alarmed.

'Don't play games, not now!' I cried. 'My daughter's in trouble and I've got to go down there! I'm sorry! I'm sorry about the e-mail, if it was a bit rude, but I don't want to be bribed! I just want to borrow the car, please . . . '

Out of the corner of my eye, I saw the envelope, still sitting unopened on his desk where I'd left it. I reached out and grabbed it, almost knocking him out of the way.

'I'm sorry!' I said, ripping open the envelope and tipping the car keys out into my hand. 'But I've got to . . . '

I threw the envelope back on his desk and ran out of the office. I ran out of the building. I ran to the taxi rank at the end of the road. I ran out of the cab straight to the lovely white Golf GTi, yanked off the ribbons and the helium balloons and jumped into the driving seat. I ran out of petrol about a mile along the M4.

★   ★   ★

Well. It was the last thing on my mind, wasn't it — petrol. I suppose I assumed that new cars were delivered to their new supposed owners with a full tank. Or perhaps I didn't assume anything, the state I was in — perhaps I just completely forgot about cars

391

needing petrol. I was lucky, of course, not to have an accident, lucky that when I started to lose power I reacted instinctively enough to indicate and get on to the hard shoulder before I stopped dead.

'Fuck!' I shouted at the car, with complete justification, you must admit. 'Fuck, fuck, fuck!'

I smacked it, hard, on the dashboard. I put my head on the steering wheel and moaned with despair. Then, whilst I was lying there, my head on the wheel, my arms flat out on the dash, I became aware of a sound coming from the floor of the car. From my handbag on the floor of the car. It was my phone! My mobile phone! Oh, YES! Thank you, God, thank you, thank you, for the wonder of modern communication! I almost kissed it as I took it out of my bag and pressed 'talk'.

'Mum?' Victoria's voice sounded odd and strained. 'Is everything OK? I just phoned your work to ask you about getting chops for dinner, and Liz said . . . '

'No!' I snapped. 'No, it's not OK. Lucy's in trouble and I'm bringing her home.'

'What? What trouble? Where are you?'

'Stuck on the M4. Where are YOU, when I need you? Why are you off sick? Why aren't you home? What are you doing . . . '

'I'm at Andrew's house,' she said in a very defensive tone.

Oh, I see. Andrew, is it, now? The Last Stand of the Celibate Army has fallen at the feet of an Andrew. Didn't take long, did it. No wonder she kept it quiet.

'Well, get yourself OUT of Andrew's house and down the M4 in that car of yours, right now, can you?' I said tetchily.

'But what's happened to Lucy? Why . . . ?'

'I'll tell you when you get here,' I returned, cutting her off.

Almost as soon as I put the phone down it began to ring again.

★ ★ ★

'Ally!' said Paul. 'My secretary said you phoned. She said you sounded upset . . . '

'I was! I am!' I swallowed hard, trying not to start crying again. 'Paul, I'm on the M4 and I've run out of petrol, and I've got to get Lucy back from Cornwall, she phoned this morning, and Neil's finished with her, and something's happened . . . '

'Hey, hey, slow down, calm down!'

I stopped, breathing heavily.

'Victoria's on her way,' I added. 'She just phoned. We'll go in her car.'

'Are you in the Golf?' he asked.

I stared at the phone. Something not quite right here. Had I missed something? A chapter or two of my life? Paul didn't know about the Golf. I hadn't spoken to him since last night, and even if I had done, I sure as hell wouldn't have told him about Ian Unwin delivering new cars to my door.

'Has Victoria told you?' I asked. 'She's told you about the Golf?'

'No, she hasn't spoken to me about it. Nor have you, yet, but I guess you were going to get round to it. But I presume it's OK? I presume you're driving it OK?'

'What?'

'I should have told them to fill up the tank. If you'd phoned and let me know it had arrived, I'd have warned you.'

'You?' I said. 'YOU?'

In my mirror, I saw a silver BMW coming up behind me, passing me slowly, indicating left and then pulling on to the hard shoulder just in front of me. IOU 1.

'You!' I said again, still weak with shock, as I watched Ian Unwin get out of the driver's seat and stride towards me.

'Ally?' said Paul. 'Are you all right? Is Lucy all right? What's happened?'

'I'll call you back,' I said, very ungraciously in the circumstances, 'in a minute.'

'What are you doing here?' I asked, getting out of the car. I couldn't seem to help the ungraciousness, it seemed to have become second nature to me all of a sudden; even now I was facing my boss on the hard shoulder of the motorway having just accused him of bribery. The Worry about Lucy, the awful, primal fear and need to rescue her, had done away with my own survival instinct and common sense.

'I was worried about you . . . ' he began.

'Worried?' I retorted. 'Worried? YOU're worried? I'm scared shitless, me!'

See what I mean — completely ungracious.

'Sit down,' he said, pushing me back into the seat of the Golf. He came round to the passenger side and sat down next to me. 'Now, take a deep breath. Come on, try and calm down. You've got yourself so worked up . . . '

'Worked up? Of course I'm worked up! My daughter's lying somewhere, battered and bruised for all I know, and that bastard . . . '

'It's all right, Ally.'

'All right? It's not bloody all right! She's hurt, and it's all my fault!'

At this, this admittance of what was bothering me, what was lurking in my subconscious underneath all the primal fear, and nagging away at me, I started actually crying out loud. Sitting there, in the front seat of a brand-new car bought for me by my husband, being comforted and — yes, now, cuddled too — by my boss, I blubbed and bawled all over his shirt until my throat hurt.

'It's all my fault!' (sob, sniff). 'If I hadn't pretended to be ill . . . ' (blub, blub) ' . . . I made it all up, I never had stress, I just wanted a day off work and Simon would have sacked me . . . ' (sob, howl) ' . . . And now you'll probably sack me anyway . . . ' (sniff, snivel) ' . . . I should never have told all those lies . . . ' (gurgle, sob) ' . . . I wouldn't have gone down to Cornwall in the first place . . . ' (howl, moan) ' . . . and Lucy would never have met that BASTARD!'

'Ally,' said Ian, taking a huge clean white hanky out of his pocket and wiping my face with it. So gentle. So bloody gentle and caring, when really all he wanted to do was get rid of me, sack me quickly now he knew all about my lies and malingering, to say nothing of my accusing him of bribery with a new car. 'Ally, please stop crying. Please, listen to me. Everything's all right.'

'No, it's NOT!' I raged. 'Don't you understand? I have to get going, now, I have to get down to Cornwall . . . '

'No, you don't,' he said firmly. 'Listen to me. Your daughter phoned again.'

She did? I hiccupped myself into silence and clung on to him for a minute, sniffing slightly, before I realised what I was doing and let go.

'Liz took the call, just after you left,' he went on.

'What did she say? How did you know?'

'I knew because I was in your office at the time. I was trying to find out from Liz what was wrong with you. I was worried about you.'

He looked at me. I looked at him. Thought about him being worried about me. Thought about him being there, listening, when Lucy phoned again.

'What did she say?' I asked quickly. 'Is she all right? Is she hurt? Did you tell her I was on my way?'

'She's not hurt at all, Ally. She's absolutely fine. She knew you were worried, that's why she got some more change and phoned again.'

'But she said he'd been violent! Neil! He's been hitting her, or . . . '

Ian shook his head, smiling.

'Mothers! Your imagination's run riot! You got completely the wrong end of the stick. He hasn't done anything to her at all. She wanted to get away quickly before he found out what SHE'S done to HIM.'

I stared back at him, my tears drying quickly, my heartbeat slowly returning to normal.

She wasn't hurt. She wasn't in danger. I could breathe. It felt good. It felt wonderful. I inhaled. Lovely. Exhaled. Lovely.

'What SHE'S done to HIM,' I repeated, slowly.

'She's cut off his hair,' he said, and his smile spread across his whole face. 'She found him with another girl. So she waited till he was asleep, dead drunk, and she cut off his hair. Then she packed her bags and left.'

Wow. I took another deep breath, and started to smile myself. Wow, Lucy, what a way to go! What a girl! Serve the creep right, the bastard, the two-timing little git. She should have cut off his dick and stuck it up his arse. But never mind, this was good, this was very good. His manky, nasty, long stringy hair that he was so proud of. Hope it takes him years and years to grow it again.

'So where was she? Where was she phoning from?'

Let me get to her. Give her a hug, tell her what a clever girl she is. Make her a cup of tea, tell her I still love her.

'At the station. She was phoning from the

station. She's on the train now, on her way back to Paddington. You don't need to drive anywhere. That's why I came to find you . . . '

'But you didn't know . . . you didn't know I'd run out of petrol . . . '

'No. I was going to keep heading on down to Newquay till I passed you. I thought at first that you'd be driving your old Metro, the one you pulled faces at in the garage, so I was pretty sure I'd pass you sooner or later.'

'And I'm not. I'm not in the old Metro. I'm in this . . . this white Golf.' I looked down at my lap, almost too embarrassed to carry on. 'How did you know it was me, then?'

'When you took the car keys out of that envelope on my desk, I didn't have a clue what you were talking about. I hadn't even opened the envelope because I didn't know what it was and I'd been busy all morning. Just as I was leaving the office to come and look for you, I thought to have another look in it. And there was the registration document for a white Golf GTi, and a gift card from someone called Paul. I still don't have the slightest idea what it had to do with me, but at least it told me exactly what car to look out for!'

'I'm so sorry,' I said, still looking at my lap. 'I just thought . . . you see, it was delivered to my house, and I didn't know anything about it, and I thought . . . after all the wine, and the fruit, and the flowers . . . '

'You thought I'd bought it for you?'

'I'm so sorry, Ian. I've made the biggest prat of myself . . . Oh, and the e-mail! I'm so sorry about the rude e-mail!'

'I haven't read it yet,' he replied, laughing. 'How rude was it?'

'I threatened you with my solicitor. But don't worry!' I added quickly. 'I haven't even got one!'

'That's all right, then!'

'It's not funny. I feel so embarrassed.'

'Don't be. I didn't buy you the car, but I expect I would have got around to it sooner or later. I probably wouldn't have moved straight from wine and flowers to a car, but I'd have built up to it.'

'Why? I kept telling you not to. I kept sending them back to you. I didn't want . . . '

'You can't blame a guy for trying. I had to try. Despite the boyfriend, and every-thing . . . '

'He's not my boyfriend,' I interrupted impatiently. 'That was just another one of my lies.'

'I knew it!' he smiled triumphantly.

'He's my husband.'

'Oh.'

His face dropped.

'Separated. Been separated for two years.'

'Oh!'

'It's him, apparently, who's bought me the car.'

'Oh.'

'Must be because he felt so guilty about calling me a poisoner.'

He frowned at this, as well he might, but was wise enough not to comment.

'Anyway,' I sighed rubbing my eyes, feeling suddenly very, very tired and wanting to go home. To get home before Lucy arrived, have the kettle on ready for her. Tea and sympathy and a hot bath. Give it a few days and she'd be over it. We both would. 'Anyway, now I've told you about my lies, about my malingering, you can get rid of me, can't you, and push off back to Portugal, and you won't have to worry any more about me and my so-called work-related stress. You won't have to bother any more about trying to keep me quiet, bribing me with flowers and stuff . . . '

'Bribing you?' he said, and his voice was louder than I'd ever heard it before. I looked up at him. There was something in his eyes that I couldn't look away from. 'BRIBING you?'

The traffic on the motorway flew past us relentlessly, at seventy or eighty miles an hour. A red car, a black car, a coach, a lorry, another red car. Whoosh, whoosh, whoosh. Past the window they went, off down the road on their way to the Midlands or Wales or the West Country. Off on their business or their holidays or to their grandmother's funeral or whatever their lives had in store for them, whilst we sat there, in the front of a brand new Golf with no petrol in its tank, paid for by my husband for reasons I could only guess at, and stared at each other, and the whole world suddenly changed.

'You weren't?' I whispered. 'You weren't trying to bribe me?'

'No,' he said. His voice sounded sort-of choked and half strangled. 'What a ridiculous idea. What sort of books do you read, for God's sake, you absolutely ridiculous woman?' And he burst out laughing.

'I'm sorry!' I said, mortified, still staring at him.

'I suppose it's my own fault,' he said eventually, trying to control himself. 'I went a bit overboard with the gifts, didn't I.'

And he reached out and stroked the hair off my face where it had got wet with tears and stuck to my nose.

'I suppose you thought I was trying to bribe you when I offered to take you out for a meal?' he said softly.

I nodded. He kissed me, gently, right on the tip of my nose and laughed, gently, right into my eyes.

'And now? Would you think I was trying to bribe you if I suggested you get into my car and I drive you home?'

I shook my head.

'Or if, instead of driving you straight home, I drove you to a motel somewhere and booked us into a room, and ordered champagne, and took you to bed, and . . . '

I don't know who made the first move. We kissed as if our lives depended on it, as if we'd both been locked up somewhere for about a thousand years where kissing hadn't been allowed and been forced to watch videos of other people doing it. I thought it was going to kill me; that the feeling I'd had building up inside me, without acknowledging it, since the day I first met him, since the day I saw him sitting in his car outside my house with his arm hanging out the window and his hand tapping to Queen . . . 'I'm falling in love . . . I'm falling in love for the first time, this time I know it's for real . . . ' — that this feeling was going to overwhelm me and drown me, that I'd go into some sort of coma and never come out of it. Feelings like this didn't happen to real people, people outside of books and films and *EastEnders*. I must be dreaming. I must already be in a coma.

★ ★ ★

'MUM!!'

'ALLY!'

The shouting, the knocking on the window, the faces staring through the glass . . .

This was real, all right. This was no dream. This was no bloody coma.

Ian and I sprung apart like two guilty children, looking at each other in amazement. How did that happen? How did we get to feel like this about each other? And when? Before we were born? Or just now?

'MUM! For God's SAKE!'

I turned my gaze reluctantly to the car window. Victoria was pounding on it, and next to her, Paul was shaking the door handle as if it wasn't locked, just a little bit stiff, and he'd soon get it open . . . The car was rocking from side to side from their combined efforts. Aha. That'd be it. I thought it was the earth moving.

'All right, all right!' I exclaimed, opening the door and letting them both fall in on top of me. 'No need to get excited!'

I looked back at Ian (well, it had been a full five seconds since I'd looked at him), and we

404

smiled at each other soppily. I KNEW, I knew it was a soppy smile but I didn't mean it, it just happened on its own without my permission.

'Oh, yeuk!' said Victoria. 'Mum! I can't believe you! Lucy's lying in some hospital or somewhere, injured, and . . .'

'No, she's not. She's fine,' I said, still smiling at Ian.

'She's fine?' echoed Paul. 'You're sure?'

'I panicked. I over-reacted. She's on her way home by train. She cut off his hair,' I said, all on one breath. 'Sorry, everyone.'

'Sorry?' echoed Victoria, pretending to be resentful, but relief oozing out of her like perspiration. 'Is that all you can say?'

'Yes,' I said, cheerfully. 'Thanks for coming to find me. You can go back to Andrew now.'

She looked slightly abashed.

'Well, I WAS going to tell you about him . . .'

'It's all right, Victoria,' I smiled. 'I knew you wouldn't make it as a nun. Black and white doesn't suit you.'

I got out of the car and walked with Paul back to the Primera.

'I brought you a can of petrol,' he said, getting it out of the boot, not looking at me.

'Thanks, Paul. How did you find me?'

'Phoned Victoria on her mobile. You didn't

call me back, and you switched yours off.'

Did I? Bloody hell. The things you do when your train of thought's interrupted by seeing a silver BMW.

'I thought I might get here quicker than her,' Paul went on. 'In fact I passed her just as I turned onto the M4. Then we both found you . . . and the BMW.'

'He's my boss,' I said. 'Ian. Ian Unwin.'

'So you said before.'

'And I think I'm in love with him.'

There. I'd said it. It was out. I'm in love with him. This is it. This is what it feels like, then, after all this time, at fifty years of age. This time I know it's for real . . .

'Be careful, Ally. Don't get hurt . . . '

Hurt? Hurt, for fuck's sake? You dare to stand there and talk to me about not getting hurt, you of all people? You, you who left me after all those years of marriage, left me for someone young and pretty, left me on my own with the girls and the cat and the bills and all the Worries?

I turned and watched as Ian got out of the car, my new car that Paul had bought me (for reasons of his own which weren't, after all, too very difficult to guess), and approached us. He was tall, and lean and smart. He was tanned and fit and gorgeous. And I loved him. He smiled at me. I smiled back.

'Do you want to poison him?' I said very quietly to Paul with a sudden flash of intuition.

'I suppose I do,' he admitted.

'I'll tell him to look out for slug pellets, then, shall I?'

'No. Fishing bait,' said Paul, managing a smile.

★   ★   ★

We were in Portugal by the time I finally admitted it. We flew out for a couple of weeks in September so Ian could see how the Faro branch was doing and we could spend some time relaxing together in the sun. I was able, by then, to look back and think about it all a bit more clearly. A bit more honestly.

'I think perhaps I might have had a breakdown of some sort, after all,' I said, leaning back in my chair beside the pool. 'Do you think I did?'

'Maybe, maybe not. Who knows? Who's to say what's normal behaviour and what isn't? Perhaps it's not so very strange to fall apart a little when everything gets too much to cope with.'

'I did have a lot of worries all going on at once. And they all seemed to build up and sort of . . . take me over.'

'That's understandable. Completely normal.'

'And to threaten your husband's girlfriend with poison?'

He smiled.

'Completely normal.'

'And . . . ' I dropped my voice to a whisper, 'To actually DO it?'

He laughed and leaned over in his chair to plant a kiss on my face.

'Totally, utterly normal, I'd say. Can't understand anyone who disagrees!'

So that's OK, then.

Isn't it.

Totally, completely normal.

Even if it was only laxatives in her coffee.

Nothing to worry about there, then.

THE END